THE IDEA OF LOVE

THE IDEA
✧ OF ✧
LOVE

LOUISE DEAN

Houghton Mifflin Harcourt
BOSTON · NEW YORK
2009

Library of Congress Cataloging-in-Publication Data
Dean, Louise.
    The idea of love / Louise Dean.
        p. cm.
ISBN 978-0-15-101385-2
    1. Middle-aged men — Fiction.   2. Pharmaceutical
industry — Employees — Fiction.   3. Married people
— Psychology — Fiction.   4. Adultery — Fiction.
5. Parent and child — Fiction.   6. Depression, Mental
— Fiction.   7. British — France — Provence — Fiction.
8. Americans — France — Provence — Fiction.
9. Provence (France) — Fiction.   10. Psychological
fiction.   I. Title.
    PR6104.E24I24 2009
    823'.92—dc22   2008050150

Book design by Melissa Lotfy

Printed in the United States of America

DOC 10 9 8 7 6 5 4 3 2 1

For Marcus

The primitive theory does not seek the reason for insanity in a primary weakness of consciousness, but rather in an inordinate strength of the unconscious.

—C. G. JUNG, 'On the Psychogenesis of Schizophrenia', *Journal of Mental Science*, September 1939

PART ONE

1

✧

LOSING HIS FAMILY was only a formality; they were never his. He'd attached himself to them believing that, being sufficiently foreign, sufficiently quaint, almost rural and almost Catholic, they were implicitly better, or at the very least — different.

He'd thought of himself as a romantic and indeed he had been insomuch as the romantic clings to the idea of love rather than daring to love. But he didn't know what love was until he lost everything.

An Englishman with a French wife, he lived in one of the small market towns that are on the crossroads of rip-you-off-Riviera and rob-you-blind-Provence. It was an uneventful and lonely place for ten months of the year. To the casual eye it was a romantic place; gorge and ravine, Saracen tower and stony riverbed, but as one grew more accustomed to the place, one's eyes were drawn to the signs of the struggle between man and nature; here and there in the middle of a vineyard or a field the stray abandoned one-room dwelling; broken down, exposed, done with.

They'd come to live there seeking a rural counterpart to his place of work; Richard's company's head office was situated in the Californian-style suburbs of Antibes with its anodyne office blocks and roundabouts giving on to roundabouts. He'd worked, when he met her, for ten years in the dismal man-made 'town' of Croydon for the French pharmaceutical group Europharm, latterly as their youthful Sales Director. He'd drunk in a pub underneath an underpass and lived in a flat overlooking a fly-over.

A year after Valérie moved in with him he was relocated to head office in Antibes — it seemed too good to be true as she was by then sick and tired of England — and so they decided to quit, for good they said, town life. She stayed behind packing his things, disposing of much of his past he found out later, while he went ahead for a month-long immersion course in business French. They meant to be happy.

When they moved out to the South of France, she was pregnant, and they gathered to them what she had for family in France, her quick-minded mother and her regretful father — and they made a home for themselves in the Var region of Provence.

He was promoted to the new consumer markets of Eastern Europe and oversaw sales of psycho-pharmaceuticals — anti-de-pressants and anti-psychotics — with the highest profit margin of any product sold, even oil. His client, the psychiatrist, was clam-ouring to prescribe these chemicals to people struggling with the transition from the old way of life to the new lonesome urban standard.

Richard knew from his work, from the pockets of madness and gluts of sadness emerging throughout the developed world, that his family would be better off living among a community in the countryside, even if he had to create it with his own hands, even if he had to spend money to make it, even if he had to fake it.

He himself was rarely at home. He was more of a tourist when it came to family life. That thought brought to mind a slogan daubed on a wall in Soweto on one of his first business trips to South Africa: *Soweto is no zoo for tourist pigs.* How pricked he'd felt on his tour bus then. Family life is no zoo either.

2

✧

HIS PREDECESSOR AS Sales Director for Europharm Africa told him over lunch that going to Africa with big bucks looking for mental illness was the craziest damn thing if he thought about it, and the thing was not to think about it.

With his knife and fork, the retiring salesman folded his last triangle of pizza into a mouth-sized piece and told Richard what he'd seen for himself out in West Africa, which was, he said, a totally different kettle of fish to East Africa; church halls packed with people claiming to be possessed. The play-acting was vaudeville.

'Hey, we aren't shrinks anyway,' he said, showing the clean palms of his hands, 'we're just salesmen. But, when you work in Africa, you can't avoid getting into bed with the government, you've still got totalitarianism out there. It's not a market economy you're dealing with. So you have to see things differently, Richard. There's not a nice way of putting what I'm driving at here.'

'I know what you're saying. You make the market.'

The girl put down before them a double-scoop ice cream in a cornet for his colleague and a cup of coffee for Richard.

The table hesitated on the cobbles before Richard settled it with his forearms and, stirring in two sugars, bent into his shadow, thinking as an aside how women were the new men, how aggressive they were in bed.

The German woman he'd been with the night before in Lyon had asked him to give her anal sex, only she didn't put it that nicely. He hadn't felt like it. It was the first time in his life he'd left a woman's hotel bedroom without having had sex. He'd had to say, look I can't do this, the first time he'd ever done so, and he'd seen then how strange it was to be there together at all, to have the cold light of day in the middle of the night.

But if West Africa was overemotional, 'spiritual' as they called it, then East Africa was much more sensible, his colleague went on. It was there, on his recommendation, the company were investing their money in relationships with one or two of the better governments, sponsoring clinics and hospital programmes, training the doctors, making the psychiatry module look swish.

Governments came and went, let alone ministers. Sometimes he'd go one week, see one guy, and the next week he'd go back and the guy would be gone. Richard would need to win brand loyalty at grass roots for the long-term safety of the investment.

His advice was to get out and about to the local hospitals, to win the medical fraternity over. The doctors would be there for longer than the politicians. Europharm should be seen to take an interest in the mental suffering of the people.

'Lay down roots for the company out in the sticks. You know, be seen to be sincere.'

Richard found, not for the first time, that he couldn't pick up the coffee cup; he was shaking. In the last year these peculiar crises came upon him in all sorts of situations, even lunches. It felt as if he were about to fail, suddenly and explosively. His chest was tight like he was having a heart attack. The scene shifted as if it no longer included him; he was central, then he was not. He

7

felt himself flush, he was going to say or do something that would embarrass himself. He thought he might pass out. The more he observed himself feeling this, the more distant he became from himself, the worse it got.

Watching his waistline, his predecessor said he was, but Fenocchio's in the Old Town was still the best ice cream in the world. It had been his haven. Worth the twenty-minute journey for lunch. He was having liquorice. Hell, we all have our vices. He didn't smoke. Or drink coffee.

He looked at the ice cream before licking it, biting it, trimming it, and he looked at it again after he'd done that, judging the work done and that to come and taking his time.

'My time's my own now. I like golf. I never thought I would. You get all these young guys who want to ask you this and that, how to make markets. Hey, look, I took anti-depressants into the Eastern bloc in eighty-nine, but I've made it plain, I'm gone. It's a long lunch every day and an easy life from now on. Though I doubt I'll get ice cream like this in Perpignan.'

'I see.'

With his coffee cold before him, and his hands clasped beneath the table, Richard asked for the bill with a nod at the waitress.

Richard would get a briefing from the World Health Organization, the old boy said. He raised his eyebrows to show what he thought of that.

'Well, Africa will have the privilege of skipping the asylum and all that jazz. So much the better for them, my friend. Of course it's tempting to see yourself as a missionary. Bringing progress to Africa and all that. Well, if you must. Look concerned, you know, though. Not everyone in Africa can be got to with baksheesh, don't think that about them. Oh no.'

The waitress stood sideways waiting for the transaction to

complete, the terminal in one loose hand, passing her free hand through her glistening curls, looking towards the sea, towards Africa.

The retiring salesman rolled the now miniature cone in his fingers. 'You'll like the Head of Mental Health at the WHO,' he said, donning mirrored sunglasses. 'She's a woman.'

3

✧

HIS RETURN HOME from work was a forty-minute drive; the scenery shifting to the rugged Wild West of the Var, its ascendancy signalled by Mount Roquebrune, which loomed like a grumpy Ayers Rock. It was here that Richard turned off the A8, relinquishing the daytime brasseries in favour of a dusk of dirty *tabacs* where old men idled, letting their cigarettes fall to the floor.

He drove, thinking how when he got in he would be able to tell Valérie that he'd be bringing home one hundred and ten thousand euros per annum.

He thought of the girl she was, Valérie, when they met. She was his opposite; dark and indolent. He was pale and useful. She was a girl with a savage haircut and dark matte skin, some swagger, almost a boy with long lashes, who sat in his flat in Croydon listening to her Indochine records and smoking cigarettes out of the window. She was the sexiest girl he'd ever met. She went braless, her nipples prominent, her back arched, her body sinuous, her face petulant. Not so very short, she had a way then, of reducing herself, of looking up to him. She hated her bar job, so he told her to give it up and she did. She waited in for him instead.

'Today I 'ave done nothing but play with myself,' she would say, sighing and smiling.

Men and women stared at her when they went out and about into pubs and restaurants together. His friends fancied her, their girlfriends didn't like her. She had a thick accent and spoke little English. She'd followed a boyfriend to England and dropped him for Richard. He'd wooed her with gifts and trips and treats. He made her entertain his friends with tongue twisters. 'I no pheasant pluck I pleasant fuck his mate.'

She was so French! She wore things Englishwomen didn't wear, like matching bras and knickers, she was frank about her periods, not remotely embarrassed about body hair and she got on top of him in bed and screwed up her eyes and concentrated very hard.

She didn't mind being driven here or there, she didn't mind doing whatever he was doing. She didn't mind staying in all day, doing 'nussing' as she said. She had a doll, the miniature of herself, with hacked dark hair, 'Marguerite'. She wanted a baby, she said.

They married in France. Their child was born in 1993. He helped her with the baby, though that was not how she recalled it later, but he remembered many nights sitting up with the infant or walking around with him, singing 'Row, row, row your boat' or 'The Grand Old Duke of York'. The birth of the child was also the end of the romance.

She named him 'Maxence'. (He'd hoped for 'Edward'.) They'd taken to speaking French between them since moving there. He'd once made her smell Marmite, and her expression then reminded him of how she looked at him if he spoke English to her.

She bemoaned their son from the day he was born. Nothing was on schedule according to her books, he didn't sleep well, he had colic, he had colds, he wouldn't eat vegetables, and all of this she took as some sort of personal indictment. *Relax,* he told her, *enjoy him.* Well, there won't be another one, was her rejoinder.

As a toddler, he wouldn't leave her alone, she couldn't take a pee without him, he was so noisy and violent she claimed, he broke things, he hit her, he hurt animals, he wouldn't settle to read or play nicely, he wouldn't go to her parents. She proposed she get a local woman to look after him during the day. The woman had other children at her house, it would 'socialize' him she said.

Richard had so wanted his wife to be at home with their children. No more children, she told him, winking as she popped her pill, waggling her finger in an ironically come-hither sort of way. She'd have Max ready every morning for the woman to collect. She gave the woman an extra three euros a day to prepare his lunch.

'What will you do with yourself?' he'd asked her.

She'd shrugged. 'It will be so much better for Max because when he is here I will be able to give him my full attention. He is a very difficult child.'

Her parents, Guy and Simone, had come to live next to them just after Max was born. He and Valérie had bought the small bungalow and they paid the mortgage. He'd hoped her mother, who was a warm bosomy woman, would have Max when Valérie needed her to, but it emerged soon after they moved in that Simone was suffering from chronic fatigue syndrome and needed prolonged periods of rest and little disruption. She tried to help, here and there, and was crestfallen she couldn't do more, but she was frail, she fell over and if she fell, well — she put her hands in the air — what would become of Guy? (He could not survive without her.)

In those early days, the family drank together more or less every evening when he got home — there was nothing else to do — and those were pleasant evenings, her mother standing, tongue out, hastily unpeeling the cellophane from a salty snack and her father bent as ever to the ground, murmuring to his dog and stroking its long hairs into the nuts and pretzels. They chatted through the good or bad luck of others. Richard liked to speak French. When he spoke French he felt like he was someone else — someone cleverer, possibly.

Guy's father was a Corsican passer-by on his way to or from the war, and Guy had a string of stepfathers until he lost his temper with one of them when he was thirteen. His mother gave him a coin and sent him away. The rest was freefall: pimping in Paris in the fifties; running prostitutes; driving for the Marseillaise mafia; he may or may not have been in the French Foreign Legion; he got Simone pregnant, to the disgust of her family, then wandered off again, and years later he came back to be a father to his daughter, to which honour Valérie seemed unmoved. She was ten then. She avoided him. She never sat close to him. They never embraced. 'She doesn't greet me,' he would moan in a stage whisper, to Richard.

His style of wooing his daughter was stealthy and practical. A basket of fresh vegetables picked and presented beautifully left on the outdoor table in the morning. The trimming and pruning of her shrubs and trees, which went unremarked until Simone mentioned it. And he gave Simone money, from his pension, to buy gifts for his daughter and grandson and told her not to tell them the money was from him and for her own reasons she complied.

'The truth is, I followed my dick,' he said to Richard one evening when they were drinking. 'That's not a problem for me now of course,' he shrugged, pointing between his legs to the ground. 'Before I was like a human being attached to a monster.'

On each of his birthdays, since they'd lived next door, Richard saw him grimly smoking outside on the terrace, waiting for Valérie to come, but she 'forgot' his birthdays or she went away visiting friends, if she could arrange it.

Richard was fond of Guy, who in a way had run to ground. He was tied to the land, and nature, would rarely venture beyond their plots and the neighbouring forest and he knew its larder. He tended to them with his herbs, his cure-all soups, his applications of cabbage leaves to swellings, thyme in the bath, and notwithstanding his arthritic hands he managed to sew lavender bags. He jested that he was a lunatic, and indeed he was very occupied with the comings and goings of the moon, the fixity of the sun and the happenstance of rain. He located all manner of mushrooms, even truffles, and made a wild-leaf salad with fresh grated garlic that would send a cold packing.

Simone was the least loved of five children, the unwanted daughter in an agricultural family, the last child, mistreated by her mother, loved though, she maintained, by her father, whose photograph took pride of place above their television, and she developed mystical powers and illnesses to secure a smidgen of attention and developed a large chest and a pregnancy as soon as she could. She allowed Guy to come back not only to the warmth of her unconditional tolerance but also to raise her up, *la dolorosa*, to tell of her life from behind her hand, askance, and to sing of it too, the self-saucing sentiment bubbling up as she hit the top notes. She sang like Piaf, all trembling indignation. She ran a number of sideshow businesses which occasionally cross-pollinated profit-wise, the two principal ones being fortune telling and selling the cannabis that she had Guy grow.

Richard liked to assist them financially and they were not greedy; a new washing machine here, a twenty-litre box of Co-op red there. They were ostentatiously helpful in return, especially Valérie's mother, who was always thinking aloud how she could help more but ceded agreeably to his protestations that she did too much. She listened to him, she praised his French, and deplored oh-so-covertly, for his ears only, the negligence of her daughter. Her hands went up at this point, resignation was her suit. Impassioned of an evening, the old boy customarily threatened the spectral rogue who dared to cross Richard or the family with a taste of his shotgun. They kept the paths weed-free.

Max got birthday and Christmas presents from them and five euros here and there, and they received his visits without much enthusiasm. Typically Max would stare into space and say nothing, waiting for the opportunity to leave. 'Well, Max, your mother will be wondering where you are.' They'd raise their eyebrows in unison as he left.

'He's not right in the head,' said Guy. 'He doesn't communicate.'

'He's a boy. What do you want?' Simone would respond taking the opportunity to kill two birds with one stone.

The low hum of chatter, as the early evenings descended, was Richard's idea of the good life, and what he kept in mind driving home. It was idyllic. Of course it was possible they were all alcohol-dependent, he admitted to himself amiably. So what? The good life, rosé, same thing. He was looking forward to telling them about his promotion and he knew Simone would rush for a bottle of Champagne and pant and sweat, all fingers and thumbs, as she opened it and they would clink glasses together. After a few glasses of Champagne, Valérie would unwind and smile and laugh and he'd put the boy to bed so as not to disturb her happy state.

They were able to laugh together, the family, and the laughter seemed to him to be like a night-light, a modestly useless accessory in the daytime, which could become so very important in the dark.

4

✧

RICHARD HAD INDULGED in plenty of one-night stands since joining the pharmaceutical business. He might have been losing his hair but with professional women of a certain age panicking all over Europe he was more than sorted for sex. He had a number of sexual encounters in Eastern Europe, some meaningful email correspondence, some of it quite touching, but he was careful to curtail it after two or three exchanges.

As a matter of taste he preferred not to lie to Valérie, and due to his travelling he didn't need to. He left this other life behind him when he took to the motorway. He considered these sexual escapades a normal part of modern life, that opportunity separated those who cheated from those who did not, and the latter dressed up their bad luck with moralizing. The rest took what they could. But that wasn't the whole story.

Just the night before, he'd sat drinking with his neighbour Rachel in her kitchen, at one in the morning, with Valérie gone home and her husband, Jeff, retired to bed, talking about sex, sex with strangers. Without going into detail, he'd alluded to his own enquiries.

'Don't tell me it's about intimacy or I'll smack you in the face,' she said.

'No, no. No, I'm like you, Rachel. It's my way of finding God.'

'Are you laughing at me?' (Rachel was a Christian.)

'No,' laughing, 'it's just that you think the road to God is through here . . .' he'd put a fingertip on her forehead, and gone on — 'it's not though, Rachel . . .'

She'd interrupted him. 'So you think you'll find God through a woman's vagina?'

'Possibly. No, seriously, I wouldn't rule it out. I think of sex as a spiritual exercise.' He was only half joking.

There was something else. He craved intimacy.

He liked talking to Rachel. Talking to an Englishwoman in English was like discovering a secret den at the bottom of your childhood garden.

It didn't matter, being drunk, whether it was true; all things might be true in drink, no one knew and few remembered afterwards. It was the only way to try on new clothes without looking foolish. He shook out the match, closing one eye, feeling the sulphur's snap. 'Maybe.'

She looked downcast, and he didn't ask her why, he let it go because he didn't want to get mixed up with her that way, he didn't want to start thinking about what she was thinking.

'Do you know, Rachel, before we acquired language communication was touch, and between lovers, of course, copulation.'

'Copulation! You fool!'

'Intercourse, not chit-chat. Think about it. Sixty years ago, sex meant so much more and words too. A word might cost as much as a penny. And sex a life. People were more sparing. Now we're verbose. There has to be some kind of a relationship between cheap words and free love.'

She mused glumly on the subject, like a nodding dog, and he got up after a while and went home.

He went across the paddock to his house, considering whether he had had too much or not enough to drink, replaying the conversation. He'd talked too much. Verbose, indeed. Sex. Words. What was it about? Approaching the house he imagined his wife's chaste posture in her pyjamas in their bed.

It was pretty much part of his job, pleasuring psychiatrists, most of whom were female and had a lot of doubts to be quelled. Being naked in bed with a person seemed to help both of them do the job. Between them they purveyed treatments that didn't treat so much as muffle common suffering in all its forms, from grief and paranoia to loneliness and despair, as well as the ordinary longing to be loved.

5

✧

STANDING BESIDE a seated panel of five other persons, an attractive woman was awaiting a projection at the screen behind her. They were in an auditorium in the World Health Organization headquarters in Geneva. As Richard made his way to the only free seat, excusing himself for treading on toes, he glanced upwards and saw five bunkers suspended above each one with the name of a language stickered on them. The translators wore headsets and microphones, they were very animated, looking at each other and making hand gestures.

The woman spoke. 'In terms of Disability Adjusted Life Years Lost, mental illness is up there with AIDS, TB and malaria. The stigma against mental illness in developing countries means that the people who need treatment are not coming forward. This Anti-Stigma campaign will reverse that intolerance . . .'

Charts raged on the screen. There was a scene of a man, manacled, wailing in a hut in the jungle with other people kicking him rather dispassionately. Arrows went all over the continent of Africa, throbbing and flickering. The scene was replaced with that of a young man in jeans and a T-shirt, talking to a doctor in a nice white bungalow, accepting a tablet and washing it down

20

with a branded soda, then helping his mother hoe the field, and giving a big thumbs-up to the camera as the helicopter-based camera withdrew at speed leaving them all just dots in the field. The image faded.

'The purpose of this campaign is to get rid of the misconception that schizophrenia is a manifestation of witchcraft. At the same time, we'll be handing out information on depression, to make people more aware that some of what they deem "sadness" is pathological and they can get help.'

'Good,' thought Richard. 'That's very good.'

A man on the panel, buttoned-down shirt and slicked quiff, received the spotlight and a microphone.

'Is it not true though, Yvette, that something like seventy per cent of Africans hear voices? I mean that if we describe mental illness in terms of this symptom we will have a long, long, long queue of patients. You know, in Italy it would be the same . . .'

There was laughter.

'Dr Frank Gitu. Regional Director Africa . . .'

'Well, now, speaking for my African colleagues, with all due respect, schizophrenia isn't a big problem for us and, as for depression, I'm sorry but you consider yourself lucky to have it in your region . . .'

Richard let himself out. He'd felt slightly sweaty and breathless in there and knew what it heralded. He decided to take a walk, to work it out of his system.

In the lobby, there was an electronic notice with the outside temperature, the date, the soup of the day and language of the week: *Cream of Broccoli* and *Urdu*. He went up the great double stairs, traversed an entire floor, setting aflutter pamphlets and circulars in in-trays, took a lift up to Sexually Transmitted Diseases and stopped to peer through a window at men and women in suits lying on recliners wearing satin eye shields. There was a handwritten sign on the window: *Bureaucrat Recycling Department!* A touch of humour.

Back downstairs, he crossed the lobby again, vaguely intrigued by the little store and its WHO souvenirs. His armpits were wet. He saw the library and decided to take a break in there. He sat down at a long desk. It was warm in there, a nice place to die. He laid his head down. His mobile phone vibrated in his jacket pocket. He quickly withdrew it and put it to his ear, hiding it with his hand, pretending to be scratching his head with all his fingers.

'Oh, Richard, so sorry to have kept you but I was in a meeting, just selling my colleagues in on the joint venture. It went well actually. Look, shall we go into town and get some dinner?'

It took him a long time to find the proper exit and once outside he was at the rear of the building so he was obliged to circumnavigate. There was an adjoining precinct for the HIV team, very deluxe, with black four-wheel drives outside it. Round the back of it was a small woody glade and as he went past it, stepping on twigs, a group of WHO employees broke cover, jettisoning embers and cigarette butts, in panic.

She drove him into town in her grey Passat. She seemed nervous, swapping sunglasses for no sunglasses and back again, swapping clipped-up hair for loose hair, and when he got out of the car she remained a moment with her visor down. When she emerged, her shirt was unbuttoned down her neck, revealing her cleavage.

6

✧

THE LAKESIDE PANORAMA of Geneva presented a staid fa-
çade with its capitalized signage and its stern advertisements for
gold and diamond jewellery, fur coats and private banks.

They sat out on a jetty, their menus folded. The tablecloth
riled against its clip-on restraints. The water was clear down below. A swan made an attempt to fly. A group of plain women
nearby clucked on about Woodrow Wilson and the League of
Nations. What a nice country, he thought; a bureaucrat recycling
centre.

Her life at the World Health Organization was very easy, she
said. She rolled in after nine, drank coffees till lunchtime, ate a
long lunch, worked between two and three, had tea, then popped
off home to the really hard work, to her kid. Her husband was an
artist. A painter.

In Switzerland? What did he paint?

'Bizarre things. Men being raped by women. He uses iconic
materials from the sixties and seventies. Cereal boxes, Action
Men, old comic books; he says he begs from innocence to pay
back corruption. That's his slogan in fact. He's sold a few works
to the Saatchi guy.'

'Oh really. Interesting. Actually, I don't like art much.'

'You don't like art? Isn't that like saying you don't like music?'

'Yes. I suppose so. It feels like showing off, to me.'

'Really?' She took a drink. 'Well, I agree with you in fact. We are very unhappy. Our marriage is a joke.'

'Oh, I'm sorry.'

She didn't talk about it normally. Amazing what a glass of wine could do. She was at the end of her tether. Just yesterday she looked at that man, her husband, and she thought: *It must be nice to be you, asshole.* She came up the hill to their house, with bags of shopping, their child strapped to her chest, and she saw him waving at her from the little window of his studio — he'd made their bedroom into his studio, it was the nicest room in the apartment — there he was waving, pleased his dinner was on the way.

'I'm sorry,' he said again. He ordered another bottle of Swiss Rolle. At her most seductive and useful she came out with it, for all intimacy requires confession, and she said it as if for the first time, that people like her, the so-called do-gooders — wrist flailing, drink spilling — were, of course, the ones who needed help. She shook as she took one of his cigarettes. She shook when she took up her glass and had to wait a moment before sipping it.

'I've always had a thing about Englishmen,' she said, by way of explanation.

He had an idea where it would lead and was not averse, but recalling his predecessor's advice, he told her he wanted to know more about the programme. She had an important position. For such a big player, she was humble, her husband was probably instrumental to her modesty. What a funny world it was at times. Especially after three drinks.

She asked him how he saw his work. He shrugged. It was what it was. People were miserable, but the pills helped. End of story.

She was six years as a lecturing professor at the Institute of

Psychiatry in London, she told him, and now she was the arch-classifier, the woman who matched the different diagnostics standards of the mental health departments from around the world; a hugely political business, for everyone's misery had to be taken into account. She had to get global agreement on what constituted an unhealthy mind. Disorders came in and out of fashion, or they failed to catch on. Some slipped away, but others you had to put your red line through. It was her responsibility to admit or refuse a symptom here or there into the lexicon of madness and to honour clusters of oddness with their own syndrome. Her standing joke? 'I'm sorry, Professor, but you're one symptom short of a disorder.'

'That's a good one.'

Then she was to take her list back to each of the countries to double-check vocabulary, to make allowance for localized disorders, from 'attention deficit disorder' to 'running amok', and she had to take into account passing fads, deleting 'hysteria', 'masturbation' and 'homosexuality', getting rid of 'nymphomania' (which was nowadays normal) and adding 'erotomania', the idea that someone you don't know loves you, she laughed.

She took a drink. She wiped her mouth. Under her watch, she said, they had launched borderline personality disorder and depersonalization disorder.

Her mobile phone shuddered. She watched it writhe, ignored it, then turned it off.

They drank the rest of the bottle and, when it was dark, he settled the bill and they went to a Thai restaurant she knew, and ordered another bottle and ate very little. He'd made sure to ask for lobster-based curries and scallops; the higher-priced items on the menu. They talked a little about their lives, they agreed that they'd never have imagined, at the outset, being the people they'd become.

She took a last man-sized drink from the glass of dessert wine, drew on a cigarette. 'It's a mad world, as they say.'

He asked her why she married her husband, and poured the wine.

'I don't know. We were incompatible in every way. I found it exciting then. He's an Australian. He might be gay in fact. I don't know. We never clicked sexually. Do you know, the first night we were married I said to him if you don't give me oral sex I am going to divorce you tomorrow . . .'

He shook his head. 'You're a tough lady.'

'Not tough enough. He never did. He read a book *Who Moved My Cheese?* or something on honeymoon. He was like a different person afterwards. He gave up work. He made a man of me. I'd rather be at home with our daughter myself.'

He called for the bill.

'What about you?' she asked him.

'Me?'

'What's your situation? At home?'

He showed her his wedding ring, splaying the fingers on his left hand.

'Happy?'

'We have a son who is thirteen. He's very bright in an unconventional sort of way. My wife finds it difficult being a mother unfortunately. I won't bore you with it. It is what it is.'

'You're so sanguine. Like with your work.'

'Oh well, yes. I try,' he grinned uneasily. 'It must be nice being me, right?' He leant forward, whispering in imitation of her, '. . . *asshole.*' He sat back, and signed the bill with flamboyant disinterest. 'She was nineteen when we married. Too young. She's a very unhappy person, intrinsically I'd say. Not that I could see that then.'

'So you saved her.'

26

That made him feel uncomfortable. Yes, that was what he was suggesting, but she didn't have to classify it right away. Put like that, it smelt like blowback from a sausage.

'Maybe,' he demurred. She was a good listener, but it wasn't going right. 'We were too young to know anything about love.'

'So do you think you know anything about it now?'

'I don't know. Maybe I'm not very good at it; love.' The conclusion. A touch of sincerity, a smattering of confession, a hint of self-knowledge, a sprinkling of bravado. 'I mean, what if I don't even know what love is?' he said. 'What if compared to most people I'm an emotional idiot? I feel like I ought to love her, you know, unconditionally even, for the sake of the boy, but I can't. I did try. But I'm not sure I can carry on without love, to be honest with you.' He was drunk. He was saying too much and for his own sake. It was like driving along and feeling bumps under the wheel and thinking, shit I've got a flat, but no, no, I don't want it to be flat, I'll keep going. Or like when you lie down and your stomach sends fluid upwards and you're swallowing like a dog, saying to yourself, oh no I don't want to vomit. He'd been through it before, this routine, about love and his quest for it; it was stale.

They went back to his hotel for a nightcap in the bar. She was a mess, bending over nearly double, laughing, and hugging herself in the low armchair, then she leant forward, her lips pouting and asked him to come with her to the toilet. He suggested they went rather to his room. The lobby attendant blessed them. They kissed in the lift. She was a dead weight more or less.

When they got to his room, she opened her handbag, and took out a foil wrap of cocaine but she couldn't quite get close to it, her heels were capsizing under her bendy legs. He used his Amex to scrape the coke into four lines on the glass-topped dressing table and they did a line each and stepped outside on to his balcony from which one could see the lake if one stood on a chair and craned one's neck. They drank beers from the minibar. He was happy to let her talk some more and she was extraordinarily happy to talk. Then after a while, suddenly, he was not at all interested in listening to her and so they did another line and she talked some more about her work and her husband, sighing all the while, and going from thrilled to stricken, sitting in her bra and knickers, taking off her tights very slowly.

He said, 'I really admired your talk today.'

'You're clutching at straws,' she said, her brow low, as she pondered the floor. She was stuck on the coke, like she'd got her hair caught in a button.

'I'm serious. I want to do this job with conscience. I want to know what I'm about. I want to do the right thing.' Was he speaking for her or for him? Was it true? 'Africa needs us to do the right thing, to know what the right thing to do is. I couldn't live with myself if it were anything less than right.'

Perhaps it was the coke talking, he felt a ghastly earnestness grip him, his eyes were so distended they hurt. He couldn't seem to stop wiping his chin with his palm.

'Well, I can help you with that, Richard. But it won't make you happy, it will just make you like me, confused,' she said looking up at him through her hair. Then she lay back on the bed. 'Make love to me,' she said.

He pulled his shirt over his head and unzipped his trousers, trod them into the floor. His forearms taut, he closed his eyes as he entered her. He hoped to God he was hard enough and that his dick wouldn't buckle. Thank God she was wet. He closed his eyes, going through his virtual folder of arousing scenes, images, situations, young girls, old women, legs apart, bending over, he was mentally thumbing through them at top speed. The German woman's cross face came to mind. This was such a performance! Maybe they should be talking. Then he felt her tighten around him. When he opened his eyes he saw that she was staring at his face and her lips were all tragic and her eyes were wet, and he was taken aback. It nearly made him stop. He should have looked at the eyes before now. What a waste! Looking into her eyes now, he felt drawn to something holy — a fire, life — it was sensational, he strove deeper inside her and felt a surge of excitement. *'So you think you'll find God through a woman's vagina?'*

And then he was done and it was as it always was, just a sticky mess. A thin sweat broke out across his back and he felt her move her fingers over him as if finger painting. He had his face squashed right up next to her. He smelt graham crackers, the smell of her and him and the sweat and the sex. He put a hand across her.

She started to talk, and he didn't mind, he was still a bit coked up, he lay alongside her, enjoying the warmth and peace and he listened to her telling him about her life, then he found himself telling her about the Var, and how beautiful the land was.

He told her how he drove out early mornings with the mist in the valleys making islands of the hilltop towns. He told her about the sky, blue all the year round, like the great Mediterranean Sea turned upside down and hung up above you. How nature there was like a kindly auntie playing cards with a child, losing beneficently. Mimosa, violets, poppies, cherries, melons, roses, apricots, lavender, walnuts, apples, grapes, mushrooms, chestnuts, olives and thyme.

He felt sadness dampening his mood.

'You're a very nice man. In fact,' she said. She squeezed his hand. He shifted and held her in his arms.

'You're a nice lady. In fact.'

'When I sleep with a complete stranger?'

'That doesn't matter.'

'Do you feel like a child again, lying here?'

'Yes. Everything seems simple, lying here.'

'Yes, it does. That's why we do it.'

It occurred to him how the lights that are on at 3 A.M. in hotel bedrooms all over the world are shining on some of the attempts of men and women to go back to the beginning.

He stroked her hair, but he was sobering up, the day would come and he started to think how he'd need to be careful now. She went to the toilet. Perhaps this was not a good start, perhaps this did not augur well for the work. Perhaps he ought not to have done this.

Illuminated. That was the word for Rachel, he thought.

When she emerged, he was lying naked on his back, with his eyes open, his mouth dry, he felt bad, he felt remorseful but for whom — her, his wife, himself? He told himself it was a chemical reaction, that was all.

She knelt up alongside him, and she whispered into his ear. 'I love you.'

He pulled her across him so she could not see his face. 'Shit,' he said to himself.

7

✧

UNTIL HE GOT the Africa promotion his weekly routine hadn't much altered. He rose at six in the morning on Monday to Friday, put on a suit, and took his briefcase to his BMW like a good boy; with bad breath all that was left of the weekend.

Then, on Saturday mornings, a different man, he'd wind the window down on the Mitsubishi four-wheel drive, pull his cap forwards, feel the tug of the engine with his feet, as he moved off to spend his own time.

On the occasional Saturday during the hunting season, like the Varois men, Richard put on the camouflage trousers and green waistcoat of the *chasseur* and went off in the four-wheel drive to meet his fellows round the back of the out-of-the-way villages. In some lay-by or other, they'd stood about with their guns, smoking and giving consideration to a plan to track, hunt and kill the *sanglier,* the black pig, if seen, arranged by size in family format.

Inevitably they failed, joyfully they failed, and then they spent the rest of the Saturday drinking in one of the little bars that were obliged to close at eight since the area became a crossroads in drugs trafficking. They went home somehow incomplete, not quite drunk enough; ill humoured by the time they got indoors.

They could afford to be. 'Your wife's for life' was the mindset round there. Each was given his dinner, and would no doubt gesture with anger at the television, no matter the programme, and spoil his wife's enjoyment. On Sunday the man endured the family meal with an eye to the window, an ear to the driveway, hoping for one of his crowd to pop by so he could go outside on to the terrace to drink and talk about the previous day's hunting; about where they went wrong.

Richard amused his comrades with his concessions to family life.

'The Englishman' he remained to them, despite his eloquence. The commonest theme of their drunken banter was that whilst they hated Englishmen, Richard was OK. His grandfather always said the French were a bunch of two-faced cowards, but he never mentioned that.

Now and again he'd skip going hunting — accepting Valérie's point about him having been away all week — and then he took Valérie and Max to Aix or to Cannes; shopping. He turned himself off for the day, used the credit card. Her purchases were futile, she'd hate them next week, and he stood in various doorways with Max, between extremes of temperature, consoling the pair of them. Lunch was the highlight. She liked to eat *palourdes* and *oursins* and the kid liked calamari, and they usually drank a bottle of Cassis and got Max a grand ice-cream extravagance.

Max, at thirteen years old, never had anything to say about school or anything relating to his actual life, but he might occasionally ask something poignant — 'Do parents love their children when the children get older?' Or something meaningless, 'It won't be last week again next week . . .' And when they pushed him to clarify, he baulked and sulked, he would just allow the ditch to widen between them. 'You don't understand,' he said darkly, desperately, 'you don't understand.'

Valérie liked to talk about how she'd lost her looks.

Family life, thought Richard on one of the long silent drives home, is one of those things that is very bad for you but which is accepted as something nifty, in the way smoking was once recommended for your throat. First, you form attachments, which once broken can kill you, or worse — and there was worse. But before you got there, there was the day-to-day wear and tear on your sense of humour and your patience; the kid's feet in the back of your car seat; the reminder that you're low on the tank of bribes and about to hit punishment and that punishment came with a suicidal accessory, a double-barrelled gun with one nozzle twisted back at you.

He could reach the kid when it was just the two of them. He dropped the hunting now and again to spend time with Max. He cut the discipline crap when they were together, he knew that it was much for show, to make the older generation feel like they were in safe hands. He liked to say to Max: *Ask me anything, anything and I'll tell you the truth.*

One Sunday in June, just back from the Geneva trip, he sat under a tree, down at the bottom of the valley near the ruins of a *bastide*, and closed his eyes to better hear the shouting of his boy running down the hill. When he opened his eyes he saw the midges dancing, the boy's ears red with the sun shining through them, he saw the green moss like a lake around the trees, springing and soft, the holly bushes squat and glistening, the big firs and pines, the scrub oak with lichen, silver-barked, secret gardens inside secret gardens and he thought: *I've fallen on my arse here.* He saw with an old man's gaze, how the afternoon rose, with the light moving up the hillsides, and the sun bowed into the valley, tipping its hat to it all.

The boy flopped down beside him.

Richard rolled on to his side to look at him, one eye open.

'So go on, ask me anything, Max.'

'OK. Why do you smoke?'

'It's an addiction.'

The boy raised his eyebrows, impressed.

'Do you know what I mean by that?'

They were lying there just as he'd once lain with his son's mother on a beach; they had a photograph of it framed in the living room, the same pose; he on his right elbow, she on her left, facing each other. To him it was the image of happiness; talking and listening, side by side.

'Uh-huh.'

'Well go on then, smart arse, what is it then?'

The kid sparked up a grin, and this was how Richard loved him most, when he took an expression from elsewhere — this one like something stolen from a bride — and Richard could see how he would be, the kid, all things going well, when he was grown up.

'Yes, I have the same thing. It's like with chess.'

'Being addicted to chess?'

'It's like when I walk away after playing it, I can't stop myself walking like the knight moves. You know?'

'Yeah, it's like that, Max. Ask me another.'

'How much money do we have?'

'I don't know. About five hundred thousand, maybe more, but I couldn't use it right away, some of it's in the house.'

'Is that a lot?'

'Well. It depends on your point of view.'

'It sounds like a lot.'

'Ask me what you really want to know, Max. About women. Girls. You know.'

34

'Oh that.' The kid sat up. 'I know what happens. But you need your balls to drop, right?'

'Well, yes. Yes. You've heard about it at school then.'

'Axel's done it with his cousin.'

'He's just having you on, showing off.'

'No. He did it. I know he did.'

'Absolute rubbish, Max. He's too young. You can't.' He remembered with some embarrassment his own efforts at that age.

'No. I know the words. Pussy. You know.'

'Yes. Right. Well, all in good time. No need to rush. The sex thing's a piece of cake. It's the rest of it that's difficult. Ha. Life.'

'Uh-huh.'

'Not much bloody use, am I?' He laughed nervily and shook his son's knee for reassurance. 'You can ask Axel for the grubby details!'

'Do you think Jesus was the Son of God? I don't.'

'No?'

'No. Not as in the only son of God. I spoke to the priest about it the other day.'

'You went to church?'

'Yes, it was empty. It always is. I like it. You know, Dad, I am the Son of God.'

'Max . . .'

'No, I am. I am. You too. We all are. It wasn't just him. Maybe he was trying to give people a clue, but he didn't have to be so like look-at-me about it. I mean we can all do miracles and heal people and stuff. If we want. Magic. After all, you know, we invented God, he didn't invent us.'

'OK.' Richard didn't know what else to say.

'I mean, I have seen him. Christ. He told me he was just a man.'

'Don't be silly.'

'In a dream.'

'Oh. OK.'

'The other thing is that I wish I had a different mother because she's not on the light side. You know, like in *Star Wars*. She's gone over to the dark side. I don't want her to take me with her so I'm going to have to do something to stop her.'

'Well, we all feel a bit cross with each other sometimes.' Richard chanced a look at his son, he could see the vein in the side of his boy's head, pulsing. 'You're a big thinker, Max.'

'She doesn't read, does she, Mum? She ought to have at least read the Bible. I'm doing that and I'm only thirteen.'

'Well, not everyone does read. It doesn't always help. Look at your grandfather. Since Grandma taught him to read he's been totally confused.'

'*Putain, this makes my head hurt . . .*' Max swung his head low, in imitation of Guy.

Richard laughed.

'It's a shame. But she'll have to go. Mother. She doesn't love us.'

'Oh, Max. Just be a kid. Stay cool, as your grandfather would say. Cool.'

They rose and dusted themselves down and Richard put an arm around his son's shoulder as they walked back up the hill. He felt a mix of wary emotions, and a touch of elation, because his son was estranged from her too and now they were complicit.

8

✧

HE WAS LOOKING SMART CASUAL, wearing a suit but no tie, at the Four Seasons hotel bar in Cairo. His company was the main sponsor of the African Psychiatry Conference. The barman pushed olives, crackers and hot nuts his way and Richard consumed three cold beers.

It was a grand marble emporium throughout; the hotel and the bedrooms were luxurious to the global standard. One only knew one was in Africa at all because of the constant telephone interruptions of the staff.

He'd sat on the toilet in his bathroom that afternoon, fielding calls — 'Er, Mr Bird? Yes, sorry for the interruption, are you aware of the functioning of the air conditioner system?' — and using the bidet as his library, stowing there the conference programme and the folders of facilities the hotel afforded.

From the bath he lay looking at the bathrobe behind the bathroom door. In all his travels, he had never taken one down from its lynching.

He stood dripping wet in front of the bed, untying one and laying the robe out with its arms wide, and he felt curiously disembodied. Unobserved, one fell apart; nothing made sense. He turned to the wardrobe. His suit on the hanger seemed strange to him too. What an undertaking it was to dress oneself in costume day in, day out.

Down at the bar, a man sat two stools down from him with a fashion-beard, colour tone *'barely there'*. When Richard lit a cigarette, he started to wave a slender hand in front of his face and Richard sat biding his time, waiting for him to say something, knowing he would. Richard smoked the cigarette with moral fervour.

He'd been up and on the pavement outside the hotel at seven, waiting for the conference bus. He'd been subpoenaed to the World Psychiatry Conference to testify to Europharm's interest in African psychiatric learning; the more exotic studies presented by the Dutch or Danish young lady docs — spirit travel amongst the Kamba — and the more practical by the young African doctors — post-traumatic distress in the Johannesburg townships. He was there to shake hands and reassure them of Europharm's commitment to their peccadillo, mostly over dinners and drinks.

The bus driver was late. An hour late. He complained to a young idiot with a clipboard who replied to him: *This is Egyptian time, sir.* The entire city passed him by distributed in family-sized arrangements on motorcycles, jeering. Ladas hooted. One honked at his ankles, and he jumped out of the way, then seeing the hand gestures and moustachioed smiles of the driver cajoling him, he got in the back of it. The driver was euphoric; with wailing radio, cigarette in mouth, he hastened into a 1950s sepia panorama, driving at the haze. They crossed the Nile and the driver sang along to the Arabic music with moody conviction.

There was no conference bus for his return to the hotel either, so he took another Lada taxi. The similarly moustachioed man in his long beige *jellaba* implied, with tilting head and sorrowful looks, that the back door handle was not working and Richard would be obliged to sit up front. No sooner were they in the thick of the ten-lane traffic, nipping in and out of each stream willy-nilly, when the man started badgering him in his language. Richard found he could understand it quite well unfortunately. It was bound to be about money or sex. He hoped it was the former. He looked out of the window, away from the driver. Not put off in the least, the driver touched Richard's wedding ring and laughed and laughed. He then used hand gestures to ask Richard whether he wouldn't like a drink with a straw, quite a thick straw. Richard pointed at the road. Cars were veering off it here and there quite suddenly, cars that had simply run out of petrol or given up the ghost, donkey carts hared into the gap in the mêlée, and boys with goats walked up the central grassy aisle of the twenty-lane road into Cairo.

He was mulling it over now, four beers in. He'd never had sex with a man. Valérie's father, who did his military service in Algeria, said he had. His life was a plausible tale until you hit Algeria and thereafter it was anyone's guess what really happened. He said he'd been buggered in Cognac, the place. They had clinked glasses. Your health! Good times, the old man said, back then you could ask a woman to piss on you and she would. It made him smile to think of Guy and his plain way of talking.

The young man at the bar spoke up now. 'Don't make me the passive smoker also.'

Dutch. Richard rolled his eyes and went to put out the cigarette.

'Can I have one, if you don't mind? I'm trying to renounce it . . .' He was a gamin little fellow with merry eyes.

They got talking. He was a Transcultural Psychiatrist, he said. 'Want to come up to the roof bar and meet my friend?'

'Is he also a Transcultural Psychiatrist?'

'The father of them.' They got up from their stools and made their way past the sad eyes of the doorman, who wished them all the good in the world, 'What about you . . . are you also a psychiatrist?'

'I'm a salesman. The mother of all salesmen. I've just been appointed Head of Sales for Europharm Africa.'

'Well, my God, then you're very important. You must come and have a drink with us. We can tell you all about Africa.' The young man pressed the elevator button. The elevator shaft was glass and gold and neon lit. They stepped out into the hot jammy air of the Cairo night.

There were low latticework tables with *shishas*, the settees were draped with *assuit* shawls, there were brass plates and goblets and ostrich plumes, lamps swinging and rock music playing. Down in the streets of Cairo below, twenty-seven million people were in different states of wakefulness and sleep, crammed in hovels. Osama bin Laden's face was on the TV screen behind the bar. A group of businessmen were sitting up there, drinking beers, hands digging into bowls of nuts.

Richard and his friend ordered a drink and some apple-flavoured tobacco for the *shisha*. A man walked over to them wearing a pale linen suit. His hair was almost blue-grey, his face in contrast very tanned and his eyes a vivid blue.

'Stefan!'

'Michael!'

'Ja! Here! Here! Join us. Join us.'

Richard was introduced and they set to drinking and taking turns at the *shisha*. Pretty soon the Transculturalists were, for Richard's benefit, discussing the tying and binding of psychotics in faraway places. They moved on to Islamic anti-female practices. They all had a lot to drink so things became more universal, less humourous. Michael told Richard that they had come up from Burundi where they were counselling the survivors of the war suffering from post-traumatic stress disorder. There were millions of people there who had seen their parents, or their children, butchered. There was a pause but Richard did not offer up where he had come from and what went on there.

Stefan had been working in Africa since the 1970s; a small man who donned big-man imagery; motorbikes, ganja smoking, he'd played the cavalry of psychiatry, lamping round Africa, claiming deranged souls for the Prince of Orange.

'They've lined me up for some doctor-shadowing in Kenya,' said Richard. 'I want to get to know the region; grass roots.' It was dreary, he thought, what he'd become, but he could never help himself saying what he thought others wanted to hear.

'Africa's one big mess. That is all you need to know.' Michael's striped shirt broke out in checks. He went right on to tell them that as a gay Transcultural Psychiatrist he'd found it very hard to get sex with a man in Afghanistan but it wasn't exactly a bowl of cherries in Burundi either.

Michael's cheer was minty fresh once he'd come out. It turned out he had arranged a date for later on that evening with a local man. He explained how in New York you could have sex with a man and when you asked him his name he refused to tell it to you, it was considered too intimate. There was a lot to this Transculturalism business, it seemed.

'It's a predicament,' said Richard. It occurred to him that all of our endeavours — work, war, charity, altruistic or not — might in fact just be ways of getting sex with strangers.

The three parted ways at the lobby, Stefan and Richard leaving Michael to try first names with a stranger, whilst they went to the dinner. The bus was pulling in, two and a quarter hours late.

Forty minutes later, the busload of ageing shrinks pulled up in front of three pyramids. Rudely woken, furry mouthed, the docs staggered through the sand to a marquee, open at the front with more low brass tables. There were a couple of camels outside and some dancers waiting in rags and sequins, bras and big trousers. Two belly dancers were checking the plasters on each other's heels.

Inside a line of delegates were standing, one by one, plate in hand waiting for a turn at the tureen. Richard bought a bottle of wine and he and Stefan went and stood side by side, admiring the pyramids — three of them and beside them, to their left, their spectral doubles, like holograms, an optical illusion. A camel pulled on its leash, swayed over to them and urinated; the two men stepped aside.

Richard thought he ought to say something intelligent, Stefan being the sort of man who inspired it; he was really bad company. He was very tired, then, of spending time with strangers; one got so far, a potted version of one's experience life-wise, and never any further, and it got more and more condensed and the only thing to hope for was that the other person knew something you didn't. He found he had nothing to say and hoped his silence would seem thoughtful. He yearned to be in a pub, in England, laughing.

Stefan put a hand on Richard's shoulder. 'I was wanting to say to you when we were on the roof—look down there, all of that can be yours. I wanted to say you must choose between three things. You can get rid of one of these from the world, you have only to choose, and all the world will be yours. You can get rid of madness, also sadness, also evil if you like to. So choose now.'

'Right.'

'OK. What do you choose?' Stefan tightened his hold on Richard's shoulder.

'Is all the fun happening out here?' It was Yvette Ducasse in a sequinned cocktail dress. She looked drunk.

'Hello there, nice to see you,' said Richard, horrified.

'Hello there, nice to see you too,' she replied, offering him her hand. She put out one leg and lowered her height by a couple of inches. She was wearing heels. 'I've just been to one of these in Stuttgart and it was even worse. You don't have a cigarette, do you?'

Shrinks smoked knowing how well nicotine worked, but only away from home. Good salesmen knew it and bought cigarettes duty-free on the way out to those conferences. Richard handed her a pack.

'Here, take it.'

'Thank you.'

She pressed her lips together, looked down at the packet and then as no one said anything more, she nodded slowly, gave a curt laugh, and said, 'Well, see you then.'

'We have history,' said Stefan indifferently, 'she and I. So. Have you chosen, Richard?'

'Really?'

'You have forgotten the question.'

'Yes, I'm afraid so.'

Stefan took another mouthful from the wine, and then he passed the bottle back to Richard. 'Think about it. The sad, the mad, the bad. These are relatives. Two we can medicate, one we cannot. That is the one that must go when the others are extinguished. For sure. That's the plan, that's what we're all fighting for. And here in Africa is a new battleground, a war which can be won.'

'Oh, but aren't they all just part of the spectrum of normal . . .'

'There is nothing normal any more. Normal has gone. The world is changing, we have many problems. Too many people wanting the same things.'

I'm not sure I care, he wanted to say. It would be a terrible thing to say. He had to pretend. He had to pretend he wanted to hear this more than a log fire, a pint and some idle chat.

Yvette was standing in the queue for the bar, looking miserable.

Two or three men jumped the queue and she seemed to go farther back than forwards. The last he'd heard from her was a Post-it note attached to a stack of reading material she sent him from Geneva. There was a dossier, complete from pre-war Kenya with handwritten notes, a diary, letters, all belonging to one man who'd served the British medical authorities there. She'd put on the Post-it note 'With love, Yvette' and added her mobile phone number. He'd not called it. She'd also sent him some very strange documents that were hardly of any use to him in his company position, quite the opposite. One was the first-ever published WHO monograph, a curious old academic paper written by the English doctor in the 1950s. It suggested first that madness, from neurosis to psychosis, did not exist in Africa until the Europeans came. Googling the man he found the trail of his influence. His work was the basis of much 1970s literature on the same theme, and Richard ordered one or two of the books. Max had taken to one of them, and he'd been pleased Max was reading in English, even if it was a strange thing to start with, *The Origin of Consciousness in the Breakdown of the Bicameral Mind.* He'd bought him Harry Potter and the boy had said something quite rude about it and taken up this book instead. It was quite a stretch, he thought, for a thirteen-year-old for whom English was not his first language.

'There's this man,' Richard said to Stefan, 'I read about, the first psychiatrist in Africa, he claimed that before the whites got

44

there, there was more or less no mental illness at all in the tribal societies he saw. No such thing as depression at all.'

'Ah shit, man! This kind of thinking is bad science. Hey. Don't shoot me in the back when I tell you this is racial bullshit. We have established the biological causes of mental illness. Enough.'

'Yes. I know. I know. But I was very surprised to find it in my briefing pack from the WHO. I mean, say it was true? I know it's not, of course, but imagine . . . Imagine selling sadness to Africa of all places, selling them pathological sadness . . .'

'Who sent it to you?'

'The lady who just asked us for cigarettes.'

'Yvette Ducasse? She's overemotional. Listen, Richard man, those papers, use them to wipe your arse. That woman, she is just a soldier. I turned that position down. And also this man you mention must, I think, be McClintoch. He had sex with lions. Ja. And also he was a racist. He measured African skulls. Completely discredited. Completely.'

'Oh, really? I didn't know that.'

'Sure. And also you drink too much.'

He looked at his empty glass. Stefan was right. They went and joined the queue for the buffet, Stefan nodding and waving at many of the doctors, falafel rolling from his plate on to the ground. Richard knelt to pick up one or two and looked across the thousands of psychiatrists squatting on short stools around the low tables. Yvette was on a bench that was covered with a kilim rug at the side of the great tent, passed out, draped over it, one arm pointing to the floor.

He went over to her and knelt down to try and rouse her, to save her the embarrassment. She opened her eyes, and took his hand in hers. She would not let go and he would not make a scene so he was obliged to stay there; like a dog stuck in the act, he cast looks about himself.

'Why did you send me those papers?' he said. She opened an eye and a grey tongue-tip popped out to moisten her lips.

'It's obvious, Richard.'

'But I'm just a soldier,' he said, borrowing Stefan's phrase.

'Yes,' she said, 'I know. But what you said about the land, it made me think you were a good person, deep down . . .' She closed her eyes. He pushed her hair back from her face. She squeezed his hand. *Like a little girl,* he thought. But she wasn't. She was the Head of the Mental Health Department at the World Health Organization. She had told him she loved him, after one dinner, after having sex just the once!

'God, I'm so sorry,' he whispered and shook her hand. He tilted his head to look from under his brow around the room at all the shrinks whose hands he ought to be shaking. He couldn't think how he was going to raise a smile and yet that was what was required of him. She wouldn't loosen her grip on him.

'I like this coffee cup someone has in our department. It makes me smile,' she whispered. 'It's got on it, "You don't have to be mad to work here but it helps." That makes me smile. It is so true. Richard, I thought I was in love with you.'

9

$\diamondsuit$

FOR THE WHOLE of August that year the Var was paralysed with heat and longing and the days were apathetic and the nights hopeful. Richard took his annual leave for the entire month. There was a new community of younger ex-pat families who had so taken to each other over the last year that they could barely be apart a night and it culminated that August in a spate of parties at their neighbours' house and everybody known ever so slightly in attendance, even Guy and Simone. The English, couples of all ages, the Dutch and some of the more well-to-do locals, and even Guy and Simone, through Richard and Valérie, were called to partake in the cosmopolitan bonhomie.

It had started with a few dinners, once every month, then it picked up pace to be weekly parties, and every other night drinks, couple on couple and so on.

The previous September he'd taken his son to school in the mornings and noticed the large number of new foreigner couples clad in rather bohemian clothes, looking shabby in a way the locals did not, standing around, shaking hands or kissing cheeks and heading for coffee together, exchanging names and histories; some talk about discount airlines' latest rates, the expense of London cabs.

Every morning his company car had crept into the village past those flushed-faced people taking their places in the cafés, waving the flag of their broadsheet English-language newspapers, toot-tooting at each other from their people movers, *'Sweetheart, I am so hungover!'*

His wife had no female friends. He'd doubted she'd take to any of the ex-pat women never mind all their bloke-ish denial of gender, their combat trousers, their swear words, their curry fixations. But they were asked as a couple to the parties and they went to each and every one, if he was home, though most happened during the working week and occurred unpredictably with phones ringing and gravel whirling, kids in pyjamas thrown into the back of the car. She'd started to go ahead of him and even without him. She said she was making friends.

Gatherings went on at Jeff and Rachel's great villa until the early hours on what was still partially a construction site with children paddling in half-filled pools and open cesspits, hurling *pétanque boules* around, lighting fires and calling each other names, all just beyond their parents' view, trailing around with shitty arses and occasionally coming into sight being upbraided by their fishfinger-flipping mummies for brandishing sticks as guns.

Valérie's parents went dressed in their best, as Elizabeth Taylor and Eminem, she in a long dress with coastal frontage, and he in his white nylon tracksuit, showing a vest where it was unzipped to the waist. Guy buoyed himself with red wine before going up, all the while deploring the fact that the foreigners spoke English in France.

They went up past Jeff's vineyard, on the lane that was lined with olive and pine trees shimmering in the thick of the heat. In the driveway they strolled past the four-wheel drives, the long Mercedes estates and the novelty 2CV that seemed so mournful, sagging into the gravel. Simone would take a bag of grass with her; it was her new business venture. Guy was growing the plants on their terrace.

Sitting down to dinner was a fuss with the chummy protocol over the boy/girl thing. The couples were flirtatious outside of their couple as the evening progressed. The rule was 'don't cross the line', no hands; only where the line was drawn was never clear. The sexual themes to the conversation were intense, and it surprised Richard coming fresh from his own secret life that they didn't find it dangerous, that it was no kind of foreplay, that they didn't get aroused, that once they got these things out they managed to put things back in the box in the right order afterwards.

These themes usually emerged before dessert. The covert search for intimacy was conducted in drink, in forcing a moment, herding everyone towards it, everyone present must come to the table of nakedness, but like the pot of gold, the intimacy disappeared before anyone could get there.

Simone and Guy began the dancing, moving together with practised choreography. After their generation, dance-wise, everything had fallen to pieces, and the younger couples joined in with some slovenly pogo-ing and breast shaking. At this point of the evening, Richard usually smoked outside with Jeff and the Dutchmen and chatted over the events of the day: the Arab kids were burning cars down in Nice, socially France was falling apart; the unions were crippling the country.

Adele, an Englishwoman, took up a broom to sing into and made them laugh at her big-lipped pouting, then she bent over and mooned them. Her husband watched impassively.

It was a return to the school disco. The outdoor stereo surging, the ex-pats converged upon the kitchen to seek saucepans and ladles and form a band and the heartbreak of a German who lived in a shack down beyond came up in his truck with a huge searchlight and beamed it on the revellers. He screamed over the hedge, 'I cannot sleep. I cannot sleep.'

The Dutch wife called back, 'You should have thought about that in 1939!' And they turned the sound back up.

On the last Saturday in that August the couples rallied in the local town for dinner, the bottles kept coming and the staff brought out plates; cassoulet for the boys and aioli for the women, the women in shining dresses, the men in Bermuda shorts. A wily estate agent had taken a break from his kidney dialysis to open a nightclub in a cellar and put in there a leftover 1960s band who took a pause from their own illnesses to play cover versions and it was there they went after the meal.

Guy was ejected from the nightclub when a wineglass smashed to the floor, more than likely because his tracksuit seemed to be wallet-less. In solidarity, the whole crew shipped out, high on inebriate principle, and the estate agent stood at the door, scolding his bouncer for his loss. It was like the UN leaving a war zone, the roundabout weeds trembled as four-by-fours took it at full speed and the party moved predictably to Jeff and Rachel's.

They stood in the kitchen, with the lights on bright and all the surfaces white under the glare. It was after two in the morning. There was some desultory dancing outside by the ladies, but the men retired to the dining table with bottles and glasses and, shortly, first Valérie then the other women followed so that the Dutch couple, the two English couples, Jeff and Rachel, Valérie and Richard, were sitting around the long table drinking together, eating cheese and biscuits and smoking pot. It was three in the morning.

'Does anyone know where our children are?' quipped Jeff, shaking his head and lighting up. The bottle was passed around and emptied, and he went to get another. No one had any intention of leaving.

'We should see this thing through,' said Simon, Adele's husband, winking, his lips puckering as he topped himself up and took a trembling sip, drawing from the rim as if it were a pint of beer. 'Here's to our happy life in the Var. God bless us all,' he said, raising his glass.

Rachel put on a U2 track and urged them to listen to it. Some nodded, some shook their heads. They were drunk and overcome. They traced the lines of the song with their mouths.

'But we're not the same . . .'

Rachel had been thinking about Africa, she said, and her eyes were brimming with tears. 'The problem of our times,' she said, 'and here we are in paradise.'

Simon played the track 'The Drugs Don't Work' as they passed Simone's weed between them.

Adele sat listening to the lyrics, lost in her thoughts, ostentatiously gloomy, biting her lip, her eyes bulging.

Rachel was describing the disparities between Africa and the USA. She was shaking. Jeff put his head in his hands. Across from Rachel, the Dutchman looked grave, Joop's chin was on his chest. A telltale snort gave him away as having nodded off.

'I had that falling off the sidewalk thing again,' he said to his wife.

Rachel stood up. She was flushed, her chest was high. She looked, Richard thought, like he felt when he was having one of his little crises. She had long red hair. Her skin was limpid and nothing was adhering to it. Her under-eyes were smudged with a ring of kohl that looked like a rubbed-out pencil mark. Her mouth was slipping off her face.

'I'm going to show you something. I said I wouldn't show it to anyone but I am going to.' And with that, she went, in fits and starts, rather like a ball bearing in a pinball machine, between sofas and chairs into a side room and came back with a DVD.

'Oh, Rachel, for God's sake, no,' said Jeff, raising his head from his hands to see the joint was out.

'What is it?' asked Valérie.

'You dirty buggers,' grinned Simon, rubbing his hands.

'Come on then, I'm up for it,' said Adele.

It was a documentary made using a handheld camera of the civil war in Sierra Leone. There were no opening credits. In the first scene, from under the tin roof of a colonnade of shops, the camera panned to take in a street with three or four dead women face forward with their arms outstretched before them, a toddler on its back with its mouth open, and it moved to focus on a teen-age boy being held by another, on his knees, his head thrust back with the barrel of a gun at the nape of his neck. You could see one of the boy's legs from the side. You could see the cross-hatched sole of the flip-flop, the button of the toe strap out; umbilical. Bang. The boy collapsed. Dead.

'Bloody hell,' said Simon.

Jeff got up, strode over to the television and turned it off. 'That's enough,' he said.

'I'm going home,' said Valérie, standing. 'This is stupid. *Je ne suis pas d'accord.* Stupid. I can't watch any more.'

Rachel put her hands in her hair. 'We must go to Africa and help them. We can't just sit here doing nothing!' The others were sobering up quickly.

'We know your heart's in the right place, Rachel,' Richard said.

'We've got to be going,' said Adele. She put an arm around Rachel, squeezed her, looked into her face and put her thumbs to the sides of Rachel's wet eyes. She hugged her, 'Come on, love, don't upset yourself.'

Simon patted her shoulder as he rose. 'Come on, love, cheer up.'

'I can't cheer up,' she said, sitting down at the table, alone now that everyone else had stood. 'Don't go. Don't leave me,' she said as they went out into the hallway. 'Don't go. Don't leave me. Don't go.'

Jeff was at the front door, turning on the porch light and bidding their friends goodnight. After the last had gone, he went to bed, ignoring her at the table, passing her by.

'You embarrassed yourself,' he said to her when she climbed into bed alongside him, and he turned on to his side, holding the edge of the bed, feeling for the lamp switch.

'I'm lonely. I don't know what the point is of anything any more,' she said in a small voice.

'You've had too much to drink. We're lucky. That's all. Like you can help Africa! Like they need your help! Go to sleep.'

'It's not just the drink. I feel this pain inside of me, I don't know why . . . Why do I feel like this? Is it loneliness? Fear? Is something very wrong? Is something bad going to happen? Do you love me?'

'It's not a good idea to talk about this stuff now when we've had a lot to drink.' He closed his eyes and lips in three firm lines. He clicked the lamp switch.

10

✧

THE SMELL OF AFRICA hit Richard as he stepped off the plane in Nairobi; a slightly oriental smell; water on the boil, mouldy rubber; the hot-water bottle. He noted the amber light on the face of the driver as they headed along the airport roads, well peopled but alien with enormous mobile-phone billboards, and the people, wandering, looking back over their shoulders, in their improbably coloured clothes — green, pink, red — matte, dark skinned, their heels triangles of coral pink, down to earth.

The driver issued peaceable words to the men at the several security checks on the way out, 'Sa-sa, sa-sa. Sawa.' He wore a cardigan. Here, so close to the equator, they dressed as if it were cold. The little kids with their red woollen balaclavas, the ladies with skirt suits and sweaters.

In the back of a rubbish truck, four people trod rubbish and grinned, holding on to the back of the driver's cab, thrilled to the teeth. The mottoed minibuses criss-crossed the lanes, glory in transit, crammed full of life, scandalous. A group of pedestrians with heavy loads passed like the dead carrying their own grave-stones. As the minivan pulled up, the sound of the cicadas entered through the open window along with the belch of modern Africa; dirt and diesel.

Soon Richard's mind would close like a daisy in the evening time, he would no longer see this in the blinding light of arrival, he would be back in the realm of his work, moving towards the white as they moved towards the black and he would no longer wave back at the children who presented him their salutes.

He was here to make contact with the Head of Psychiatric Services for Kenya. He sat, his fist at his mouth, considering the meeting. He had found the best approach was to hold back. He would set out his stall by proposing to sponsor the department and the training module for new psychiatrists specifically. He had with him ten laptops loaded with the drugs trials and stats and psychiatric reference material. On the next visit he would be offering them brand-name compounds at special rates conditional on monopoly.

The Head of the Psychiatry Department at the government teaching hospital, Dr Wainanga, would want more than a laptop before giving any sort of commitment. This was how it always ran. His driver's questions went unanswered while he thought about this. What could he justify? He struggled to bring the figures to mind; *Year one, a market base of... a market penetration of* . . . He saw himself suited before the board, 'Brand share, ladies and gentlemen, one hundred per cent.' Where else was this possible? He could give the man an early Christmas present.

The next day he visited the hospital and presented the psychiatry department with the laptops. A former patient took the photos of Dr Wainanga and Richard holding each other's right hand, smiling for more than five minutes, almost as if in the process of transfusion, before the doctor cried out with impatience at the useless photographer. The boy had come to them after his brother reported him for stealing his potatoes. He was, however, in fact

55

schizophrenic, said the doctor through his teeth, still waiting for the flash. So many of them were. Undiagnosed. As yet. Flash!

'Bingo!' Dr Wainanga quipped, sliding his palm free. 'Will you be adding a safari to your trip?' he enquired. His staff and students, biscuit nibblers, were circling, the laptops on tables were open and shining, a technical kid at each of them with his memory key out like a thermometer, checking their health.

'No,' he said, 'I'm only here for work.'

'Such a shame,' the doctor brightened.

One of the first things the British had done when they got to East Africa at the turn of the century was to build a railway. That done, they built a lunatic asylum, the Mathari. When the photo session was over, Richard and Dr Wainanga went up to view it.

They traipsed round the bungalows and their animal runs looking at the inmates, with a bit of guidance from the doctor tour guide as to the exhibiting disorders. The men wore blue calico trousers and the women wore shift dresses, A-line, made of the same hard fabric.

A woman took Richard's hand. Her hand was sticky. Her two front teeth had a cliff line of calcium across them, they stuck out of her mouth like doll's legs. Her face was warty. Eight years in two bare concrete cells, and burnt-out women came and went, as lifeless as she, swept in and swept out. They came empty-handed and stayed that way. All they carried was in their heads.

One round room with five decrepit beds. One oblong room into which big round plastic bowls were brought, one with rice, one with stew, and big plastic containers of water and plastic cups, three times a day. One cooler wall, one hotter wall, concrete between them. Gardening work down by the slums, a chance to look over the fence.

The doctor translated the whispers of the woman who had

Richard's hand, her grasp now tightly congealed. He was not generally a hand holder. He never even held his wife's hand.

'She says she's in here because she's ugly. She killed her children in fact.'

The woman gazed at him romantically. He felt a coursing sense of shame and revulsion; it was hard to say which came first.

The doctor was an intern. He was young. He had questions that would not wait. 'Excuse me, Mr Bird, I just wanted to ask about this World Health Organization programme which I know your company is sponsoring. So much money, you see, and if you are from this country and you see what I see and where money is needed, then you have questions. Please forgive me if it seems rude to ask why so much money is being spent persuading our peoples that they are mad . . .'

'That is not the case,' put in Dr Wainanga quickly, 'there are plenty of people in this country who are severely mentally ill. Just as in Europe. You will be sure to see that in Nyeri, Mr Bird, when you get to visit my friend's clinic there. Yes, you will be sure to see those long, long queues for the outpatients clinic. It is a fact that every bed on the psychiatric ward is taken one hundred per cent of the time. This service is oversubscribed. So you see we are thinking, naturally, here in Kenya it would be a good thing to get to our people those drugs which will allow them to lead normal functioning lives from their homes. This is a very important thing for you to know. You must write this in your notes. Please do not go back and forget what you are seeing here in our country.'

The intern was from Nyeri too, he said. The White Highlands, it was known as once. The people there, his people, the Kikuyu, were once used as indentured labour, then they fought back. The

British medical establishment in the colony described them as 'psychotic'.

'Of course things changed after the war,' Dr Wainanga grinned. 'And after independence the ringleaders became the first government.' He laughed and Richard smiled. 'They were political protestors not psychotics. And that was a long time ago, before we knew about the biological bases of mental illness,' he added hastily, mopping his brow.

They were standing in the heat of a corridor, looking down to the few patients tending the vegetable patch before the high wall. The intern continued doggedly.

'I am concerned that our conception of the mind, as Africans, is based on a map drawn by a world that was empire and colony. The African mind is different, that is true, but the reason for this is of course cultural and not genetic and what may seem to be aberrant to a European may be quite normal within the context . . .'

'What has that to do with Mr Bird?' Dr Wainanga exclaimed. 'He is a businessman not a philosopher!'

They passed back alongside the wire runs of the African patients, with Dr Wainanga continuing to recover ground by explaining the diagnoses of the patients held there, poking fun at the young man slightly by referring to his 'learned friend', whom he suggested would of course offer a more modern diagnosis — such as 'depersonalization disorder', he threw out, to show that he too knew his stuff. His cheeks were round. He rocked back and forth on the balls of his feet. He was a survivor, Richard thought, just the sort of man he could work with. He would never be able to work with someone like the intern. The intern would be a pain in the neck.

They made but a brief tour of the final ward, in which a number of the beds had only three legs, like shipwrecks. Richard could not imagine what contortions were required to sleep on them. Dr Wainanga insisted on showing him the latrines.

'Lamentable,' he said, in the doorway.

One young man, naked apart from a raincoat, followed them out, stood up at the fence grinning and calling out, 'Manchester United! Queen Elizabeth! David Beckham!'

They stood in front of the verandahed whitewashed bungalow offices that had once belonged to the colonial-era chief psychiatrists.

After a brief enervated exchange in Swahili with the intern, Dr Wainanga excused himself for a few minutes to get them some soft drinks.

'Mr Bird,' the young man began, and from his earnest expression Richard could tell what was coming was going to cause him discomfort. 'I am a young man who loves his country and his people. Personally, of my own efforts and using my own salary and time, I am trying to put together a programme which offers local people free counselling. If your company were able to help, it would be very little money for you, and of course we'd name the centre after your company, whichever you prefer. Please excuse me. I am most passionate about this. Could you help us, please?'

'Indirectly, possibly.'

'Indirectly?'

'Yes, not directly. With supplies. Drugs. Possibly. If it were to meet certain criteria and conditions.'

'Oh. I see. But we need tables and chairs, you see, and to pay the rent on a small building, just one or two rooms. I wonder if you could see this as some sort of publicity, whereby your company would be associated with recovery, perhaps that's it. What is your company's objective here in Kenya, Mr Bird?'

'My company's objective is to make a profit for its shareholders,' he said stiffly. He turned around to look for Wainanga.

Shit, he said to himself. Shit.

Nobody said anything as they went into the administration block. The three of them — he, the intern and Dr Wainanga — sat with the matron and other members of staff who'd been summoned, on wasted sofas, sipping warm Fantas. It took him quite a while to realize that the visit was over and they were all waiting for him to announce his departure.

11

✦

RACHEL BIT INTO Jeff's leg when she pushed their daughter into the world, then she counted the fingers and toes of the baby and got out of the birthing pool, dried and dressed herself and took her daughter home while Jeff slept on, on the birthing bed. When he got in a few hours later she was already established as a mother, feeding the baby, crying at the news on TV and so it went on for what seemed to Jeff like a very long time; Rachel in a night-dress, leaking love.

He fell by the wayside. He stole out early evening to find a more complex kind of life in the dark of nightclubs, watching people be sweet and saucy, wrapping themselves around each other. He'd come home and piss the bed and be sorry about it.

It was the baby's old-fashioned looks that touched his heart, not to mention the crazy leg-kicking when she saw his bony face. He put her little fat hands on to his rough beard and spoke to her with wide-eyed affection.

Rachel met Jeff at her place of work in Manhattan, where he hung morosely, the Creative Director of a small ad agency, a forty-two-year-old bachelor, high and dry due to the repeated obfuscations of his friend and business 'partner' regarding the 'partnership'.

His boss, Don Abrams, was a multi-rused multimillionaire who ran on Diet Coke and spleen and made Jeff's life a misery of want, tempting him with some celebrity acquaintances into thinking he was going to have a life worth watching. And Jeff was easily tempted.

Because the boss said he liked Rachel, it gave Jeff the idea to take her to bed, several times, and he even told her she had nice lips. But he never did say that he loved her. Rachel omitted to take her pill and Jeff, perhaps jaded with picking off the floor his gay neighbours and perhaps embarrassed about having been picked off the floor himself when the recreational drug went up the alphabet from *e* to *k*, decided to move in with Rachel. He came with very little of use or worth to live with her in her stifling top-floor apartment in Brooklyn. She cooked, she washed and ironed, she kept beer in the place, she took care of his needs in order to keep him there.

She was determined to save him. Her mother had killed herself. She wasn't going to let anything like that happen again. She could see he could go one way or the other, so she offered herself as an example to him. She went window-shopping for a small loving God, and found one convenient to their home, a nice Dutch Presbyterian church, and she herself was very stirred by the communal prayers and coffee mornings. *We are all in this together,* she liked to think, lumbering up and down the hills in the bitter winds with rice cakes and peeled miniature carrots and juice boxes for the mothers and children's group.

She kept taped copies of the sermons from church and Jeff listened and tapped her knuckles with his fingertips at the good parts. He could see their point; God wasn't all bad. She asked the pastor to marry them and when he interviewed them he informed Jeff he would be marrying a Christian woman. Any questions?

'Why do I cry at communion?' asked Rachel, and the old pastor smiled at her with his Ray Charles head-wobble.

'The Lord is with you then,' he said.

She felt a most highly favoured lady with all the love that was coming into her and going out of her. She was wrecked physically with the additional weight, some forty pounds of overenthusiasm, and when she went to see the doctor just the week before she gave birth on account of her haemorrhoids, she learnt a new word. '*Yowzer.*'

About six months into little Maud's life, Don Abrams turned up at their door. He was a man with a lot of friends who didn't like him. He was wealthy, a little tight-fisted, but the combination kept people on their toes and he was dubbed 'charismatic'. He was attractive, ugly as he was, huge and volatile and he insinuated himself into everything he could, in counterpoise to Jeff who hesitated and stood apart. Whereas Don knew he was master, Jeff never knew he was servant. They were like bread and butter, and they needed each other, and after they met, Jeff never went free of him. He knew he should mistrust him, all the women in his life told him so, but being better than the man seemed like such a pittance he couldn't be bothered with it. He just wanted to stand in that man's wake, in the sidelines, penniless but possibly superior in some way.

Don Abrams, founder of several advertising agencies, came there with disaster on his hands. His only son, a teenager by the second of his four marriages, had taken his life in a cupboard in their place in the Hamptons with one of his father's handguns. Don had found him and handled the necessary. It was August, he'd been up there on his annual vacation. It would hit the papers the next day. He wanted to hide, he wanted to drink. And so Rachel and Jeff hid him, and gave him drink for a week, and the three of them talked every evening after supper, lying on the floor with heads on the bottom of the sofa, in that single girl's apartment, side by side, and they managed to get the big man through his bad week.

Don in turn humbled himself prettily, did the dishes, and amused the baby by pretending to drink from the bottle. And they marvelled at their handiwork, the fruit of compassion, in bed together they reviewed the man's true qualities once under their roof, and Jeff was impressed with the magic of Rachel's Christianity and what it could effect. He told them everything, Don, about his life, his regrets, he said he had done some bad things. He doubted he could change.

'It was the worst of times and the best of times,' said Don on his way out. He added, 'She's too good for you, you great dope.' And gave Jeff a little mugging slappity-slap on the side of his jaw.

Jeff tipped his head out of the way and stepped back. 'Yeah, yeah, I know.'

'I'm serious. Rachel, when this guy lets you down come see me.'

They laughed.

He looked at the two of them and his whole face seemed full of tenderness for them. He put his hands on the doorposts. It wasn't love that caused him to speak, it was something else, which made him angry and gave him the sort of pain that is better to cause others than to feel oneself.

He said, 'You kids shouldn't be here. We're all going to hell here. I bought this plot of land last time I was in the South of France; a pal of mine took me to see it and I fell in love with the views and all and I got this architect to start making plans. I sort of thought me and Tyler would get over there sometime. But what about if you guys went over there and got it built for me? You've got a flair for that kinda thing, J., design and all, you could oversee the thing, make sure it comes off according to the plans and even do the décor. You'd get it right, I know you would. We have the same taste in women after all! And you know what, you guys? You could bring your kid up someplace she can run about . . . somewhere a kid can be a kid.'

'What about the business?' said Jeff.

'Don't you worry about that, man. You know how easy it is these days to stay in touch, email and whatnot.' His mobile phone rang and, much consoled, he shouted into it all the way down the stairs, abusing the caller with ribald humour until the door closed on him.

And then after the eleventh day of that month, with ash filling the skies and tumbling into their backyard in Brooklyn, they decided to take Don up on his offer.

Jeff was a cartoonist and a poet on the side; he kept a small notebook in his man-bag for his preferred thoughts. Often he forgot it and was obliged to use Rachel's mind to make notes; he'd relay the essence in cryptic style, using no more than four trigger words as if afraid to let her have more in case she robbed him, as if somehow his penny-gags would give her a head start up the tree of life. Back at home he'd take out his pens and draw it up. He'd submitted some to the *New York Times*. He'd had a few published. He hoped to make something of it, undisturbed by the demands of his day job. *Make people buy new underwear; make people drink Gatorade every day; make people go on a cruise.* The last one he drew there was a 1950s mom and pop, standing with their arms around each other looking woefully down at their cute-looking kid, who had a cowboy comic book in his hand. The caption read: *Son, we are the bad guys.*

'I think we're done with America for the time being,' said Rachel, as they drove to Newark airport, Nice-bound.

'We're going to create our own way of living, baby,' said Jeff.

A stray dog was running along the turnpike traffic, its ears back, a stupid grin on its face, cars braking all over the place, and the dog just jauntily larruping along. It nearly gave Jeff an idea, he reached for it, he could feel the knot of it, but as happened sometimes he couldn't untie it in time to see it before it went.

Rachel saw the dog too, and she saw Jeff watching it with his mouth slightly ajar, his hairy long fingers twitching on his knees, and she thought to herself: *Well, we'll be better off in the countryside. He won't stray . . .*

The first year or so there, Jeff and Rachel persuaded themselves that they were cannily managing the appointed construction team and were keen-eyed enough to spot the inflated prices, and they took the manager to task over it; so much so, he took other work and they were forced to use an assortment of sons of friends of friends, mostly Simone and Guy's, with Simone insisting she oversee their payment in cash and dashing out of her bungalow the moment she saw more than two men assembled about Jeff to 'negotiate'.

Most jobs began in earnest with fifty per cent up front and were abandoned by the next bank holiday. A crack team of losers went about the place erecting walls, knocking down walls, and generally fouling up the architect's grand plans, but eventually a house emerged, though what lay beneath it was anybody's guess.

One elderly, very feeble team of olive pickers, charged with the plumbing, simply threw an assortment of cheaply bought plastic tubing underground, ate their lunch slowly, and left, the better off for their day out.

Each new team bemoaned the corruption of the last and so Rachel took to sitting with her tea, supervising, from the concrete interior, the sediment of the area's male population acting out construction. A dwarf was winched past an open window with roofing materials. He returned with gravity's full assistance and she took him to hospital and bought him chocolates. The bashful JCB driver, new to the machine and overjoyed with it all, drove over the newly laid outdoor electrics and watering system and the crane operator swung a palm tree into the balcony and produced an avalanche of tumbling rubble. The bank manager allowed his friend, who ran the first construction company, to lodge a false cheque to the sum of thousands of euros.

All of this melodrama kept their friends amused in the evenings and after a few drinks they'd suggest it was time for them to give a hand themselves. Jeff agreed, and there was much baseball hat slapping all round; he pretended he saw the funny side, it was not his money, after all. But he sat biting his raw thumbs in the cold of his 'works office', what would be the utility room, losing his bonhomie. *Am I a racist or am I a misanthrope?* he wrote on the first page of a virgin notebook. He sat back and blinked. He knew it then; he hated people. They drove him crazy. All of them except Maud. But one day, she'd drive him crazy too.

And then, at three times the budget and over eighteen months, the structure of the house was up, and Rachel brought some local cokehead gypsies to the site to finish the work, and the campfire evenings outside seemed almost idyllic with the young traveller women juggling or spinning ropes on fire and the gypsy leader of the band playing his guitar and tempting the middle classes with Latin-style lovemaking.

The icing was put on the cake by some gay friends of the Dutch who came down from Rotterdam in campervans and painted and decorated the place in the manner of a tart's boudoir, bringing from the junk shops all that their sense of irony could stomach; gaudy chandeliers, broken chairs, Victorian chaises longues, all to be painted red or black and covered in velvet or silk.

One way or another all their friends worked on the project, crafting hopeless cupboards, hanging cheap doors. One or two had bad experiences with electricity, the better tools went missing, the hospital repaired the flesh wounds at a good price, and a child's electronic toy, trapped inside the wood decking by the pool, bleeped for months every day at 5 P.M., reminding them to open a bottle. By the end of the second summer, the road to Ikea was strewn with the debris from the open-topped 2CV and baskets and curtain rails bumped in and out of the convoy of campervans following, and they had friends, plenty of thirsty friends. Their home, Don's house, was like the common room for the expats in the area. They were never alone.

The house was done, but Don Abrams did not come and see it. He sent very little in the way of work, but he kept them with enough in the way of funds for them to tick over, enough for Jeff to dabble in a little winegrowing with a farmer across the way. He liked to drive the tractor. They both took to the place. It was the land; God's own, they agreed.

And on beatific mornings under the lovely sun, Jeff stooped to study the vines, to feel the grapes, and he listened to the old winegrower, all the while squeezing with his palm from the dog-eared phrase book all the words he could find in his defence and little Maud behind him, retching down her stripey front the bitter grape skin and pips. That sticky hand in his, stuck fast, made him feel like a good person.

12

$\diamond$

JEFF AND RACHEL TOOK refuge from their home and its stream of visitors by going next door, where Richard was received into his home with tipsy hilarity and some piss-taking regarding his suit and shiny shoes. The three of them were smashed, the music loud and distorted.

As Richard went through to the bedroom to change he saw that the sofa was a mess of magazines, the beds unmade, and he felt anger reveal itself; he wanted to break something. He looked at his hand on the handle of his son's bedroom, all knuckle, and instead of allowing the door to open as it should he shoved it and saw a fragment of wood break from the latch.

Maxence was playing his Game Boy in bed. Richard told him he had to go again to Africa next week but he'd be back as quickly as he could and with a present; he could have a stone from a pyramid, a lion's claw, a bag of camel dung, or a Pygmy's loincloth. His son put his arms around his neck and Richard put his hands on the boy's back and whispered in his ear what he always said to him, 'You're my boy, be the little man now and sleep tight,' and then he went to the bathroom and stood in front of the sink, holding on to it. He looked at her earrings on the window ledge and swept them to the floor.

Earlier that week, when he came home from work, Valérie was outside in the car. She'd been there since she brought Max home from school.

'Does she think she's bloody Princess Diana?' Richard had moaned to Max, referring to her sense of melodrama.

'She's alive though,' Max said with circumspect logic, and he continued, talking at his father in his usual rambling way, a flicker of a clever grin sometimes showing itself when he ventured into the philosophical, while Richard nodded and assented, occasionally raising his eyes to give a show of interest.

He told Max he wouldn't go out to her. He would make the supper himself. He cooked the steaks and made pasta to go with them. He opened a bottle of good red. They took their supper without her and after they cleared away he went outside to get her. It was dark. He found her, head sideways on the steering wheel, arms hanging limp, in the act of listening with complete absorption to a hip-hop track, which finished with the sound of thunder and lightning.

'Who's that you're playing?' he asked her, his hands together on the roof of the car, his forehead against them as in prayer. She pressed a button, extinguished the music.

'Puff Daddy.'

'Puff Daddy,' he repeated, deadpan.

She looked at him. 'You're killing me, both of you, you're killing me,' she said. Then she got out of the car and walked inside.

'It's the time of the month,' he said to Max.

His son was sitting in the pink and blue neon thrall of *Star Academy* on the television, his teeth at rest on his lips. Richard sat down next to him with his head in his hands and Maxence moved forwards to sit on the floor, right in front of the screen, turning the volume up, the remote outstretched, shaking in his hand as he willed it louder and louder.

'*Ri-schard!* Dinner! Are you deaf? *Merde . . .*'

He joined the three in the kitchen. He wanted a whisky. When he opened the cupboard Simone's stash of home-grown weed in a carrier bag fell out. She'd used their electronic scales to parcel it out in August. She'd made a loss with the ex-pats never having money on them, and so far not one of them had returned to pay her for what they'd taken. He poured himself a large drink. He might as well play catch-up.

Jeff and Rachel had been to see the head of the rugby team in L'Argens. Rachel was flushed with wine and excitement.

'He used to be the rugby coach but he works for the social services now, he's going to be our mentor for the adoption process, which is endless of course . . .'

'I'm fine with that by the way,' quipped Jeff, taking his place at the table.

'It's just a question of getting all the paperwork together but also, you know, I do realize,' she threw a look at Valérie, 'I mean I do know it's his job to slow things down, in that very, uh, Gallic way, it gives him time to check us out, how certain we are and that.'

She finished her glass and he refilled it for her. There was a dark line on her lower lip, red wine sediment.

'He thought we were strong candidates. We already have a child, we're young, we're married . . .' She counted off their virtues on her fingers. 'I said to him that I see us with a little African girl about Maud's age, you know.'

Valérie served the moussaka. 'Richard, he think he have had a very bad childhood. You know. His mother ran away with an American singer . . . maybe it was Elvis.'

'His name was in fact Albert Hall.' Richard received his own plate, noting the burnt bit was his. 'I was close to my father. He was a good dad. I can't remember missing her overmuch. She must have been very unhappy.'

'Oh Richard,' said Rachel.

'Take your plate, honey,' said Jeff.

'He fed me, clothed me, paid for my schooling. He loved me. And now he lives in Devon, with a very plain, very kind woman.'

'The only woman who would have him,' put in Valérie.

'Yes, maybe. He's happy, though.'

Rachel sat looking disrupted, while Jeff and Valérie ate. 'I feel sorry for that boy, for the little boy who had to grow up so fast.'

No one had ever said such a thing to him. He looked at her. Her eyes seemed somehow as useful as hands. *It's a good thing God didn't make you beautiful or you'd be really dangerous,* he thought.

Valérie put her fork down on the plate, a hard note.

'You've gone to a lot of trouble, Valou,' said Jeff.

'It is a very difficult dish, it takes me too long, I don't know why I make it. I haven't done it in years. Oh,' she sighed, 'I don't know, this adoption plan of yours, it depresses me. Perhaps I am jealous.'

'Jealous? Why?' cried out Rachel.

'Of your nice intentions. But for me I do not agree. For me there is the love that is natural, which springs from the interior of you, this love is passion, it comes from somewhere profound, maybe dark is the right word in English, and then you have the love that is all here,' she tapped the side of her head, 'which is work, just work, you know, it is about what people think of you . . . charity I think you say in English but we don't have a word quite like that in French and maybe this is why I cannot understand.'

'Oh no, I mean, it might start that way, but it changes, doesn't it? It grows . . .'

'Like with a dog or a cat, you mean.' Valérie hid her mouth with her glass.

'No! No, but it's like, well your husband isn't your blood relation, is he? But you grow to love him . . .'

'It begins with passion. Not charity, I don't think.' Valérie glanced at Jeff and smiled.

'Jeff and I were friends really, weren't we, darling? We worked together, that's how it started. Anyway, people are different, I suppose. I know that I could love any child. Really.'

'Even a psychopath? Even a crazy child who burns things or kills things, who hates you?'

'Don't exaggerate,' Richard said.

'But *Ri-schard,* she doesn't know what kind of a child she will get and these kids in these crazy places have seen some terrible things, they have done some terrible things. Some of them have been soldiers, some of them have been raped . . . Nobody knows what has happened to them. We have seen the film. Maybe Rachel gets a boy who shoot another boy in the back of the head.'

Max came in and put a remote control on the table next to his mother. *'Y'a rien a' la télé,'* he said.

'Hi, Max,' said Rachel. The boy looked at her. He was standing like a pregnant teenager, tummy out. His pyjamas were too short and too childish for him with a SpongeBob cartoon on them just discernible but cracked like mosaic, they were faded and pilled. 'You all right, sweetie?'

Valérie stood up and took a glass from the draining board which she briskly filled with water from the tap, then handed it to her son. 'Go on — bed. It's too late for all this.' He went out.

Valérie took the chair across from Rachel, where Jeff had been sitting until he got up to spark up a joint by the back door. They faced each other, pale and dark.

'I don't think it comes from being polite, love. I think that love is very *malpoli*, it is rude. You die for someone you love. You kill for them. You put them first even at a big price. I mean, do you think the Nazis didn't love? I think they were maybe great lovers, they love their own people so much that they kill others.'

Richard was shaking his head as he lit a cigarette. *Oh do shut up,* he was thinking. He caught Rachel's eye.

'And who is a bad lover? Let me think? Maybe Gandhi, yes, maybe the Abbé St Pierre . . . maybe the Pope he is a very bad lover . . .'

Jeff laughed, at the door, sucking on the spliff, blowing smoke into the night, the light on his face from the porch lamp.

'You see. You see . . .' She was leaning over the table, a hand curled around the glass, enjoying herself, and she spoke quickly. 'Love is a very dangerous thing, . . .'

Richard shot another look at Rachel, who looked right back at him, and he could read her thoughts in her eyes.

He looked at his wife, unleashed, in full vibrato, her hands moving; hands in her hair, hands in the air, fingers moving.

He looked at Rachel; her head now bowed, her hands crossed on the table. One woman trying so hard to sit up straight, he thought, and the other trying so hard to fall off her seat.

From across the room, Jeff piped up, pointing the spliff at them as if it were a conductor's baton, bringing himself into the music, 'I don't think it's fair to bring Catholics into it. I resent that. I mean, take my family, we're Catholic, and I know we don't have any good intentions at all . . .'

He closed the door and brought the little paper end of the joint to the sink where he ran water over it. His head went from side to side and he said in his creaky tones, 'Well, Richard, you must be like some sort of Don Juan with what you do for a living.' He turned round with the wet stub, looking for the bin, and laid it on the table.

Jeff did not look Richard in the eye; he pretended he was looking for a cloth to dry his hands.

'I'd like to be a good person actually,' said Rachel. 'So that makes me really unsexy, I'm sure. In fact I don't think you could get less sexy than that, could you really?'

Jeff put a damp hand on her back. 'You're OK, baby. You're not a good person yet. There's still a chance for you.'

'But this is not all about you, Rachel. You know? Will this child, this African child, be lonely?' Valérie tore the petite strip of plastic from the pack. She was smoking Marlboro Reds these days, like Jeff.

'I don't think so.'

'Will this child, will it feel it is in the wrong place with the wrong people? So, you will give it good food, and nice clothes and everything will be so nice of course, but is that enough? And of course he will still be black and you are very, very white.'

Jeff made a face, swilled the wine around his gums. 'Whatever. I mean it might not even happen. That counsellor guy did say it was better for these things to go slow; the slower the better.'

'He told us how this one couple actually brought a child back. He said it just about finished him off. I mean can you imagine? They said the kid hadn't told them he *loved* them . . . I mean that's just so screwed up on so many levels.' Rachel shook her head.

'Me, I can understand that they brought the child back,' said Valérie, 'it is too much to bear the feeling that you are not loved. I can understand that anything — even failure, even guilt, even the hatred of others — would be better than that.'

No one said anything.

Suddenly, breaking the silence, Jeff laughed out of nowhere and apologized.

'What?'

'Sorry, I was just thinking about the Pope.'

In filling his glass, Valérie emptied the bottle. 'Maybe Richard can bring you back a child from Africa . . .'

'I won't come across orphans, I'm afraid.'

'Come on, those kids have got to be depressed,' smiled Jeff.

Rachel laughed in spite of herself. 'Oh, Jeff, that's terrible.'

'Well, I wish it was a funny business.' Richard was feeling humourless. He was very tired. 'But it's just business.'

" 'Business"!'

'Yes, Rachel. That's the truth of it. Business. It's another way of doing good, you know. Maybe the only real way.'

'Open another bottle,' Valérie said.

Jeff started to laugh again. 'Sorry. You guys give me the giggles. You Brits, you're so . . . pompous sometimes. You kill me. The realist and the believer.'

'I don't think Richard is a realist. Not really,' said Rachel.

'Well, I can tell you he is not a romantic,' Valérie put in.

Richard stood up. 'Well, goodnight folks, the bad guy needs a night's sleep before he goes off to rape and pillage.'

He looked at Jeff and put out his hand, and Jeff took it and shook it and winked and mouthed at him from behind his sleeve the words *ball breakers*.

Max was standing in the doorway, he might have been there a while, Richard only saw him as he went towards it.

'Max! Come on, son, I'll take you to bed.'

But Max had his magician's kit with him. His grandmother had bought it for him for his birthday.

'I have a trick to show you.'

'Oh, go on then,' said Rachel, 'go on, Max, I love magic.'

'It's past his bedtime,' said Valérie, extinguishing her half-smoked cigarette and going to open a window. She stood looking out of the window.

'This isn't very good,' said Max, his teeth just showing on his lip as he opened the box.

'What about *Ladies and Gentlemen*?' said Jeff, pouring himself another glass. '*Mesdames et Messieurs . . .*' he effected a little drum-roll with his fingers on the table.

The boy put the box on the counter, took out three cups and placed them on the table.

'Ah it's the old cup and pea trick,' said Jeff, 'a classic.'

The boy sat down where his mother had been. He fiddled a bit, squinted at the cups, sizing them up, and said, 'Here we have three small balls . . .' He put his right hand on the table to unwrap the three small fabric balls, and out of his sleeve dropped the fourth.

'Whoops.'

'Too bad, man.'

'Start again, Max, no one saw anything.'

'No, we didn't see anything,' said Rachel. 'Start again, love.'

Max sat back in his chair, his shoulders slumping, eyes out of focus, his mouth open. Then a tear emerged from one eye and rolled down his cheek.

'Come on, Max, it's not important.' Richard put a hand on his shoulder.

'It is,' Max said, 'it is important. You can either do magic or you can't.'

77

Valérie came back to the table. 'It's time for bed.'

'I don't want you to go to Africa, Dad.'

'Why?'

'In case they kill you.'

'They won't kill me!'

'I don't want to be left with her,' he said.

Richard watched his wife's eyes transform; the brown centres deepened, the whites seemed to yellow, a barrier of brine formed. She put a hand over her mouth.

Before he turned in, he went into his son's room to breathe in the full-cream goodness of the sleeping child that he still was. He sat down and looked upon that slightly satisfied face, virtuous in sleep, smooth and sure now that Christmas was coming, and everything was getting better; his hands folded like a martyred priest.

We are quiet faithful creatures hiding inside noisy faithless bodies, he thought. He wondered whether Max would one day be in his shoes, drinking with friends, coming and going, worrying at the bathroom sink. Losing his hair. Losing his nerve.

As on other nights like those, Valérie had the music in the kitchen running high into the early hours while Richard clutched his pillows, sweating out the red wine, and when he woke his mouth was dry and the sun was prising the sides of the shutters from the window frames and his wife lay mouth open, still fully clothed.

13

✧

BEFORE TURNING IN, Valérie stood swaying ominously in her kitchen. The last one out, Jeff's hand remained on the handle of the door as he looked back over his shoulder, closing the door softly, slowly. He saw her there with her head back, her eyes shut. He bit his lip.

Until she was sure they were gone, Valérie remained in this apparently enraptured state. Then she snapped to, threw the casserole dish into the sink and let the hot water from the tap fill it.

She sat by the back door and looked at her reflection in the glass as she smoked a last cigarette. Perhaps he would come back and if he did she would kiss him in the doorway and they would never be apart. In the reflection there were no wrinkles on her face at all and she liked the way her eyes looked large and dark and her jaw and neck were sleek and hard. She twisted her hair in her hands and held it up at the back.

Jeff walked up the hill, behind his wife, his hands in his pockets, looking up at the sky, loafing, imagining all sorts of temporary things, shopping for poetry. The stars cavorted for him. He was a happy drunk.

His wife was waiting for him in their hallway and he let her kiss him.

In their bedroom a fat and furious fly buzzed around, fretting itself senseless. Jeff rose uneasily, to fetch his dirty socks from the top of the laundry basket in the corner. Rachel touched the sheets, felt them with her hands. He moved about the room with the socks, missing in the air, merely ruffling a cobweb. The man was always too late wherever he was.

Then it occurred to her, watching him, that she had no idea what would happen next, not in minutes, hours, days, weeks or years. The bedsheets were red, the pillowslips were red. The illumination didn't stretch into the next second and she became suddenly aware of the quiet, the fly was gone, done in, legs in the air underneath the radiator and Jeff got back into bed and set to scratching a leg and a film gathered over the surface of the feeling, and though they were comfortable together, side by side, she felt return all the pretenders from her past, all the men who'd turned her away, and the feeling of being there with a fly to swat and memory-less and future-free was gone.

'She can talk the leg off a donkey,' he said, pulling back the sheet from his side and putting a knee on the bed.

'Do you think she's beautiful?'

'Valérie? She talks too much. Way too much.'

He lay down beside her. They held each other and she kissed his chin.

'You're doing well, J. Here.'

The red wine was like antiseptic, it helped a lot, in quantity, early evening. It made him docile, besides which there was nowhere to go. It really was the best way to avoid temptation, to live in a place that closed at seven.

When they were asleep, their daughter came and stood in her nightdress, looking at them, the tears in her eyes stopped by the sight of these two. She stood there for a moment or two and then perhaps she thought that as they were so still they might be dead.

She cried out loudly and they woke and took her into their warm bed between them and though they told her there were no monsters, it had seemed to her just the moment before as her eyes had got used to the dark and failed to find them that the dark itself was monstrous, that everything that was night was terrible and that the main thing was not to be alone. She went to sleep in the middle hearth, between the fires of both of them.

14

✧

Max sat in the car with his mother in a sulk. Purple, a sniffing fury, his eyes downcast, his hood up. All that gave him away as a boy, as her boy, was the sprinkling of freckles across his nose and cheeks and the long lashes downcast. His mother drove at top speed to loud music. She barely spoke to him, she was impatient, she hated him to speak and necessitate her turning down the volume. She would frown, tilting her head in exaggerated listening, 'What?'

'I hate this music.'

'Don't be so miserable.'

Other times he'd chatter on, careless, issuing wanton prophesies: *'I think I'm going to get locked up when I'm older.'* Making boastful claims: *'I might be great. I might be a magician, or a rock climber, the world's best.'* And joining the two: *'All that separates me from being that, you see, Mum, is persuading people to say it. I mean why don't you say it, just say it? Max, you are the world's greatest rock climber. No, go on. All right, well don't because I might want to be something else, I've got to think about it. But words are really powerful. They're magic, right? It's not I think therefore I am, it's if they say so, then I am.'*

He looked unattractive with his now slightly spotty skin, the wisps on his upper lip, and the soft puppy fat; neither child nor man.

He made repetitive noises about the house or in the car, a pen lid clicked up and down in his hand until she screamed at him, the door of the TV cabinet kicked against the wall and kicked harder and harder after she asked him to stop, and then she'd lose her patience and lash out at him with a smack. In the mornings, before school, he kicked a ball against the kitchen wall, over and over again, a dull thud. He was less and less content. The cereal was wrong, his hair was wrong, his clothes were wrong, he was ugly, everyone hated him, he was useless at sport; thus ran his conversation.

'Oh, stop it,' she said.

Then suddenly, out of nowhere, when she was cooking or speaking to someone on the phone, he'd want to dance with her, he'd take her hands in his, old-style, and try to turn her round. He spoke to her through the bathroom door, it could never wait and yet it was so trivial what he wanted.

'Did we buy the towel with the dolphin on it at Marineland?'

He asked that one of them sleep in his bed with him or that he come in with them.

'You are nearly fourteen!' she accused him.

'He needs you,' Richard would say to her.

But she wouldn't concede. When he was in bed, she went to look at him and stood in the doorway. In the gloom, he'd open his eyes enough to see her but not so much as to be seen looking. Then one evening he sat up and told her he wished she wasn't angry with him. She told him he must not annoy her then.

'Don't you love me?' he asked her.

'Of course I do.'

'Kiss me then, kiss me goodnight.'

When she did, he took her hand in his. 'You have beautiful

fingers. Oh, did I do that to you?' he asked, tenderly, running his thumb and fingertip over a burn on her finger.

'No. I did it on the oven.'

'Oh. I thought it was me. I'm sorry,' he said and he kissed it. 'There. All better, now.'

'I wish you were dead,' he said to her other times.

'You shouldn't say things like that to me.'

'Why not?' he'd ask, genuinely interested. 'The words come into my head and I have to say them. I don't know if that's what I want or whether I want you to say something to me so that's why I'm saying it.'

'I'm not playing games with you, Maxence.'

The days were busy enough but she had nothing to do with them. She was never alone; the painter had come to do the front room, and when the painter went, the plumber came, delivery men came, there was the postman at midday and Guy came up for a smoke, hoping for a chat here and there; Simone came up to help with the ironing and rearrange the drawers and drink and smoke, and then there was Max back home and then Guy came up again to watch her getting supper ready, then Richard came in and she had little peace or time for herself, but at night she held her nose and plunged underwater to attend to her proper life.

Her dreams returned to her in pieces throughout the day. She thought about Jeff. She had seen the way he looked at her. She was going to tell him that she was in love with him when they were alone.

She lay in bed with a hand between her legs and waves of feeling came from her head, flooded across her breasts right through to her nipples and went down between her legs, ending in an angry little thud, and she burst into tears. Music was bad for her. Drink was bad for her. People were bad for her.

15

✧

THE PRE-ADOPTION counselling pamphlets remained on their neighbours' kitchen counter for a couple of weeks under canteen tickets and leaflets and rubber bands and keys until Valérie put them in the bin. By then, Rachel had grown impatient of waiting for the rugby coach to procure her another child to love and had taken the business into her own hands.

She scoured the internet for orphans and found the website of a young Christian man who had traversed war-torn Sierra Leone like a Pied Pastor collecting orphans. There were Polaroid photos of each child with their names handwritten on them in black felt tip, some forty or so, for whom he provided. There was a particularly beautiful five-year-old girl, the only one not smiling, with huge solemn eyes that called out for a mother; Salamatu.

She felt called. She decided to pray about it. She wondered how He felt about her there on her knees. What kind of love was it if it was love? Was it paternal love? Or dread of his most difficult creation? Fury, pique and patience, these were all in the mix of parenthood but none as much as the task of simply cleaning up after the child.

'Father, here I am,' she said. And she waited, and said it again, and she felt a small stirring inside of her.

She bought the plane tickets — Nice, Gatwick, Freetown — from the small sum of money her mother had left her in a bank account in England and then she told Jeff what she'd done. She asked Simone if she would look after Maud for five days. No one said not to go and she was glad of that. Jeff was non-committal about it all. The party juggernaut was motoring on towards the Christmas tollbooth. Rachel sat drinking without conviction, wondering why she wasn't getting drunk.

Rachel went over to Simone's to have her tarot cards read on the eve of their departure for West Africa. Beware of a black man, Simone said dourly after shaking her head at each card she turned over, each one apparently worse than the last.

Thanks for the advice, said Rachel. She left Maud with Simone, so that she could get on with the packing. As she went out, passing by their kitchen, she glimpsed Maud standing on the dustbin doing the washing-up and Simone behind her encouraging her with the dirty stringy cloth as the little girl took into account the tap, the windows. She heard Simone's lovely unfettered laughter ringing out free and true and she felt chastened by it and stopped and looked up at the vast sky; she felt like a small bad person, a creeping thing.

That night she woke on the floor and called out to Jeff who wasn't there, he was drinking with the Dutch and the neighbours.

She got back into bed, afraid, and her heart felt heavy as a car battery pulling her down to the bottom of a pond. She fell into dreams and said to herself: *I must open my eyes.* It was as if her eyelids were sewn shut; she kick-started her heart and opened them. She wondered why it had been so hard, what part of her had urged her to open them and what part had held her back?

Downstairs they were drinking their way through the American business partner's cellar. The opening chords of 'Smells Like Teen Spirit' rose through the ceiling.

'Go home and entertain yourselves,' she whispered, pulling the pillow up around her ears, feeling better for having spoken out and shamed the dark.

16

✧

NAIROBI REMINDED RICHARD of the geography books of his school-days and how they depicted modern life in the Commonwealth, Meccano-constructed office blocks, painted pale-blue bungalows, and the government departments with their Peg-Board black-and-white notice boards. Except, there were long lines of people along the length of the road back to the hotel, with picks at equal spaces, men and women, digging to lay a new cable. Less-employed men stood singly here and there, burning rubbish, and the cattle mingled with the traffic.

He was back this time to 'shadow' Dr Wainanga's friend in Nyeri, to see the 'shocking lack of medicines' according to the doctor's last email and to note 'and convey please most forcefully the number of very mentally sick people in our country being just the same as in your own'.

'There are other drug companies,' the doc had said coyly as he shook Richard's hand at the airport, 'but none we like so much as yours so far, nor as generous, but you see, Mr Bird, we must like each other, trust each other and know each other.'

Say what you like, old pal, Richard had thought, handing over his passport to the airline desk, he'd noticed people felt better for a spot of rhetoric before they signed these sorts of contracts.

So here he was again, playing the white man. It would be the last time for a while anyway. Once signed up, he'd not be back for a year or more. Next stop, Uganda.

That evening he took a beer in the bar at the Norfolk. There was an open fireplace, a leather armchair and sofa, it was all rattan and polished wood, fake leopard-skin rugs and black-and-white photos of the 1930s. He took the armchair and the waiter put his head alongside his in a confidential style as he poured out a Tusker beer from its bottle.

An Englishman, slightly camp, dishevelled, sat down on the sofa opposite. He ordered a beer too, kicked out his legs.

'Staying here?'

He was, himself, for three more months no less. He had already been there nine months. Making television shows, very popular, millions of viewers. They were sponsored by a condom manufacturer, racy little episodes, a week's anticipation culminating on Friday night, with *a sort of, well, a sexual scenario really,* he put it cheerfully. Condom comes to the rescue. Wonderfully successful. The chap who owned the company used to make porn magazines, but this was much more profitable. Poacher turned gamekeeper. The British government co-funded it too, and the World Health Organization.

'My company helps fund one of the World Health Organization's projects out here too.'

'What are you up to?'

'It's a big drive to eliminate the stigmatization of mental illness in Africa. No television shows. But that's a good idea.'

The Englishman had straggly greasy hair, a weather-beaten face and a rather juvenile ethnic bracelet tied in a knot around his wrist.

'So you're shopping madness and I'm shopping promiscuity. Cheers to us.'

'I suppose they've always been around.'

The man started to laugh, took a drink and then laughed again. 'What a business,' he chirped. 'I used to make movies but I sold out. I'm a sell-out! I love it. I live in Vietnam now; great place, great girls.'

After dinner, Richard returned to the bar.

Travelling was unravelling, falling apart, too much drink, too much food, and the acid stomach of something being amiss. Nightmares about infidelity, not to mention the strangers in and out of his own bed who made him prone to such suspicions. He took a whisky and then another.

When an Englishwoman came and sat up at the bar, Richard bought her a drink. He was feeling increasingly disconsolate but nevertheless he was prepared to be cheered in his usual way.

She was a journalist, covering the elections. She had led quite a life. She was happy to tell him something of her sexual adventures. Politicians; *useful,* she stressed with emphasis. She said she'd slept with hundreds and hundreds of men and though she'd tried 'relationships', she used her index fingers in the air here, she found them disappointing, *not* knowing a person was so much more interesting than knowing them, she smirked.

He didn't like her but he did find her attractive. She had long ringlets, a mass of curls, hard lines on her forehead, bangles on her wrist, she was noisy and she was thin. It was no surprise to either of them that she came back to his room with him and they had sex. She was businesslike. She took her underpants off but left her top on. That was a new one.

He gave her his best, good long strokes, and she clutched at him for a bit then pushed him off and climbed on top. She certainly knew what she was doing. She put a hand under his chin, pushed his head back and almost as if in some unkind imitation, mimicked a man fucking a woman. She put a fingertip underneath his balls and pressed hard as if trying to find the choke button. With or without him, she appeared to reach some sort of climax and he conceded his own. When she came she said 'urgh'. Then she got up, went to the toilet, came out, pulled on her underpants, belted her skirt and said, 'I always feel depressed afterwards.'

Not as much as your prey, he thought.

'Do you want a drink?' he said.

'Not now, it's too late,' she said. She got up and put her wallet in her back pocket. 'Thanks anyway,' she said.

He was still lying there, in the same position, on his back, crumpled and dejected with his cock sheepish in his genital hair, as she gave him one last glance over.

'Listen,' he said, 'listen a minute, let me ask you something.' He switched the side lamp on. 'I'm interested, that's all. You say you've slept with hundreds of men, but what I want to know is why, I mean it can't be that different . . .'

She sat on the end of the bed, facing the door but turning back with a gentle face. There was pity perhaps, as if having to include in the bedtime story a little word of warning.

'When you get a man into bed and out of his clothes, you see the boy, you see who he really is, that's why. I'm interested in the boy not the man.'

He made a face.

'It's primitive. I suppose it's my hobby, like stamp collecting. Only I like to denude powerful men. In general.'

'Don't you feel cheap afterwards?'

'Nope.'

He felt the bed lighten again as she stood and he closed his eyes.

'Well, I'll say goodnight then.'

'I don't even like women any more,' he said when he heard the door close, swinging his legs out of the bed and going to the minibar.

Maybe he had created the world he deserved. 'I don't believe in hell,' he'd said to Rachel, one night when she was proselytizing. 'It's a stupid idea.'

'It's not an idea,' she said, 'it's right behind you.'

'You would say the same for heaven then,' he countered.

'Yes, I would,' she said, 'it's not pie in the sky. As long as you know it when you see it.'

'I'll take what I can in this life, Rachel.'

'But that'll be all you get, Richard.'

And what about you? he thought bitterly. *Have you got what you want?*

He closed his eyes and saw Rachel's face. He felt his heart move and he felt sick and afraid. He opened his eyes.

He posted the cigarette butt into the empty can. Two A.M. He couldn't sleep. He needed someone to talk to. *'Hi, Rachel, I know it's two in the morning but I wondered if you wouldn't mind just talking to me, telling me something preposterous, old-fashioned, and unlikely . . .'*

Oh God, he needed a friend. He needed someone who loved him. He needed to love someone too. He put the bedside lamp on. He turned it off.

His wife did not love him! Was there one single piece of evidence he could bring to mind that she did?

He reflected on the last few years. She accepted his flowers with a 'moue' of disappointment. She was too *logique*, she claimed, for such gestures. Roses depressed her — she hated to watch beautiful things rot and die — and as for her former favourites, lilies, she decried the chore of them, those vainglorious paprika shakers that ruined white shirts and expired in a melodramatic swoon; she called them 'cheap'. They'd given up on birthday and Christmas presents. For his last birthday she'd offered him fifty euros. He considered asking for seventy-five, for a joke, but they didn't share the same sense of humour. She'd taken to wearing a beret, pulled up, it looked like a microwaved bag of popcorn on her head. It was navy blue and dusty, and it made her ears stick out. She looked like Marcel Marceau but God knows she wasn't miming. She had pretty much told him everything he needed to know. He was a useless father and a bad husband; or so she said.

Her disarray was out in the open like the washing she put on the line that went through various rains and winds before being released from its distress, and washed and dried in the conventional succession by her mother. She kept a tragic theme tune on tap, agonized numbers that she played in kitchen or car incessantly, and he'd want to scream: *Change the fucking track, I've got the message.*

He thought of what his son had said about her. 'Max, are you safe? My boy. Are you happy?' He lay there with one hand reaching across the bed, open-palmed.

The next morning, idling by the pool with a Coca-Cola and trying to feel better, his eyes sore behind his sunglasses, he saw the Englishwoman. She looked over at him from her sunlounger and raised her glasses. The expression on her face was straight-laced.

Her legs were well crossed. He sat up and called out good morning. He told her he was heading on after lunch and she nodded. He told her he was going to visit a clinic in Nyeri. He was coming back in a couple of weeks to spend a whole week there, shadowing a doctor. She nodded again, evincing no interest.

'You out here much longer?'

'Who knows,' she said.

'Right.'

She called out to the waiter and began a conversation in Swahili.

'Well, see you,' he said.

He went to the toilets to put his clothes back on and took a look in the mirror. He was shocked. The skin under his eyes was very lined, his forehead looked like glazed ham, sliced into, there were stray hairs sprouting from his nostrils, and they were ginger. His mouth tasted of nicotine.

That afternoon he checked into the hotel in Nyeri, sat down at six for dinner, and a Kikuyu marching band arrived before the vista of a cloud-obscured Mount Kenya, in tribal dress, singing, the sound of cymbals coming from the metal-purse knee pads that were filled with ball bearings. They were sporting skins, headdresses and face paint. Their legs were daubed with limestone stripes. The girls walked dumpily, down at the mouth. Behind them this land was comely red earth, divided into greenish smallholdings.

Before dinner he wandered to the church and graveyard, hailed by those going home from their work, and followed the pathway which was lined with the signs bearing the Scout movement commandments to Baden-Powell's grave. *The nearer to Nyeri, the nearer to bliss.* This was the quotation of his they cherished above the reception desk in the hotel where he was staying. But Baden-Powell's stone bore the simplest inscription Richard had ever seen. A circle with a dot in the middle, like the bull's-eye on a target, one single shot to the heart of the matter; he remembered what the sign meant from his Scouting days—'Gone home.'

That night, with the disco music in the background, he opened the French doors and walked out on to the lawn. The middle of the night under his toes, he looked into the distance and saw twinkling lights from homes on the far hills, like fairy lights. It made him remember how Christmas felt when he was a child, when his mother was there, and it came to him with a rush: *Here I am, in the middle of my life, in the middle of the world* . . . He was standing on the equator. A circle with a dot in the middle of it.

When he woke the next morning, it was quiet, and he had the bloom of a dream still close. It had opened in the first light; lovely, fragrant and fair. Rachel was leaning over him tracing an eyebrow of his with one finger, saying: *What is it that you want?*

17

✧

TO GET INTO THE CAPITAL, Freetown, they had to board old Russian helicopters on an island runway off the mainland and once inside they crouched, unseated, holding on to straps, looking out through the open windows, passing low over mangrove swamps. With them was a plump, foppish-haired businessman in a lightweight suit, an unlit cigarette in his mouth, frowning into the twilight.

The first thing that hit Rachel was that everywhere it smelt intensely orange, a lethal kind of human sweat which had her reeling as she and Jeff were manhandled, pushed and bossed forth by scores of men in blue overalls, hoping money would rub off on them as they passed the foreigners along the line to their bags. Their bags were removed from them, it was no use protesting, their fat wallet was taken too, thrust across a single counter and emptied of its pounds sterling and changed into local currency.

Pushed to one side, Jeff was struck dumb. Rachel had a hand over her mouth, wide-eyed. Here and there each man took a note, a boy too at the very last minute, and finally the throng dispersed and left them with one single man who had their bags on his back. They followed him and he gave the bags to a man standing by a car and the wallet to them at last. Finally they had it back, the notes as limp as autumn leaves, stinking.

Jeff said something like they weren't in Kansas any more and she smiled back. She saw the crooked tooth that came from behind, that clasped the canine and overlapped it, when he was nervous. Their driver opened the door for each of them in turn.

'My name is Mohammed,' he said.

He took them to a bombed-out hotel. It was the best there, according to him.

The lobby was bare apart from a wooden desk set in concrete.

There was a plastic letter board on the wall behind it bearing the names of foreign currencies with consonants missing and the figures scant. There was the scar of where the name of the hotel had once been on the roughcast wall.

It was as if it had just been evacuated. The open corridors gave on to rooms with doors wide open. In the courtyard, tropical plants were overgrown and there were empty cement bags hanging from them. Everywhere they went, people attached themselves to them: the receptionist had a family member who needed surgery, a barman had a child who wanted to go to school, and on the street, a shoal of grinners accompanied their cross-channel swim to get to the National Bank.

A photographer had told them on the plane, how the people who go first into a war zone, photographers and aid workers, weren't heroes, to his mind, but adrenaline junkies. But those days were over, the junkies — or rather the vultures, he grinned — were gone, and now it was a mopping-up job, small pickings for journalists now. There was no media market for 'Salone', but the Congo, now that was big. The relief agencies were pulling out, those still there were doing some partying before the next disaster.

In their room, she opened the door to the minibar and saw the wall. The sink sagged in the bathroom from one fixed and one loose bracket and the toilet was seat-less and already filled. The covers on the bed were bandages, bearing cigarette holes. The horizontal strip blinds had been punched toothless.

But outside there was the Atlantic. Local people sat on their haunches before it as if waiting to see what its tide would bring in from America; families squatted among the undergrowth with small fires and tents in the sunset.

'It's not so bad,' she said. 'It's quite beautiful in a way. It's sad. Like the end of time. Like a disaster movie. You know, to have so little, but to have fire and each other. It's very touching. Come and look.'

He stood beside her a moment and nodded. He went to unpack the bags.

'Man, this toilet's really bad news,' he exclaimed from the bathroom.

She was still standing at the window.

Mohammed had waited outside. He'd offered to stay with them for the week for a good price. They went outside early evening and found him there, leaning against the car door, smoking contemplatively. He snapped to, dropping his cigarette. There was nothing to eat at the hotel, they told him, so he took them a short drive to what he said was the most popular bar with the foreigners. He bade them go in, like a parent taking his children to a party. 'Go on,' he encouraged them, 'have fun.' And he lit up again.

Inside, short Bolivian UN soldiers were teaching taller European women how to dance with a man. Pakistani bureaucrats, who were settled in for the long haul, nursed rum drinks. The local hookers sat around the sides of the bar, pulling at the chinoed legs of a group of businessmen, offering to blow them for a soda. Ordering a couple of malaria-aware gin and tonics, Rachel heard a girl saying, 'I'd like to suck you.'

Jeff shook his head in admiration. There were no rules in a place like this. It was the sort of place you could find out how like other people you really were.

The following day they met the pastor, Alpha Bangura, a young, blue-black, very thin man with a hard jaw and large eyes. He was formal with them, all nervous energy, hanging off their words as if trying to learn them by heart. Each member of his voluntary staff made a formal presentation of themselves before the children were assembled.

While they gazed upon the forty or so faces of the children, who had arranged themselves in three rows by height, Rachel glanced now and again at the attending adults, feeling their gaze, and she saw how each was keeping an eye on her particularly, the mother figure. The kids were instructed to sing, and they began a song with dreary conviction, eyes rolling to the ceiling, hands loose, with the smallest of the children, some just toddlers, coming up slightly short on the words but as solemn as the oldest.

> No mummy; mummy gone,
> No daddy; daddy gone,
> Who gonna love the orphan pikin?

The children swayed and put their hands out to Rachel and Jeff at the end of the chorus. Rachel stood during the song, facing them, shimmering, out of focus; the smile on her face taut.

One little girl in the front row was exceptionally beautiful, her eyes shone. Salamatu. The poster girl who'd beckoned Rachel across the sea.

'Well,' she said to Jeff, as they sat in the back seat of the car leaving just before dark to return to the hotel. (They had waved through the back window all the way to the main road.) 'It's clear to me. Much as I'm taken with little Salamatu, it can't be some sort of beauty parade can it, this whole thing? We can't just lift one kid out of this hell, we'll have to do something for all of them. We'll have to build a home for all of them, here. That's what we need to do. That's what would be right.'

They shared hand-wipes. Jeff wiped his face and Rachel followed suit and they showed each other the rust colour on the tissues.

She put her hand on his. 'Whew,' he said. 'Whew.'

'What do you think?'

He didn't say. He'd got a football out and kicked it about in the dirt yard outside with the boys while the girls lined up to receive clothes from Rachel: a T-shirt, some shorts, some underpants each.

She'd taken the time to ask each one in turn about themselves, while a member of staff either side of her urged the child in their own language and smartly filled in the gaps of understanding, with anxious laughter at some of the children's misconstructions, correcting them in English.

'This child is ignorant!'

The girls had hair in thick crusts like plaster, set with dirt and dust, and their arms and legs were mottled and dry, there was nothing soft about them, the younger ones smelt of urine, the older ones of sweat, and they touched her face and her wedding ring and earrings and the older ones tried to whisper things to implicate themselves especially in her affections.

All of their characters were fixed, it seemed to her, from the coquettish five-year-old to the surly unhappy seven-year-old; they were either winning or losing, in a way, and it was hard to know from their stories whether this was due to experience, but it seemed so. The most kittenish of the little girls kept running to the legs of Uncle Abu and was gently but firmly pushed away from him.

Rachel organized a game in which she told a story and had the children play parts. They fell apart laughing at the preposterous notion of goats going over bridges, and bears in beds, so she asked them to make up their own.

The oldest girl, Jakka, took charge, hissing at the little ones who went ahead of instruction, beating a boy who played the fool, and her story was both intricate and morally grandiose; she used all the children available, had the heroine — herself — going forth saving souls, doing good, and being countered at every turn, and all those who did her wrong were avenged, they fell down groaning and moaning and she stepped righteously towards victory. For the finale she took the remaining unused little children in her arms and had them call out (after much angry enjoinment to do so and some pinching and smacking), 'Mother! You have come for us!'

Rachel stood outside in the dusty yard, wiping the back of her neck with her hand, letting Jeff photograph her amidst a sea of little black faces milling round her. She had her long red hair pinned up and curls stuck to her damp nape. 'Their storytelling is amazing, I suppose because it's an oral culture. Jakka's so impressive really. So ferocious. So bright. I can't think of a child I know back home who would be able to hold a story like that.'

'She probably rehearsed it a few times.'

A couple of the little ones clasped her and hugged her to them and she bent down and was nearly overbalanced by the tide of children.

When they rejoined each other for the finale, a Christian song with hand clapping, they shouted out their thanks to the Lord and named each member of staff and cheered loudest for 'Uncle Jeff' and 'Auntie Rachel'.

'We love you!'

'Shit, who wouldn't be touched by that,' said Jeff, quietly. 'That's quite something.'

'Where are they going now?' Rachel asked, wiping her permanently sticky hands on her trousers, watching them file out.

Uncle Abu said that some were staying with him and his wife. He had a winning smile, rich in patience, and his eyelids fluttered when he spoke. A thin woman stepped forwards with one dead arm that she held with her other hand and nodded stiffly. His wife didn't smile.

'She has bad teeth,' her husband explained.

'I have fifteen living with me,' said Sister Rose, pushing through to the fore. She looked like Whoopi Goldberg, Rachel thought, with her craven smile. 'Fifteen! One bag of rice a day!'

18

✧

THEY WENT BACK to the room after a beer in the hotel bar. She was elated, she couldn't stop talking about the children. In their room she would not sit, she stood, talking. He wanted her to have sex with him and so he said, 'Come on, honey, let's get naked.'

She paused.

'Come on, honey, share that love.'

She took her clothes off, lay down on the bed and looked up at the electric wires hanging from the ceiling — spare, useless, potential. As he started to go faster inside her, she looked aside in the sliver of mirror remaining on the cupboard door and she saw there was a melancholy to her face.

He didn't kiss her before or during sex, he only began it by looking lovingly at his member, taking it in one hand and tapping it against her thigh, as if to rouse it, and then he entered her and followed his own directions to find the way out, asking no help from her. It was a route he knew so well.

She spent most of the night awake, thinking, making lists of things for the children.

'Are you awake?' she asked him, at one point, halfway through the night.

'Yes,' he said, but nothing more.

She put a hand between them, on the shared sheet, to find him and he rolled over on to his side, facing away from her.

At breakfast the next morning, over papaya and boiled eggs she said to him, 'I can't wait to see Salamatu. Well, all of them actually. I want to play some games with them, old English ones we used to play like Kick the Can. And we can buy them all a fizzy drink today, I thought, and give them some crisps or something.'

He ate slowly, carefully pushing the plantain aside. She took it and popped it in her mouth saying, 'It's not banana.'

'I know that.'

'It's plantain.'

He pushed the plate to her and looked out to the Atlantic, his fingers over his mouth, his nose resting on the tips of them. She saw his eyes cloud with the onset of a thought; to her he looked so handsome like that, pensive and fragile, and she wished he loved her as much as he loved whatever he was looking at.

'Are you OK?' she said.

'Sure.' Interrupted, he fell into being downcast. He dribbled the sachet of coffee powder into the tepid water, stirred it and looked at the table next to them.

A white businessman in a linen suit was sitting with a fat suited black guy in sunglasses and batik shirt and a prim-looking elderly white woman in khaki, ski glasses on the top of her head. The guy waived the offer of a cigarette from the black guy. 'I don't smoke,' he said, though the evening before they had seen him smoking at the bar.

Jeff tilted his head, then dipped towards her to whisper, 'This is something else, this place. I never imagined it would be this, well, fucked I guess. Man, it's like another world. I feel — what's the word — all discombobulated.' His smile disappeared as soon as it formed.

She began talking about the layout of the home they would build. She sketched it out on the back page of his notebook. 'I always had this dream of a big house with loads of bedrooms, you know, and I used to doodle all the time this sort of dolls' house, and now I know why. This was always going to happen. I can do some good now.'

The businessman rose and shook hands. The prim woman sat looking very worried, while the black guy turned in his seat, ordering up another coffee.

Jeff looked at her T-shirt: *International Mercy Movement.* 'American,' he said, under his breath.

'You are a very good woman,' the black guy said, in basso tones, 'God has brought you to us, Mrs Kemp.'

She didn't reply. She dabbed her lips with the napkin, rose and shook hands with the man.

Jeff moved his chair to allow her to pass by. Looking up as she passed, he smiled at her, the flat, regretful smile of sympathy. He was taken aback by her look of disdain.

Before going to the Christian Mission's quarters in Kissy they decided to take a look at an orphanage in Freetown. They'd been told by the staff it was the best. It looked almost clean, from the outside it was all primary-colour painted wood and breeze-blocks — supplied by the Swiss. They looked into all the dark classrooms, stabling their glowering learning beings. In the last, there was a male teacher shaking in the dark, gritting his teeth, sweating over a natural law. The orphans were uniformed and smiling. Rachel chanced a wave at a small boy up front and he showed his teeth with glee.

Behind them came the less-tutored noise of a disturbance. The teacher raised his voice. A tall woman was being restrained by two security guards, who looked more doubtful than sure. There was a small child, red underpants, with a sticky-out belly button, dusty woolly grey hair and the cellophane snail trail under his nose, crying. The guards were shouting at her and pointing at the child and shaking him by his shoulders and pointing at her and pushing the child to her. But she was resisting taking him back. She was turning her neck, shaking her head, cowering and turning away, looking for the road. She wanted them to keep him.

Mohammed, their driver, sat solid in his seat as he drove them away. 'You're here on God's work,' he said, looking at them in the rear-view mirror. It was said without irony, but it sounded odd to Rachel, having just heard another man say the same thing. On the sunken back seat, they bounced along to the rap music in the tape player.

'Corruption, corruption. Pack and go. Pack and go . . .'

After miles of potholes, and a steep incline, Mohammed got out to retrieve the exhaust and stick it in his boot. He pointed towards an old mansion long bombed out, ivy clad. 'You change money here.'

Jeff got out and went over to where, in front of padlocked gates, some other foreigners stood hairy legged, exposing their wallets, while the turbaned money-changer went through his pockets, pulled out wads of treacle-soaked brown notes. Jeff was laughing with the other white people, showing the notes to them and shaking his head.

They were going to give money to the staff of the Christian Mission, they wanted them to buy the children clothes and to keep them fed until they came back with more. They would tell them to start looking for land for the home.

Mohammed sat head on the headrest, hand on the car window ledge, waiting for them, his taped music on a loop, 'corruption, corruption', occasionally greeting somebody with two lifted fingers. Before him the kaleidoscope of the town changed its patterns every few minutes, renewing orange with red, blue with purple, yellow with brown, moving, stirring, bewildering, and he faced it with indifference.

Jeff stood at his window with the notes.

'You pay me later, no problem.' Mohammed turned the key in the ignition and the music started up again. *'Corruption, corruption . . .',* and off they went to the lilting tones, the steel drums and electric organ, the windows rolled down, inhaling petrol fumes. Alongside them was a fleet of running children; bellies and lungs, sprung on legs, deliriously excited for as long as they could keep up with the car.

The day before they were to leave, they arranged buses to take all the children to the beach for the day. The kids lived only twenty miles from the sea and had never seen it. The excitement was wild, all the kids bouncing at the windows of the buses, shouting and singing. Arriving, they went en masse into the water, charging and cheering, then retreating in shock, then advancing again, splashing and crying out.

'Like pepper the water, like pepper!'

'Like pepper in the eyes! Like pepper!'

This was a change from the maudlin crooning, the torn petticoat-holding, the swaying before benefactors, and Jeff and Rachel were pleased to see the children being kids and not in their usual role of 'war orphans'. One by one they came out of the surf, to wipe their eyes on T-shirts, and then they raced right back in again.

Jeff had brought out a baseball bat and he organized the kids into a game while Rachel had her hair plaited by some of the older girls and a little one on each knee. She asked them questions about their lives. She was careful; the kids had seen some terrible things. When they first met, she had asked the pastor for the story of each child and he summarized each case study with casual brevity; mother raped, father murdered, mother lunatic, father amputee, mother missing, father missing.

Before they left the beach, they opened great plastic bags of gifts for the kids, a T-shirt each, a bag of sweets, some new flip-flops and, because the violence of the pandemonium threatened to harm the smaller kids, Rachel commanded them to stand in lines by size and let the little ones choose first.

Salamatu didn't get what she wanted, she had whispered her desire to Rachel on the beach, and so Rachel persuaded Jakka to relinquish a doll in favour of a pair of shorts. The twelve-year-old girl went off in a sulk, and cast Rachel looks all afternoon, making sure she saw her hurt. But Rachel kept her eyes fixed on little Salamatu, who sat and hugged her dolly by the side of the snack hut.

'It's like me and my mummy,' she said.

'Oh, sweetheart, do you miss your mummy?'

Sister Rose limped up in her long skirts, telling the girl to join the group for the lunch.

On their last night they took the staff for fried chicken and there was some dispute about who would get the chicken bones that were left over, Sister Rose was scolded by the pastor for pulling the bag from the hands of the junior pastor's wife, but the evening ended in reconciliation via prayer with the pastor offering thanks to Jesus for Auntie Rachel and Uncle Jeff.

'All of our hope and faith now rest with you, Uncle Jeff,' said Sister Rose throatily into his ear as she embraced him on their way out. 'I have fifteen children living with me. Don't forget me.' She held his arms in her hands as she pushed him away to see him better, and with a beatific smile she enquired of him, 'Who you think need them bones most? You can send me something, you can do it when you get back. Some dollars.'

They had a last beer in the bar. Jeff said he felt bad.

'Are you ill?'

'No,' he laughed derisively. 'No.'

'Then bad about what?'

'The whole thing, Rachel,' he said.

He looked sick. They sat there with a beer each, scratching their arms and legs. She gave him his anti-malarial pill. He pushed it back at her.

'Fuck it, it makes me want to retch,' he said to her. He finished his beer. 'I feel bad,' he said again. 'I don't know that I'm up to this. I can't work out what's good and bad like you can. I can't figure it out. There's no, like, tool or anything for that. I'm out of my depth.'

'Don't say that. It will be fine.' She tried to touch him.

He moved his arm away. 'Like we're such paragons, Rachel! Well, maybe you think you are, but I don't think I am.'

'Come on, J. They need us.'

'Yeah, but that's not enough.'

'Of course it is! That's everything! I don't understand. Are you going to let me do this on my own? Because I will.'

'I never asked anyone to count on me for anything! I never did! Not in all my life. I never asked for all of this!'

'You've had too much to drink.'

'Hey, I can't even count on me.'

'What do you mean?'

'I know who I am, Rachel, and what I am. I can't pretend to be some sort of saint. I'm selfish. I want to be happy. I'm sorry these people live like this but I'm not sorry enough to swap places. I can't follow you around Africa like . . . like some sort of . . . like . . . like I mean it.'

They looked at each other. He raised his beer bottle.

'I feel better for that.'

19

✧

MAUD ASKED TO STAY the night with Simone; they liked to watch television until midnight, eating toffee chews with Maud's head in the crook of Simone's button-up housecoat, the two of them lying side by side on the sofa. It was their secret that they stayed up so late. Guy went to bed before eight most evenings.

'We won't tell,' the old girl said to her.

'*On ne dit surtout rien,*' Maud would confirm. And Simone's eyes would cloud as they did so often when she held the little girl who was all hers, whom she had taught to speak French, who spoke her own words back to her, who listened to her so intently.

> *Ma petite est comme l'eau,*
> *Elle est comme l'eau vive . . .*

Maud would sit in the bath, humming this, Maud's tune, passing the flannel over her legs, wishing for a mermaid's tail.

Rachel had gone to London to meet with lawyers who were going to act pro bono to establish a charitable organization to raise money for the orphans' new home.

Jeff stood outside the great villa that evening with a glass in his hand. At night the yellow mustard green of pines seemed to ripen, and nature seemed to approach, a version of *who goes there,* don't look or else. Two or three birds sang their last good songs.

He felt the excitement of knowledge that wine brings diffuse through his throat and abdomen. He looked down to his neighbour's house and he thought: *You and me and the green on the tree, willing spring or anything, to happen and to happen to us.*

Then he went down there with a bottle in his hand, feeling the plastic wrap around the cork willing to give.

He and Valérie drank the bottle. He told her that he'd been presented that morning with a letter, by his wife.

'She prays morning and night, that's the problem.' *('You're driving me nuts,' he'd said to her between gritted teeth, looking at her on her knees, at the foot of the bed, praying.)* 'Why does she have to do it here in front of me? Some things should be private.'

Like his own assignations in the shower every morning. But before he could get to the shower that morning she had that letter ready for him, and he took it into the kitchen and sat, reading it, picking the corners of his eyes, stale mouthed, wiping up the milk that Maud spilt from her bowl with his shirt-sleeve, overly harsh with the kid when she upset her glass. He took her on his lap when she cried and kissed her head, and read the second side.

It might be because you don't feel the same way about God that I feel so lonely with you. In any case, although I care for you, as a 'neighbour' as a brother, as a fellow, I feel that I need to follow Him and love Him with all my heart. I don't want to have further relations with you until God's love is in this marriage . . .

He'd walked into the bedroom and sat down while she teetered round, wet haired, clutching her little breasts.

'*You've lost your mind.*'

'*Sorry.*'

'*Maybe you need to see a doctor or a shrink. Get something.*'

'So she leaves me this damned letter on the bed, you know, because we can't even speak to each other any more now we've got not just the one kid but fifty fucking three or whatever it is. She's like some kind of religious maniac. Basically she's saying the relationship is over. Oh no, wait. We're to be like Mr and Mrs Billy Graham or something. You know, it's the piety I can't stand. Talk about holier than thou.' He laughed through his nose. 'I like sex, I can't help it. Is that so wrong? Jesus Christ, I might as well be a eunuch.'

Valérie opened another bottle.

'Thank you for listening to me, Valou,' he said almost shyly. He was on his best behaviour; the decorous old-fashioned Yankee Doodle dandy.

They opened a third bottle and emptied a packet of cigarettes.

'Just to be touched, kissed . . . I mean is that so wrong? Is it? Yeah, it's great about the orphans. Great. But if it's all good, why do I feel like shit? Why does having orphans mean my services are no longer required? Oh, man. I like sex. Shoot me!'

When she began with her own cautionary tale, he cut in and got back to his. But she didn't mind. She knew she had only to listen to him to get what she wanted.

'I like sex too,' she said.

'I mean, come on, we're only human . . .'

'I like sex. I like it even when it is wrong,' she said.

'It's not even like we used to . . . What do you mean by wrong?'
His mouth stayed open.

She put out her cigarette.

'*Crimes passionnels*,' she said ever so slowly, enjoying the moment.

'That's not wrong though. Is it?' he said, his brow knitting.

'If it's bad. If it's really bad. You know.'

'What do you mean by bad?'

'That it is not right, that it is not right to do it.'

'You mean like, well I don't know, I mean like something people don't normally do, what do you mean? Like something weird?'

'No.'

'Oh, come on! Don't leave me hanging. What are you talking about? Anal?'

'No.' She laughed and threw the empty pack at him. 'No, I don't mean anal.'

'What then?'

'No, I mean need. Something, you know, really savage. And hungry.'

'Oh, man. I'm hungry,' he said. 'I'm thirsty too, and I don't know how it happened. I used to have a great life. She got pregnant and I did the right thing. I had a great job, I was riding high. I was somebody. I gave that up. She wanted me to give up the life I used to have. I did it. I did it for her and the kid . . .'

He was off again.

'I'm sorry, but you will have to think long and hard,' she interrupted him, 'about what you will do now. Right now, I mean.'

'No, no, no. I don't want to think. I want to drink.'

She stopped him with her hand on his face, three fingertips on the cheekbone, she was looking at him with clear intent. 'I'm afraid of falling in love with you,' she said.

114

He took her fingertips from his cheek and uncurled them and kissed the centre of her palm, looking up at her and he said, 'Fall in love with me, please. Please fall in love with me.'

'Come to bed and I will.'

They kissed and held each other, moving their hands over each other's skin. They averted their faces from each other to breathe; her lips moved against his razor-neat cheek, and she gave small ordinary gasps.

'I love you.'

'I love you.'

Then he put his hand over her mouth like a soldier raping a girl, and she looked at the half of him she had not seen before, the strained face, that looked at her with anger.

'Don't go home. Stay here with me,' she said afterwards as he moved off her and she reached for the side lamp and switched it off.

She lay on her side with her buttocks in his groin. He put his arms around her and held her breasts. He kissed her hair. He whispered, 'Voltaire said that it is in the face of the lover you see God.'

But it was completely dark in that shuttered room and he was asleep within seconds, while Valérie lay there, creating love.

20

✦

THE NEXT SUNDAY lunchtime was the last they would spend together, as couples.

Guy and Simone joined them all up at the Abrams villa. The meal was slow coming. They drank a couple of bottles of Champagne before it appeared. Bored, Guy took up the bowl of Camargue salt that was on the table, and threw it in his mouth, swallowing it down in one, then sat coughing and spitting, all done in. Simone assured them he'd done stupider things, he'd eaten live frogs for example. He retired a few minutes later, to the pool maintenance shed, to sleep it off.

Rachel had just come back from London. She was distracted, Richard thought. She forgot to turn the oven on, and the leg of lamb sat for an hour in the gloom.

On the terrace in the sunshine, Valérie manufactured a conversation concerning love and, on her insistence, each person was enjoined to put forward a definition. Jeff closed his eyes. She woke him by spilling her glass over him. He opened his eyes and dried his trouser leg the best he could with a napkin, making no comment.

Simone was chewing on her cigarette holder. 'Love is sacrifice,' she shrugged heavily, 'for a woman. That's what it is. Putting yourself second. You do it for the children and sometimes for the man. The cart cannot go faster than the horse.' She shrugged again. 'When I was running the market stall . . .'

'What about you, Jeff?' said Valérie, seeing his reptilian face settle again into the pretence of slumber.

'Oh, I guess we all see things very much our own way, you know. I guess we think about ourselves first, don't we? And what we want, and then we go and get it . . .'

'I think that is pathetic.'

'He's being honest,' Simone said, just as quickly, with a nervous smile, uncertain as to which way the wind was blowing and what, if anything, it carried for her and hers.

'It is so *égoïste*!'

'Yup, that's me. Prime asshole.' He closed his eyes again, but he was not smiling.

'Well, love is the belief that there is someone better than you, worth putting ahead of you, like Simone said,' said Rachel. 'Of course it's very close to idolatry, really. If you think about it. *I am a jealous God . . .*'

'It ain't me you're looking for, babe,' Jeff sang, pulling his baseball cap down.

'Why are you asking anyway?' said Richard. 'Are you trying to teach something or trying to learn something?'

'It's for a book I'm writing.'

'A book? You're writing a book?'

'I knew it!' said Simone.

'Oh really.' Jeff opened his eyes. 'How does it end?

'I don't know. I haven't decided yet,' she said, rising. 'Badly, I suppose.'

After lunch the women went to do the washing-up, the men dallied with their wineglasses outside. Simone glanced through the windows at them from time to time, her experience had taught her that when two or more men gather in any place, they are avoiding something.

Simone was at the sink, like a school-bus driver, casting looks behind her to see who was on board, sleeves rolled up, and Valérie drying and Rachel putting the leftovers into the rubbish bin and piling plates.

When Jeff stole past with a bottle, Valérie let a plate drop on to the floor. He flinched but kept walking. Simone spun round with a spatula in a cloth like a robber with a gun, saying, 'Nobody move.' Then she bent to pick up the pieces of the plate with hasty assurances, concerned for their feet, saying all the while, 'Stay still, you're wearing sandals, stay where you are.'

'Je rentre,' said Valérie, stepping past her mother, leaving her tea-cloth on the counter. 'I am going home.'

Simone carried on with a dustpan and brush, fussing and sweating and laughing and talking, talking, talking. It would be hard to sweep away, this one, and she knew it so she kept her head down, seeking specks of glass. 'I'm thinking of the children,' she said, 'they come in and out with bare feet.'

Through the open door Rachel watched the dark-haired woman walking loftily past the two men on the terrace. She had taken the long way round. It would have been quicker to go through the front of the house.

Rachel poured herself a glass of water in the kitchen. She looked at Maud in profile, sitting on the kitchen counter, playing with an Alessi corkscrew, opening and closing the arms on it. Her lips were slightly parted, her eyes still, she was utterly absorbed in this opening and closing until she tapped a glass by mistake, liked the sound and made deliberate music. She caught her mother's eyes and smiled. Rachel's eyes were full of tears.

Maud put down the corkscrew and opened her arms to her mother. 'Don't cry, Mummy, don't cry. Have a glass of wine.'

21

✧

PEOPLE LIED. People stopped talking to each other. Rachel was disappointed by the ongoing disputes from the construction of the villa, some of which were now going to tribunal for work not done, work badly done, and there were other spurious rows, some based on tittle-tattle, which gave those paid in full up front, sometimes friends, the excuse not to complete the work.

She asked Jeff, on the flight back to Freetown, what was wrong with the world.

He suspected she thought she knew and that frightened him. Jeff disliked fundamentalism. He kept a lid on what was wrong, and focused on what was pleasant; like Valérie with her top down around her waist as they kissed in the lawnmower shed, the evening before he left.

'Her big mouth, always hanging open, it annoys me when I see it. It seems to me so false, you know,' Valérie said to him about Rachel and that had made him nearly as nervous as what Rachel was saying now.

He had a lot on his mind, and still she talked, and talked and talked. He turned away from her, drinking his beer from the can, and he put on his earphones, studying the tiny screen intently, regular in his sips.

She looked at him, at the peevish turn of his lips. He was only there begrudgingly.

In getting pregnant, she'd aimed to capture the essence of him so that the living fact of him would be less and less important to her. She had to get over his smile with its slight underbite, the rough-shaven chin, how his face came together when he smiled, how he was never serious by choice but when he was forced to be, how he was bemused, somehow left behind in the game. He must have been a lovely boy, he must have made his mother's heart sing, he must have been naughty and daring, he must have called to her from high branches, from cold rivers, from under the bed, he must have cheated and cheeked her, he must have stolen and been sorry, he must have smoked and been sorry too, he must have messed up at school, too dreamy to get good grades. And then one day he'd come home, dumped out his schoolbooks which were a mess of graffiti and bad jokes and brought out his artwork, a pencil portrait of another kid, graded A. And his father would have come in with his cap set back one time, fresh from the park, his brow sweaty, and he would have told the mother about the boy's swing, and his eyes would have been slightly teary and the mother would have held her hands together tight and hard, not daring to clap.

Jeff handed four empty cans to the hostess and nudged her elbow so that he could pass her and go up to the toilet. She stepped up to let him pass.

The WC door opened and he allowed a man to exit, then ducked inside himself. He stuffed her gift for the journey, the little paperback edition of the book of Job, introduced by Bono, down the waste shute and sat down for a shit. When she talked to him about charity, the proper meaning of the word, a love that did not prefer, *true love,* she called it, he felt like killing her.

I hate lies, she said about the disputes, as if it were all that easy.

Oh yes, we all hate lies, sure, why not? Apart from the fact they're very, very useful. People lied and cheated not because they were fools, as she seemed to think, but because they were between difficult things, obstacles, caught hard and the only way out at all was under the wire, on your belly.

'You think you're better than me,' he said to her, sitting back down, swinging on the forward passenger's headrest to manoeuvre himself into the pew. He opened a fifth can of beer that he'd grabbed from the hostess station. 'It's the arrogance of it that kills me.'

She didn't say anything.

'Where's Jesus in it? Huh?' He pulled the ring, released a fine sour mist. 'Say you don't think you're better than me . . .'

'I don't.'

'OK. OK. So. Are you chosen?'

She said nothing.

'Come on. Have you been chosen? Rachel? Have you been chosen? Did God choose you?'

'I don't know why it upsets you, me being a Christian . . .'

'Ah, sweetheart . . .' He made a spitting sound, kicked his feet out, pushed his knees into the seat in front of him. He took a drink from the new can, wiped his mouth. 'Part of me just wants to watch your fall from grace.'

The old Russian chopper with its floral sofa seat coverings was the same. They flew low over the river ways and inlets into Freetown again. The hundreds of hands reaching and grabbing at the arrivals were all the same as before but the two of them emerged fairly relaxed with their handful of exhausted banknotes into a small group waiting for a minibus in the car park. They were with three American businessmen who were making much ado about staying at Mammy Yoko's, they'd been told to stay there, they were set on it and the bus pulled up every place else where the driver had some sort of interest and at each stop attracted new woolly-hatted hangers-on, useless and helpful, self-important, some furthering other causes and others devoted to the cause of the three men's stay at the Mammy Yoko.

The minibus drew up again and again and at each stop there were long-winded futile discussions.

'I believe I'm in Africa,' said one of the three men.

'You bet,' said Jeff warmly. 'Listen, guys, I bet I can get you in at our place. It's not so bad, some Indians run it, it's kind of clean. Showers in every room.'

'Sounds good to me, partner,' said the man, offering Jeff his hand.

The sari-clad owner's wife arranged the rooms and Jeff and the Americans went to the bar.

Rachel stood in the room alone with the bags of gifts and toys. 'Father be with me,' she murmured. She went to the window and opened it, she saw the nets on the shingle beach, the seaweed, the empty coconut husks, and she saw the twinkling lights of the small huts at the coastline on the other side of the harbour. 'Sweet Salone,' she said, using the local nickname, then she went to join him at the hotel bar.

The Special Court was in session and the bar was full of white people this time, the barman jumping through hoops; the diamond dealer was back again. Jeff was holding court, buying beers for his new friends. When they asked him what he was doing there, he gestured with his thumb at Rachel.

'Ask her, she's the good one. I'm the no-good non-believer. I'm here for the beer.'

22

$\diamond$

THE QUIET MORNING was rising and the last of the UN cars and trucks moved along the streets. There were groups of lucky children in dark-green uniforms going to school.

Mohammed told them the kids were 'hungry' to see them, he'd been by to see them just the week before. He hadn't changed the music in the car.

'Corruption, corruption. Pack and go. Pack and go . . .'

The kids were this time more joyful than shy, in their new T-shirts and flip-flops, they were ready with songs and dances, the older girls giving the younger ones harsh shoves when they moved too slowly, the boys cocksure.

Mohammed came up the steps of the church hall and stood outside, watching them. He leant back and raised a hand lightly to acknowledge Rachel's glance.

Salamatu was pushed into her arms and Rachel took her on her knee as well as Olive Jean, who was the tiniest child there. She called out to a plain girl of about seven or eight who would not join in with any of the games but hung back in her ragged red pinafore dress. Her hair was braided in three pigtails that came out of her head like a version of the Hydra. She had a squint.

'Hawa?'

The girl looked at her.

'Hawa? Why don't you smile?'

'I am ashamed,' she said. She raised her chin, then she turned away and went to sit on the steps of the wooden building to look out across the dust that blew through the yard between the shanty dwellings.

Rachel brought the staff up to date with their progress in establishing the fund-raising charity and they announced that they had found the land and needed, as they had correctly estimated and communicated already, about a thousand pounds to secure it. This sum Rachel and Jeff had deposited upon arrival in the national bank with the pastor as co-signatory.

Mohammed stood in this doorway too throughout. He seemed to be taking an interest in the venture.

Rachel told them she wanted to sit down with the kids one by one again and get as much biographical detail on each as she could elicit. She intended to take the details to the UNICEF office to check that none of these children were being sought by their parents. It was due diligence, she said.

The Christians exchanged looks.

'That will be hard,' said Uncle Abu, grimacing awkwardly. 'The children, they are not always remembering, not always truthful either, I'm afraid. It is best you take from our notes please.'

Some of the kids she was speaking to about their histories for a second or third time. She sat with her notebook, turning pages back and forth. Their stories changed; Jakka's mother was bitten by a snake and died in Conakry, was raped and killed in Liberia, shot dead in Hastings, and was also a lunatic a few doors up from the church hall.

Rachel told the staff she was confused.

'It is as Uncle Abu has said,' Sister Rose ventured, a hand curling upon Rachel's shoulder. She went between the white woman and the black children, translating the stories with her style of bashful brutality, smiles and stick, willing her charges onwards and backwards.

In the afternoon, the stories were translated by the spruce and humourless younger pastor, whose large pregnant wife had wrested the chicken bones from Sister Rose. His translations were unfathomable. He'd lift his head and say in clipped tones, further to a small boy's earnest account in Krio, 'I'm sorry but this is nonsense. This is of no use.'

Besides the six- or seven- or eight-year-olds who seemed so lucid and sincere, were the surly older kids, less than cooperative, and then there were the bewildered babes, saying little and looking off-stage all the time, turning their heads to the door.

'Where is de mama?'

The coquettish little girl giggled and put her hand over her mouth.

The young pastor stiffened, his jaw clenched. 'Where is de papa?'

Olive Jean pointed at Uncle Abu and laughed.

'Joking,' said the young man. 'She is joking. She is a bad girl.'

In the afternoon, they left the children and went in two cars with the staff to inspect the plot of land. The owner showed them the land with pride, touching the sugarcane as he passed it by as if shaking hands with old friends. They came to a clearing. In the distance were low-lying red mountains.

'Africa!' said Rachel.

The staff formed a circle and they all held hands there while the pastor said a prayer. Before they left, Jeff picked up a red rock, volcanic-looking, and gave it to Rachel. She held it in her hand, her palm taking the blessed heat of it.

The negotiations with the landowner were brief. They sat with his wife in a small room, painted blue. Mohammed joined them, again at the doorway, in mute surveillance, an eye on the road, an eye on the room. The landowner approved their scheme; it was a good thing, the children would be happy there.

After they all shook hands, he took them down the mud pathway towards the river creek, his garden. They passed under a laden avocado tree; he gave them miniature bananas. She'd never tasted a banana like it. She said to Jeff, 'They taste like a rainbow looks.'

Some men were digging a latrine on the way down the hill and they grinned at their visitors. Hoeing the soft mud beside the river were the owner's family members, children more or less naked, and women with babies on their backs. They waved up at them and Rachel was struck by the scene. Suddenly, tears coursed down her cheeks.

'I'm sorry, I can't help it,' she said.

The pastor looked at her but said nothing. The Brooklyn pastor might have said to her that it was because God was with her, but this pastor said nothing.

Two of the owner's grandchildren brushed against his pressed trousers and, as he bent to sweep them, Rachel noticed the Armani brand name on the band of his boxer shorts.

In the car she took the rock to her lips. Mohammed saw her in the mirror. He wore mirrored glasses, she did not see him looking.

Jeff offered him a cigarette.

'Thanks. I like these cigarettes,' he said. 'You like that land. You're pleased with it?' he asked, blowing out smoke.

'I think it will be great for the kids,' she said, her eyes outside, going from wandering child to wandering child.

'The kids, kids, kids. All she think about is the kids.'

'That's right,' said Jeff.

'You poor man. She must give you very hard time to make money for the kids, the kids, the kids. She got you working all the time, right?'

'Yeah,' said Jeff, 'that's right.'

'Oh yes,' Mohammed drawled agreeably. 'Just like my wife.' The traffic was still. He turned off the engine. He made a call on his mobile phone. It was a brief and happy exchange. He took off his glasses as the smog and dirt merged with the early-evening darkening of the shantytown landscape.

'Your wife?' asked Jeff.

'No.' He laughed.

'Your lover?'

'No, not her,' he returned with pride, 'no, it was a friend of mine. I'm going to take you to meet him. He's a very old man, very wise. He can help you. You'll like him. A very respectable man, very religious. He's in the government. The only man who is not corrupt!' He put a finger in the air, started the engine, and the usual music.

'*Corruption, corruption*, huh?'

'You said it, man.' He put his glasses back over his eyes, extinguished the cigarette, and was quiet for the remainder of the drive. He looked at the two of them more than once; the man relaxed and loose, and her with her hand at her chin, in a fist which suddenly broke open like a bird's wing when she saw a child to wave at. He couldn't understand why she was not with her own child; he kept his eyes on her when they were shaded.

He deposited them at the offices of an Italian children's charity. This time he stayed in the car, in his usual pose, one hand tapping out the beat of the music on the car door, waiting for it to be over.

The Minister for Children's Welfare arrived on a motorbike wearing a long white *jellaba*. He had his bike to get round the potholes, to dodge the loopholes, to make quick getaways. There were not enough chairs and so the pair of them sat and others stood, like bouncers ready to bounce them, around a table outside under an old stone pagoda affair, a relic of colonial days. The woman who ran the charity was something like the mediator. She had a notebook opened at a blank page and began by asking them to explain what they were doing in Sierra Leone. They did.

He looked old, the minister, but as it happened he was more quick than dead.

'I will look into this group of war orphans, but I doubt they are what you think they are. We have, I think, managed to get something like ninety-five per cent of child war refugees back to their villages, where they will be looked after. There is no such thing as an orphan in Africa. It is quite unlike the West in that way. The community is the only wealth we have. The children you saw at the school you mention were left there by their ambitious parents. We have seen already three orphanages built in Freetown and with all of them it is the same and so we discourage such things. We do not want two systems here. And that is the least of it frankly. My next job is to call my counterpart in Holland, there are four hundred of our children there, shipped over for the sex trade. They had been kept in an orphanage near the border, as a holding centre. So you can see, there are many reasons we do not allow orphanages to be built here. So now, please give my office a list of these children's names, will you?'

They stood, chairs scraped dirt. He was back on his bike and away leaving them with the word 'orphanage' sounding suddenly so communist, the pagoda cringing away from the baked earth.

That evening they met with their orphans and their sponsors, the Christian Ministry of African Brothers and Sisters, for a half hour of song and prayer in the church hall. Afterwards, they followed a few of the kids back to their 'foster' parents, brothers and sisters who, indeed, looked very much like them, and whom they called mummy or daddy. The orphan children, the ones they'd come to house, school and feed and to remove elsewhere, were being made by their families to sing for all of their suppers.

Mohammed knew the location of every possible place they needed to go but, given there were so few roads, wherever they went they were obliged to sit for hours on the same main through road in the traffic fumes and fog, sweltering hot, filthy dirty, sore-throated, thirsty while Mohammed turned his engine off for minutes at a time.

On the long road home, an hour's drive, every time the pedestrian or street hawker they set off alongside would pip them on arrival, a footfall ahead. From the car she saw people pawing through the garbage dumps, hawkers selling green liquid drinks in bags, donkey carts pressing on, picking their way through the chaos, and everywhere you looked someone was watching you back. Jeff sketched a tall boy with his bundle of sticks, leaning against a workshop, looking at the mêlée as if he saw open fields, daydreaming. He titled it 'Ambition'. He caught perfectly the boy's poise, the will of his conjuring eyes.

In the morning, she stood by the window. Jeff woke, saw her there and sat up. 'Rachel. The young guy, you know the apprentice pastor or whatever, he said to me yesterday they'd need a motorbike. I said sure, what, like a moped or something? He said, no man, I mean like a big bike, a Honda, 850cc. Don't you think his wife's kind of fat for Sierra Leone?'

'I honestly don't know what to make of it,' she said, looking down to the sea. *Like pepper for the eyes,* she thought.

23

✧

SHE TOOK THE 'pastor' to task over lunch. Was he really going to have these children taken from their parents? He considered his bowl of cassava. Sensibly, he ate while she left the sticky bottle of soda untouched, annoyed by the mosquito bite beneath the line of her ankle socks, reaching down to swipe and scratch like a chimpanzee.

If he was tired, then he was tired. He looked like he'd taken better beatings elsewhere. There was an edge of defiance he was keeping clean for the next time, she could see that; only a portion of him was present. He was already thinking 'internet'. He polished off his lunch.

And what about her? So she took the upper hand and threw him off. But what had she left behind her moral line in the sand? Just a gulf of understanding; slightly deeper.

Both of them saw through her at the same time now; she was quiet in the car, defensive in the bar. Jeff tried to make it better, over beers, he tried out some jokes. Black humour.

'What SUV do you think the pastor drives?'

It seemed sweet, somehow cinematic, only the day before

when they drove down the hillside, tossing handfuls of wrapped sweets out of the car window to the children running alongside.

She sucked at the brown beer bottle, the backwash sweet and frothy. They'd put a whisky bottle up on the bar shelf earlier this week and there were peanuts in a dish. The war was over, but the UN were almost done pulling out and business was bad. A lone black woman in a miniskirt sat without a drink, carrier bag at her feet.

There was a radio plugged in now, its aerial broken, its message a confusion of languages, bleating about evil between candy-cane beats.

Jeff was drawing something in his notebook, quickly absorbed, his head low, one elbow out across the table, pencil point going fast, his wrist a tremor. She sat there, looking at his left hand sketching away, the hairs on his hands, the movement beneath them of the nerves; he didn't look at her, though he knew she was looking at him. And then he got up, stretched, sighed and said, 'Going back to the room for a meeting with my maker.' He took his notebook with him.

From the bar she could see all the drivers waiting in the hotel car park down below, behind the breeze-block wall and barbed wire, standing about, smoking. White sports utility vehicles; the UN. A couple of brown Mercedes, ancient things, for the use of the rest of them to peruse the damage in terms of human collateral.

Mohammed had said goodbye to them. He wasn't surprised when they told him it was all a stitch-up, even the land they'd bought to build on. At the Land Ministry they had the tax receipts for the sale of the same land seven times in the last three months. Rachel kicked the car wheel down in the car park.

She'd looked at Mohammed. 'We don't even own the land!'

Yes, he said. *Yes. I know.*

If he knew he could have bloody told them! She didn't ask him why he hadn't. She gave him his money and some extra for his daughters.

'Thank you,' he said. 'See you next time, I hope.'

She went up the steps to the hotel, her hands in her pockets, wondering whether he was in on it too. She thought of him standing in the doorway at every meeting. She leant over the balcony and watched him go, his brown Mercedes minus its exhaust pipe groaning up the steep hill. The weighted white iron gate swung back into place, the sentry jumped out of its way in alarm.

She said to herself: *It's OK not to know everything.*

She never thought about Mohammed again. But he thought of them, and the other white tourists he drove sometimes reminded him of that young couple; the hand-wipes, the cigarettes *('I only smoke when I'm in Africa'),* the tips and the cordiality. If he could help it he never drove a black man.

When she got back to the room, Jeff was on the mobile phone. He closed it up right away. He looked at her, both impatient and crestfallen.

Nothing was said.

She lay down on the bed, looking up at the wires where the light should be, with her feet crossed. The door to their room was open and outside there were two cleaning ladies squatting near a marbled coloured plastic basin. One had her eyes closed and the other had her tongue in between her front gum and upper lip, ruminating.

Rachel closed her eyes. In her mind they were already in reverse, drawn backwards to the port, to go to the airport by boat, going past the Cotton Tree, backpacks on their laps, an amputee's stump retracted through the open car window. 'Long sleeves', they called it, when it was just above the wrist, the stump bound like a salami.

You get diminishing returns from love and horror, she thought. *You get wiser. But is it worth it? What do we lose in return for seeing clearly? There's no choice, in any case.*

She saw in her mind's eye her so reserved father look up from the chair in the living room, pencil hovering over the crossword. The hoods of his eyes coming down and, before he spoke, deciding against telling her what was on his mind. The death of his wife one more obstacle. He did not love like lovers love. Why? It scared him — very well, it scared her too. It had scared her mother. Love required embracing absolutely everything, not just the fairy tale but the monster too, the light and the dark.

Now she knew that nothing worth having came of guilt or pity; that you had to be tough to love, not sorry, sorry, sorry.

24

✧

RICHARD WENT TO Kenya the next time to learn the market from local doctors by shadowing, but he was the shadow who saw his own form. Everything else that happened came after that.

A driver came to take him to the local hospital in Nyeri. The minivan paused at the traffic light in the small town of colonial leftovers, the streets were ruinous, the shops shambolic. Beside the vehicle six men had green sturdy chairs for others to sit on while they polished their shoes. A dwarf was using his stubby hands rather adroitly to polish a pair of shoes. His customer looked up at the white man in the van and smiled.

They moved forwards slowly. Women walked at the same pace along the side of the road, in crocheted wraps their infant children were secured on their backs. Boys came along with bundles of sticks tied and attached to the seats of their bikes. School children walked past in twos holding hands. Posters advertised condoms or Jesus.

They moved along the cusp of a hill. He looked down to his left and swallowed hard. The view extended for hundreds of miles. Africa beyond was inexorable, vast, glistening. Giraffes moved across the plains like churches with nodding steeples, and beyond them he could see a herd of elephants, stately, among the flat-topped acacia trees. To the east, Mount Kenya loomed, its peaks concealed in cloud.

He sat, dumbstruck, stuck by sweat to the seat, trying to find space for it all.

'Africa,' he said. The driver nodded.

Out the back of the tinpot provincial hospital was a separate bungalow nominated the psychiatry department. As Dr Wainanga had told him, there was a long queue of young people and their parents waiting for their turn in the outpatients clinic.

He was shown through to the small stuffy consultation room and bidden to take a seat at the side on the bench. A schoolgirl was shown in with an adult.

In front of her was the big old wooden desk, a single chair, for her, on which she was enjoined to sit, and there were the two doctors before her, behind the table. The younger one was in a white coat. The other wore a checked jacket and had a newspaper spread out before him. To the side against the school-paint-blue wall on the bench with Richard were three nurses, with tiny white starched triangles attached to their corn-row braids, sitting with their knees crossed the same way.

More boys and girls, in their school uniforms, came and went. Each received medication, and the adult with them received some serious instructions after a few curt questions.

The chief doctor, Dr Wainanga's friend, was courteous enough; he asked the patients to present themselves to the 'guest' and each did so. He asked them to address themselves to the guest in English and each made a good showing. An elderly woman came in, bent over like a crone, and raved in a distraught fashion, occasioning the outright laughter of the nurses and doctors.

The young doctor explained in English that she said she was six hundred years old, and that her daughter was four hundred years old and that even allowing for the difference, he smiled, she would have been well beyond her childbearing years when she gave birth.

The nurses looked at Richard with glee, and he obliged them with a breezy smile. The older doctor told her to greet the guest too and she turned to him, and as if the language required a different role entirely, she said with dignity, offering him her hand, 'Good day to you. I'm very pleased to meet you. I hope you are enjoying our country.'

The next patient was a very thin little girl, bone-chested, in a gingham frock, her auntie said she was twelve, and she came in as though nailed to the cross, her head back, eyes scanning the ceiling, her neck and arms stiff, her face awash with tears. All she could respond in answer to their questions was, 'I am all alone in the world.'

Dr Wainanga's friend explained that this effect was produced by over-medication, too strong a dose for too small a girl; she was suffering the side effects.

'Acute dystonia,' nodded the young doctor.

Another medication could counteract that, which they would prescribe. No wonder she felt she was all alone in the world if all she saw were ceilings!

They shared a smile.

The girl left as she came in, startled, her face wet with tears. The doctors asked the nurse at the door to give them five minutes for their notes.

Richard went outside to smoke a cigarette in the warm damp air. The little girl was standing out there, her unfocused stare like that of a blind person; she was waiting to be led away by her aunt, who was in discussion with the nurse on the front desk.

'Will I get my eyes back?' she asked him.

'Yes, you will,' he said.

'I never dreamt I would meet a European.'

He blew out, his shoulders sagged, his stomach sank over his belt.

'I would be a good daughter to you,' she said. She smiled with a sudden radiance that stopped the flow of her tears.

He didn't know what to say.

She had not seen him, she had only the idea of him in mind. Was that sufficient to make such an extravagant offer? Her hopes humbled him.

The aunt came and took her, guiding the girl by the arm, and they went above him to his left, then farther above him to his right on the zigzag pathway that took them away up the slight incline through to the main campus.

He put out his cigarette and wandered down the alleyway to a fenced compound arraigned with young bodies prone, face forward often, in their calico patients' robes, stretched out, in medicated stupors on the grassy dirt.

They were kept this way, their days must surely pass as slow as a hundred lives, the dreams or visions that moved through their heads as unreachable as the clouds above them.

The little girl believed that there was goodness. She asked for some. But there was not enough to go round. There were too many people asking. The thing was to stop them all asking at once.

He told himself he could both do his job and satisfy his conscience by making a note to get these people the new generation of anti-depressants and anti-psychotics at a fair price, a price they could afford. That would be the best solution. They could function that way.

He looked at all the bare feet at right angles to the earth. He looked at the knuckles. He looked at the thick-nailed fingertips, making their claim upon the earth.

He took off his jacket and undid his tie and put it in his pocket. He rolled his sleeves to above his elbows.

'Jesus Christ,' he said out loud.

Back in the consulting room, the nursing trio changed knees in unison, something like medicine's answer to the Supremes. Supremely happy they seemed, and the next patient to come in, another young girl, couldn't help but smile at them; a shot of that pubescent joy fed on its opposite, apprehension.

She was a very pretty girl.

Her father, browbeaten and muddy, took his place, perching on the bench on the other side of the room, the least confident. He could not make his mind up whether to sit or stand so he hovered between the two. When asked, he described her malady unctuously, moving farther forwards on his seat, his intentions shared between the doctors, his betters. It was as if he'd come for a loan.

The suited older doctor turned the pages of the newspaper — perhaps he was looking for a certain car. The younger one wore a forced expression, in stark contrast to the other's amused and relaxed air. The father recounted his story.

All the while the girl, from beneath her long hair, with delighted jaw jutting, was seeking something from the nurses and from him, Richard, with bashful lashed looks. She was quite different from the last little girl; this girl was on the brink of delight, so sure life would go her way and that this was a temporary silliness.

She was disobedient, the father counted out her sins on his fingers, *she laughed when alone. No, there was no joke to laugh at, she just laughed.*

The doctor closed his newspaper and looked with serious interest at the girl. *Laughing alone?*

The young girl was like a modern princess in a foreign land, all uncomprehending delight. He couldn't help smiling back at her, they had a moment of complicity. He wanted to say, *Don't worry, don't worry . . .* and it was as if she were saying, *I'm not, I'm not.*

He wanted more than anything in the world for her to go on out of there with a spring in her step, into a good life. She was not scarred, she had nothing to carry on her shoulders, she was the lightest of all of them. She reminded him of the girl he married.

She read in her room. Books. She would not do as he said. She laughed at him openly. Yes, she was doing fine at school.

'Anything else?'

She was disobedient; she did not do what he said.

'Is she elated?' asked the fine doctor, raising his eyes, looking somewhere past the nurses, taking them under the wings of his authority.

The young doctor frowned, licked his lips. 'Yes.'

'Is it catching? Are we elated?'

The intern was quick. 'No.'

It was the sentence. The nurses stifled themselves. Knees dampened down. The older doctor closed his newspaper and served the father at last.

'Your daughter will go no further at school, she will never have a normal life, she will need medication all her life. She will probably never marry.' The young doctor opened the prescription pad. They had but one medication to give. He looked at Richard Bird. And not much of it. Chlorpromazine. An old drug. This was the injustice they lived with. They had just as much mental illness as in Europe or America, all the same disorders.

The nurses lowered their eyes. They had heard the doctor say it in the corridor that morning, before the visitor came, angry, while his patients milled around dumbly in dark-blue calico, eyes glazed.

They would prescribe the medication and she must take it daily. She must not miss a day. Did he understand? He must pay for it too.

Yes, yes; this episode was waiting for him, the father, somewhere at the back of the shamba, his garden, inside the order, outside of the order, something connected with his planting, he knew to prepare for it. He knew that when it came he would be straight and ready and right.

The girl untwisted at speed, uncoiled, put out long hands, her eyes rounded and darkened, her eyes sought the nurses but they weren't there any more, their eyes, their matching teeth, their cake-shop paper crowns, all gone. The intern disappeared next, the father evaporated, the doctor fizzled out. Gone.

And all that remained were the girl's eyes, waiting for the stranger to say something to save her.

He sat there, silent. He sat there dumbly.

Goodbye, girl. You have to move along now, shuffle off, go on.

But Richard felt that if she went from his mind, some of him would go with her.

He was finished with the job, he knew it then, and moreover, he was finished with the rest of the life he'd fabricated.

PART TWO

25

✧

ONE FRIDAY EVENING at the end of August, just after supper, he picked up the phone to hear Jeff's wife's voice.

'Richard.'

'Yes?'

'Richard.'

'I'm listening.'

'Richard.'

'Rachel, is something wrong?'

He'd raised his eyebrows at his wife, pointing at the phone. Valérie was leaning against the kitchen counter holding an empty glass at her lips. He mouthed the name of the caller at her: *Rachel.*

Her look did not match his. She looked afraid and also excited. She didn't move. She waited. And so did he. He waited but he already knew.

They'd lived next door to each other for four years or so, but it was really in the past year, drinking together, that they'd become friends, he and Jeff.

Richard was out of step with everyone else around there, because he was working for the man unlike the locals and the foreign 'lifestylers.'

143

After a good many *apéros,* dinners and impromptu into-the-early-hours drinking sessions, he'd gone and told Jeff something about his other life.

It was a departure from the usual programme. The anecdotal salesman, much travelled, Richard had a book of life arranged in chapters to which he referred normally over business lunches and dinners: *Saint Petersburg Nightlife; Meeting Mick Jagger; An Embarrassing Bowel Accident in a Ski Lift.* He was no longer sure if these things had really occurred but the telling and retelling took a consistent enough form, his audience was rarely the same, and from each tale he emerged unscathed. But in drink and in this man's company he went beyond the script.

The thing was, he suspected now, that was what really finished it all; telling Jeff about his other life. Until then he'd kept his two worlds apart.

The old adage about shit and the doorstep was worth observing.

He woke after their drinking sessions the same way: face forward, saliva oozing on to the pillow and over his cheek, and in his thorax, between the ribcage and skin, a pain. He assumed it was the booze. When he recalled their conversation later in the sober light of day, on the motorway generally, he had a curdling feeling in his chest, which he later knew to be the tickle of a tiny treason. He told himself he was allergic to wine and swapped to beer.

The women had left them to it, to the barbecue, the fire, the roast, to the opening of the bottle; their manly play. Jeff did offer a good turn in self-deprecation; that he was washed-up, with the implicit addendum that he had found 'the meaning of life'. The ring-pull used to sound the end of one story and the beginning of another.

He never knew whether Jeff's anecdotes were based on any

truth, they were entertainment, they seemed improbable enough, combining famous people with outlandish drugs in high-rolling places, fantasies most likely, campfire tales that got more spooky, more twitchy later on in the evening. He would finish with the flourish of making off with the stash, the booze, the money, and the girl, perhaps, if Rachel and Valérie were absent. He could tell a story, he kept a smile on his face and didn't mind admitting his mistakes.

Jeff had sat on Sunday afternoons in Richard's kitchen, his head bobbing under the hanging lamp, eating salty snacks, *cornichons, saucisson,* going to the fridge for the both of them, slow as an old horse, for another beer, for more of the same.

Their mutual confidences mounted in the springtime, as he and Jeff spent more and more time together. Their friendship showed itself in the hand on the shoulder as they parted ways. Fishing trips, camping trips, holidays in Sardinia were mooted. Jeff showed him his poetry and his cartoons, he took him through the vineyards, had him taste the first wine he made. Richard had got to like the man's quiet joy. Now he knew something of its source.

He'd even gone and told Richard how he screwed his business partner's wife. (This was the guy whose house they were drinking in. It was this very Don Abrams who was paying the bills.) She was an opera singer, Don's wife, she made such a noise, the major domo (as he described the servant) tried to break into the bedroom by shouldering in the door.

He laughed in slow motion. He took his time and there was some marvelling at himself in it, some callousness too.

Sometimes people tell stories for a reason, as a warning, as a way of spilling the beans, as a way of trying to part company with the bad, but the story is always bigger than the storyteller.

26

✧

HE PUT A SUITCASE into the boot of the car on the Monday morning and stood looking at it with slowly dawning detachment, as if it were a person whose name he could not recall. He was having lots of moments like that since Valérie left.

A month after he returned from Kenya, he was going to Cairo again for another conference. It would be the last time he went away on business. In the interim his wife had left him.

He closed the boot and took off his jacket. As he stooped to put it behind the driver's seat, on its rightful peg, he checked through the window the place by the kitchen door where she used to stand watching him go. It occurred to Richard now why it was she stood there watching him go. Nevertheless, there she remained, in his mind, paused in the act of caring that he went safely, soundly. Yes, in his head, his wife was leaning for ever more, leaning against the door with a cup of coffee between her hands, contemplating him as if he were the suitcase; with objectivity, one might say. She used to offer up a half-hearted wave, a faint-hearted fair-lady folding of the fingers on to the palm. She'd looked exhausted, worn out. But that was the look women wore there. Her mother bore the same. *La douleur, la souffrance.* It was the ancient order of things round there.

His son ran out of the house and came round to the passenger door. He leant across to push it open for him. His wife was attractive but Maxence was not a very good-looking boy. The smallest thing and Richard found he had tears in his eyes that day — it was as if a cobbler had sewn his heart to the back of his throat with leather cord. Richard kept his head low so it pulled less.

He had already told Max he'd be away at a conference for a few days. He drove him to the village to school; a bold morning, the sun striking hard, the elderly buildings and trees embarrassed by its mercilessness. Visor down, he drove in silence up the single street of the village that ended at the school.

Hey, he said as Maxence got out of the car. The kid gazed back at his father with great foolish eyes and buck teeth, poised on comprehension. *Hold on, what am I thinking? You're too big to kiss your father now!*

Richard watched him run up the steps. The boy didn't look back and that hurt, but he said to himself: *That's good, that's good.* He had the impression that everything he said or did mattered in a way it never had before. As he drove he looked from time to time in the mirror to see who he was and who was behind him.

At the airport, in one of the departure lounges, there was an enormous group of orthodox Jews fussing about, all untied, womanless, waiting for their flight to Tel Aviv, muttering and mumbling. Richard didn't mind standing and looking at them. He didn't mind if it made them feel strange to see how strange they were to him. There were things he needed to find out about human beings; clearly there was a lot he didn't know.

He was sick of being a foreigner. All the pretence of being French! How irked he'd been when some shop person replied to him in broken English after he'd used his best local accent! He'd been a long time away from himself. It went back further than

France. It went back to how he left school and went straight into commerce, chopping and changing jobs, going to competitors for salary hikes. How he could talk his way into anything. Eye contact. It went back to his accent even in English, how he could be either plummy or working-class. It went back to how his mother left them when he was seven and his father took them from council house to oast house and women came and went with Easter eggs and high heels, wearing that year's perfume. It went back to how his father had shoved him up the class ladder and in through the window of private schooling. It went back to how as a child he had to learn how to be a child by imitation. It went back to how surprised he'd been to find that girls wanted him to touch them between their legs, and how much their willingness depended on his own idea of himself.

His wife once said she didn't know him, but he'd assumed things had changed since she'd not mentioned it in the fourteen years thereafter.

To all appearances, suited and smart, perfumed, clean-shaven, he was the man he used to be, the same man who flew this route back in spring.

He passed amongst his former sales brethren unremarked. It was embarrassing to him now to see how pharmaceutical sales reps conducted themselves. Freeloaders. Jackets off. Backpacks emblazoned with drug brand names. He stared at people because he wanted to see what was in their heads.

Rachel had told him once that if he looked, he would see that every single thing is a piece of God and that in any single event there is everything we need to learn. He was counting on it now.

She'd told him it at 1 A.M. the week before when they were sitting drinking in her kitchen, with the shining sincerity that two bottles of red can bring about, and he called her a silly cow and touched her face. It changed just as he touched it, as if by transubstantiation; the wine became blood.

So he was going to Cairo to have his head occupied with the clever thoughts that belonged to other people. He would listen to them talk about the mind, although what was getting him up every morning was the idea that he might understand something new about the human heart.

Just a couple of weeks ago, a fortnight after Valérie left them, he and Maxence went off fishing together one Saturday. He had stood by the side of the river bludgeoning a trout with a stump of wood when he saw himself. *This is supposed to be father–son bonding time — and we're beating this creature to death,* he thought. He looked at Max and thought: *Why am I even doing this? This is bullshit.* Max's face, the expression on it, reminded him of the whole of his childhood, all fixated patience, trying so hard to see the sense in what the adults were doing, waiting to see the point.

He said: *Enough hunting, enough fishing.*

'Is this how we're going to get to know each other?' he asked Max.

Max took the fish in his hand and bit the head off it. The boy stood there with fish blood and bones in his mouth, the body in his hand, the head on the toe of his sneaker. He spat out what was left in his mouth two or three times and said, with a full grin, his eyes shining, 'Done it.'

Richard nodded, kept his cool; he looked around to see if anyone was watching.

'Is that what your grandfather does?' he asked Max in the car, recalling the stories. The live frogs consumed whole. The pig's heart still warm.

'No,' said Max. 'I'm better than him. Can I have a Coca-Cola now?'

27

⟡

ARRIVING IN EGYPT, Richard smiled like a son of a bitch, at everyone and everything. He wound down the window and opened his mouth. From the sweat and heat, he went into the cool marble lobby and had his bags taken from him; he impressed the staff with his smiles and thank-yous. He treated them like friends, better than he treated his friends. This was the mainstay of his travel routine, and all of his life was a travel routine. His policy was being polite, being nice to stay safe and not because you were nice.

After dinner alone, having tried the Egyptian wine, and praised its virile fortitude, having got along very well with all the waiting staff and the door handlers going in and going out, and thanking them all and grinning hard, he went to his room to go to bed and when he got inside he dropped the trousers of his smile, he locked the door and put a chair against it.

The opening session at the conference was an address by the head of the World Health Organization. He had once been a noted psychiatrist, he'd written tens of books. But this whole thing was a front, paid for by pharmaceutical companies, including his. The old hack got straight to the point.

'Advances in Psychopharmacology: New drugs for new disorders.'

He was wearing a brown suit, he was very thin and old, he stood with one hand in his pocket. The glasses, lightweight frames. The tie, a garish red and purple, a sort of visual hologram. A Swatch-type watch on his wrist. His hair dyed too brown for his pale shiny face, he looked like a crème caramel. The migraine-conducive lighting meant that they were all looking at him with various other images imprinted across his chest, the things they'd glanced at before they looked at him.

'It is our endeavour to classify the world and simplify it. A child is born and knows what is a dog, then it sees small and large dogs and gradually it understands that there is not a single dog but creatures which have in common their bark, of course, and other features like a bone in their penis . . .'

Nobody stirred. But really this was a strange thing to say, and for the opening address too. One could only suppose he said what he liked because no one was really listening to him and he was used to that.

Richard scrutinized the other attendees, sitting there with their free folders and fliers, the crib notes to be stowed in the Sanitoxat-branded satchel. He looked back at the brown president. His shoes were of thin leather, you could see the shape of his toes.

It seemed to him that life was loss. Sometimes in drips and drops, sometimes by flood. What was it his son had said the night before he left?

'I've lost so much lately.'

She didn't deny it, Valérie, 'the affair'. She packed and moved out. They went away together, the two lovers, somewhere modest in terms of a drive that cost a fortune a night. He got the credit card statement in the post. If only that were all he got in the post.

Rachel came round and told him she was going back to England with Maud. Before she left she said, 'God comes into your life. They tell you to ask Him to and He will. They don't tell you He can bugger off again.'

He'd stood to open the door for her. 'Take care of yourself. You're such a good person.' It was all he could say; it was true. She tried to be and that was more or less the same thing; the only thing. Her look said: *But so what?* And that made him feel sad, and he was sad about it the next day and the day after and even after that until he had forgotten what it was that had made him sad.

Valérie left him the boy. He stayed in and drank heavily while Maxence played his Game Boy. Then she came in one Sunday lunchtime, with mascara under her eyes. They stood up, he and the kid. They stood to attention. Richard looked at his son to see what was on his own face; chin in, reproachful, afraid of this woman who for so long had been hiding how little she knew either of them.

She looked at the dirty dishes on the counter but said nothing.

'I don't think he loves me.' Being French she cut to the chase. An Englishwoman would have sat minding her p's and q's, counting the pennies, folding the smalls before getting to the point.

Her lower lip went like it used to, when they first met, wanting something, as yet unpronounced. You just had to wait to hear what it was. You just had to wait.

She prepared a meal and they sat to eat it at the same places they had sat since Maxence was born.

'I think he has been with another woman.' She handed Richard the olive-wood salad bowl they got for a wedding present, with the utensils pointing towards him and the underside of her forearms hairless and pale, tending to him. 'I want to be back with my son,' she said. 'I miss him. I need to come home.' Then she wept.

'I assume your home does not include me?'

She looked at him with pained reproachful eyes. '*Ri-schard . . .*'

When they met, her big hero was Daniel Balavoine. She liked the saddest song of all, the most popular one, '*Mon fils, ma bataille.*' With its naïve, merry tune and its distressing words.

'*I am going to break everything if you take my son from me.*'

But he doesn't say 'son' he says 'fruit of my loins'. So primitive, but it wasn't too much to put it that way, perhaps, thought Richard, for someone as sincere as Balavoine, though of course, like many things, it's better to sing it than to say it.

'You know the gobstoppers that change flavour? We found them at Super U,' Max said suddenly, standing, poker faced, his eyes startled. He looked like Bambi with the butterfly.

'Do you remember, your mother wanted to see how many I could get in my mouth, when we were on the motorway? I nearly choked to death.'

'She put one in your ear.'

'What? What's that?' Richard tapped his ear and shook his head.

Richard poked his fingertip in his ear in staccato motions with his eyes wide and father and son, they ducked in and out of each other's laughter.

The kid sat, and they each took a mouthful of food, then Richard looked at her. He let his knife and fork drop on to his plate.

'If you need a home then have this one,' he said. He took up his glass and drained it and put it back down in its place; empty.

'No. No. She can't come home now,' said Max, shaking his head and repeating the phrase again, his head bowed.

She put her head in her hands and started to weep again.

The salad bowl sat, untouched, two wooden arms outstretched.

28

✧

He went to that last conference, hell-bent on attending as many of the psychiatry seminars as he could. He was on his own. Empty; every conference room, chairs in rows, pointing the right way, but lacking weight. He went from session to session. In each, suited speakers spoke through their studies, making an occasional aside for the benefit of the faithful, the one or two colleagues or the assistant who pressed the button for the next slide.

The supposed audience, those thousands of attendees, doctors and sales reps, were all either absent on one of the tours, or down in the 'information centre'-cum-casino, or sleeping off a hangover in a hotel room.

He went to the vast hall that was the information centre. It was a futuristic marketplace, with its lightweight exhibitors' stands, stacks of pamphlets and coffees on offer. The rubbish bins were filled with the pamphlets. The air hostess representatives of Big Pharma, with their sashes and smiles and shaved eyebrows, were calling the docs over to win. A game show host was wearing a headset, leaning over a circle of consultants in suits whose heads were bent to computer screens. They were being asked the question: *Which drug is the only drug on the market that may* reverse* *or inhibit the development of paranoia-like symptoms in schizo-phrenia?* (* Or may not.) The answer was emblazoned on the canopy, behind the host. It was on the coffee cups and on the computer mouse pads.

Richard took a small plastic receptacle of scalding black coffee and watched them pressing the mouse that makes no squeak, like techno-cats, one-claw winners.

It brought to mind the psychological experiments that are contrived so that no one wins apart from their inventor. You can-not win, you have the illusion of winning in the first game and thereafter you lose whatever you press. The point is the explana-tion one gives for losing. The depressive will say, with some ac-curacy, that there was nothing they could do, they were bound to lose, they always lose. The paranoid will say, with an even greater accuracy, that the whole thing was rigged. Only the 'normal' per-son falls short of any accuracy of surmise, claiming they're the architect of their 'achievements'.

After Valérie left, he went up to the Bar des Chasseurs a couple of times with his former hunting comrades. He had explained the experiment there, and held the attention of the drinkers, and he had even done so after four or five glasses of pastis. He may have got the mental types confused but they got the idea. *Putain,* they exclaimed, baffled, morose. Denis Sabène, the butcher with the Porsche, had gone so far as to say that in this world the sane were mad and the mad were sane and Richard had praised the insight, being drunk.

He went into that butcher's two weeks later, after he'd been ar-rested, and the guy stood with his hands behind his back, a mus-lin cloth staunching the blood dripping off the counter, and gave him no eye contact, and Frédéric Barret, the tobacconist next door, another one of the *chasseurs,* gave him his cigarettes most carefully, making sure the warning was face up. '*Smoking kills*'.

So suddenly he was English again, after they'd all pretended for so many years, when the drinks were on him, that he could pass for a Frenchman. He could have passed for a Chinaman. One of his friends, Maurice, an ex-cop, picked a row with him over some slight given to his dog by his in-laws, in order to escape the wider association. The English he'd partied with for the last year crossed the street to avoid him and his bad luck. Only the Dutch shook hands. They were busy people.

His home was not his home in any meaningful way at all, beyond the bricks and mortar.

The point is the explanation one gives for losing.

29

✦

THE MUSIC OVER THE LOUDSPEAKERS in the hall seemed
to speak to him. American songs pressed him to find the hero
inside of himself. He wanted to fill his head, so he wandered on
from session to session. He entered a small back room. The
speaker looked anxious when Richard walked in, paused, then
went on.

'And so a male rat is introduced into the cage of a rat whom we
know to be the dominant male and he is forced by the dominant
rat to lie on his back. This is a very stressful experience indeed. It
is only being returned to the cage amongst his own group that
lowers his dopamine level. It may have risen as much as six hundred per cent. Now the extraordinary thing about this is the
proven link of elevated dopamine levels in the schizophrenic,
and of course the hypothesis here is that social defeat is a risk
factor for schizophrenia, especially over a prolonged period, and
this of course may be one factor in a multifactorial scenario for
increased levels of schizophrenia in migrants. Thank you.'

So succinct, it was brilliant! Richard applauded. One or two
others joined in his clapping, with less conviction, and when he
could hear only the sound of his clapping, he knew he should
desist.

'Thank you. Thank you,' the speaker smiled, shy as a jockey.

A discussion started and Richard left to go to the toilet.

'*Hello, Mr Cuckold.*'

His urine ceased. He zipped up. He washed his hands. Then the voice began again.

'*Your wife's pussy goes so wet when I get my cock out and then I fuck her really hard in her hairy little box or sometimes I give it to her up the ass. She says you never pleased her. You never could. You are too afraid to come and fight me because you know I'd kill you. Too scared to go to work, too scared to move, scared of your own shadow. Prove me wrong. Mr Nobody.*'

That was the letter he received in the post. The words had leapt from the letter and infected him in seconds, moving pathogens through his bloodstream to poison every part of his body and make it shake. Those kind of death throes can give you life.

The next time she came by to get clothes and remind him of his offer to leave the house, he ran after her car shouting as she drove off and then he came inside, told Max to do his homework and took charge of the house. He vacuumed, and he did the dishes and he had a turn at the washing machine, all the time his heart was beating like he was on the front line.

'I'm not going anywhere,' he said to himself. 'I've changed my mind. She's the one who left the house. How many houses do they want?'

They had an emotional afternoon, he and Max, watching a movie about a baseball star who had to choose between the duty of his gift and the love of a nagging woman. Max cried. Richard held him in his arms.

'He's like you, Dad.'

'Do you think so?'

'Yeah, you're a hero.'

'Oh, I wish I was. But I'm not.'

'You are.' He put his arm around his father's shoulders like he was the father. 'You should have hit that guy anyway.'

'Who?'

'Gérard.'

'Who?'

'Him.' He nodded towards the neighbour's house. 'You should kill him.'

'Jeff, you mean?'

Max nodded.

'Well, it wouldn't be a smart thing to do. I could go to prison or something.' He pushed his fingers through Max's hair. 'But thanks for the thought, pal.'

He took Maxence to McDonald's that evening and because the server was such a miserable prick and Richard was a professional salesman, he asked him a question about how he thought he was doing, and when he told Richard to fuck himself, Richard pulled him over the counter and held him by the ears and head-butted him across the bridge of his nose.

He was not a violent man. He'd never been anything remotely close to violent before. It made him feel a lot better.

He had to stop to pee by the side of the road and it was then he saw the blood on his shirt. Maxence was sorry the order was only half filled. He moaned that he was missing the chicken nuggets and it made Richard laugh and cry, and when he wiped his face he spread more blood on to his sleeve, but he knew now to use a higher temperature on the washing machine.

'I think I will come out of this shit all right, Maxence. I promise.' That's what he said to him.

His teeth resting on his lips, Max held his paper bag on his lap, saying nothing.

30

✧

HE OUGHT PERHAPS to have paced himself, but he decided to take in as many sessions as he could. Coaches circled and withdrew in the car park, and he watched them with increasing anger, standing at the glass windows of the main lobby. There were signs on the front windows of the buses: 'Giza', 'Nile Tour', 'Old Cairo'. The salesmen were sitting on the steps with their packed lunches in the sunshine, going through their Happy Meals looking for the free toy, pens on strings around their necks.

Next to the toilets there was a session full of African psychiatrists. They were the presenters, six or seven of them, friendly as a sports team, handing each other slides, conferring. Ten minutes or so later, and no one else entering the room, with dignity, their chairman addressed Richard; their entire audience.

'Thanks for coming,' he said with dignified economy. 'We're going to take you through the results of findings from the world's largest psychiatric survey, of sixty-eight thousand persons over the last ten years, in rural Ethiopia.'

The way the man was fixing his attention on him puzzled Richard. He looked behind and saw that it was because there was no one else there. The team all laughed at that. It must have looked comical. Richard smiled to help out. But it was not funny really that he was the only person there.

'Are you OK with English, Dr . . . ?'

'I'm all ears,' he said, his arms enfolding the satchel on his lap. He nodded. 'Ready when you are.'

Jeff answered her mobile phone. He said, 'Listen, man. I didn't send you any damn letter. What do you mean, *do I love her*?' He'd never heard Jeff speak that way; he sounded wrathful and small like a goblin whose name had been guessed. He should have gone over to Jeff's house and beaten the shit out of him when Rachel called; he should have given him a pasting, it would have done them both good. 'Yeah, you should have done that, only you should have done it before now. And it wouldn't have changed anything. She left you. Get over it. Let it go.'

'You sat at my fucking table, you sat there . . .' He could hardly get his words out. 'Tell me how you could *sit* there . . .'

Jeff did begin to tell him, but the mobile connection was lost at that point. So now he'd never know. He threw the phone down the toilet. Then had the task of retrieving it with the barbecue tongs.

Valérie got a letter too. She came back for more clothes and to issue a final warning regarding his removal. She showed the letter to him. It was just as disgusting as the first one, and he'd been surprised enough by the language of that. This one told her she was going to have an accident in her car on her way in to town one day. Watch out, it said. Just because you have a pretty face, you shouldn't think you're anything special. Keep your legs closed in future. He read it through twice. Valérie was shaking and smoking as she stood watching him read it. She had that look on her face like when she got bad news about other people, her

162

cheek muscles taut, reining in pleasure, the thrill of the bullet missing you.

'Obviously, it's Rachel,' she said.

He gave it back to her. He didn't say what he was thinking. He didn't look her in the eyes.

'Well, what do you want now?' he said. 'What about your lawyers, what are they planning?'

'I don't know if what I am doing is right,' she said.

Perhaps she meant it. He examined her as he had examined the letter. It was actually quite ugly, her mouth. It expressed, to his mind, a revulsion wider than the matter in hand.

'When are you moving out, Richard?'

'I'm not going anywhere! I've changed my mind.'

'*Ri-schard . . .*'

And to think he used to get an erection when she said his name.

The youngest man on the team made the final presentation. Richard had applauded each of the three preceding presentations, all very interesting. The final paper would discuss psychiatric illness amongst the extremely poor, those who could not claim to own more than twenty possessions. He was on the edge of his seat. It was important stuff. How to compare it to his own troubles? There was no gold standard to compare these things, no exchange rate for them.

All he could do was to care, to care with all of his being, since only he was present. The duty, the responsibility, the honour, made him sit tall. He concentrated; he was the right screwdriver for the screw.

31

⟡

HE WENT ABOUT HIS USUAL BUSINESS, cleaning and doing the laundry. He was storing the bills in an old washing-powder carton in the laundry room so as not to see them. He had begun to dread opening the letter box, mostly on account of the credit card statements listing Valérie's spending throughout the French Riviera. He decided if he got another of the handwritten letters he would leave it there, he wouldn't even touch it.

He trudged up to the house with a handful of bills, wondering what next. Before she left they had taken out a large loan for a new car for her and a holiday. Then there was the mortgage. His salary just about covered it. Plus, he needed to keep Maxence happy. He knew it was no kind of solution, going shopping, but he didn't know how else to pass the time now they weren't doing outdoor things. Inside the electronics store they forgot everything. They bought a PlayStation and took to playing 'Grand Theft Auto' with all the residual machismo they had left between them. Max said he was having the time of his life.

Among the bills, there was a letter from her lawyers outlining their suit for the tribunal. The next day a bailiff served him formal notice of his required appearance. She was going for full custody of Maxence and he would have visitation every other weekend. She was to have the house.

He called his lawyer. He told the lawyer she could have it all, the house and so on, but not the boy. The lawyer said it wasn't that simple; the mother always got custody. Even if she was the one who left? Even if she left her son behind? Yes, even if she drugged herself, sold her body, no matter what. Even if she was dead? The lawyer said she didn't hear that. She said he should prepare for the worst.

He did. He opened a bottle of whisky. He asked Maxence if he wanted to try some. Max said, Don't be stupid, I'm a kid.

Grow up then, Richard said.

Max took a sip, tasted it carefully, made non-committal noises of vague appreciation and then he took one of Richard's cigarettes and lit it and smoked it.

Richard gave him a quizzical look as he exhaled the first puff and sighed. Guy.

'Papi,' Max explained. Guy.

'You know what?'

'What?'

'You're my best pal, Max. My only pal.'

When he woke, Maxence was lying asleep with the game console between his hands; the screen paused, blinking, panting for more crime. It was 1 A.M. Maybe she's right, he thought, maybe he shouldn't be with me.

He put the boy to bed and lay next to him, making the pillow wet and dirty with his tears. He would put the pillowcase on at sixty degrees the next day, he had a whole load of whites to go in with it. He lay there with his nose in the nape of his son's neck, in that mousey sweaty hair, the fine hair that infuriated his mother, being so prone to head lice. 'He's got a colony on his head!' she used to yell, sitting with him between her legs on a stool in the bath tub, combing, gritting her teeth, knees wet, clothes wet, gripping his neck. 'Let me do it,' he'd said. And he sat down himself behind the boy and took each hair in turn with Maxence asking his bizarre questions that came from nowhere and led nowhere, from sharks to oddities of science to questions about love.

How crestfallen he was when he could no longer find one of the slick comma-shaped *bestioles*. He had enjoyed it and, by God, he took his time, every beast, every egg, gone; he truly knew every single hair on his son's head.

He regretted he hadn't spent more time with his son. Now he and Max were not doing anything as touching as lice-picking, but still there was a wealth to the indifference of their time together. They sat in cafeterias in supermarket malls, just the same way as mothers and children did, heads averted, each away in their thoughts, content. That was parenthood; idling side by side, the gorgeous profligacy of doing nothing much. Time passing; one growing, one fading.

Now he would be reduced to a scrounger, driving the boy to this theme park or that water park, getting him lashed up on soft drinks and French fries, pumping him for information about school and his mother, forcing his future with bon mots and strictures, never short of clichés, even rummaging through those of his own father, demanding a show of affection, purloining an audience to witness for him, *sign here please,* how good they were together, mussing his boy's hair when people looked, chucking him under the chin — *'Always do the right thing, kid, make me proud of you'* — and at going-home time pressing him for a show of love. Checking for sadness and loss and needing it to be there; this the very worst thing of all. And afterwards, he would be ashamed of himself.

He was crying loud enough to wake Max; he wanted his son to wake and comfort him.

He heard a band start up; they were playing the melody so cautiously, just for him. Out of the wardrobe stepped that cherubic high priest of popular music, Daniel Balavoine.

'*Ça fait longtemps que t'es parti maintenant . . .*'

He didn't skimp. This was his anthem. The father deprived of his child by a mercenary mother. She'd ripped his guts out. Nothing said about him in court would matter to him, it would be nothing as compared to the smile of his son. He gave it everything he had, Monsieur Balavoine. He had his microphone in his hand, and he brought it to him, his face aching out loud, his brows livid. Shouting.

He sang through each pledge, each threat, a second time to underscore them, turning an open supplicant palm into the warning of a pointed finger, repeating, *she shouldn't have gone.*

And then he withdrew back into the wardrobe.

Richard knew what to do. *Je vais tout casser.* The whisky inside him rose up like a serpent with its fangs bared, and let loose a ludicrous wolf-whistle.

32

◇

THE TALLER AFRICAN DOCTOR in his navy-blue suit stood
behind the projector, tapping his pen on the key points. They had
arrived at a figure for depression in rural Ethiopia among the
poorest of the poor of 4.4 per cent; this compared to a figure of
10–17 per cent in the United States and Europe.

'The implications,' he concluded cautiously, 'seem fairly obvious.'

'Yes, they are,' said Richard.

The first speaker gently enquired as to Richard's provenance.

'Are you in practice or teaching . . . ?'

'Me? Neither.' He folded his hands, shook his head. The ques-
tion hung in the air. 'I am a salesman, I work for your sponsor.
I am here supposedly, apparently, officially on behalf of Big
Pharma.'

'And you come to sessions like these? Are you new to the job?'
There was some laughter.

'No, I've been working in it a long, long time and I've never
been to a session like this. But I stand corrected. I have learnt a
lot today. You know, my company's sales objective is to grow the
market for anti-depressive pharmaceuticals by twenty-five per

cent this year. My own region is Africa. My job is to grow sadness.'

His voice cracked. He stopped and put his head in his hands, he had lost control of himself. The Ethiopian doctors grouped around him, and one of them knelt and offered Richard a drink from his water bottle.

There was a hand on each of his shoulders. He was smiling and crying, like the sun and the rain. He saw a rainbow on the projector screen, and thought: *Shit, I'm having hallucinations too now.*

Oh God, he thought, *what a fool I am. Oh God, look down on me and pity me.*

He pulled himself together enough to speak.

'Please,' he said, 'don't get to the conclusion yet. I know what's coming but I need to get myself ready for it. Give me some time.'

The presenter looked at his colleagues, as if to say: *What's the form here, with these overemotional white salesmen?*

A fly traversed them, each man in turn waved a hand over his face, first the farthest right swiped, then the next left, then the next left, then finally the tall presenter passed his hand in an arc.

'How long do you need, Richard?'

'A lifetime,' he attempted to laugh but merely dry-choked. 'No, no, not a lifetime. Give me like twenty minutes or something to pull myself together.'

With that he exited the room; the fly went with him.

The Ethiopian doctors shook their heads, and the shortest offered his hand to the tallest and then they laughed again.

'Well, we'll wait. Do you see anyone else listening?' said the presenter.

33

✧

AT 2 A.M. ONE MORNING, the week before the custody hearing, the telephone rang. He was in bed. He had no idea where he was when he woke. He'd been drinking.

'Ri-schard.'

'Hi, honey. Where am I . . .'

'Ri-schard, I keep thinking about Max; you know, he is not normal. I've been thinking about him, about how he was as a small child, and I've been reading and I know now he's not well in the head.' She started to cry; she whispered, 'I've decided I am going to take him to see someone . . . but I want to come home now, for his sake. He is so disturbed . . .' She started to sob more heavily, 'Please, Ri-schard, you have to help me to do this, for Max . . .'

He put the light on and sat up. He knew then where he was and who she was and who he was.

'So you're telling me now you think he's got some sort of mental problem? Well, if he does it's because you've fucked him up! Look, Valérie, he's fine, he's happy with me. I can tell you that. We're cool. Leave us alone.'

'I shouldn't have been the one to leave the house. Max. He needs his mother.' Her voice broke again.

'Oh pack it in, will you? I'm a better mother than you are.' He got up, the phone under his chin, and pulled on underpants, socks, jeans and then he slipped his shirt over his head.

'But, you are not a mother, *Ri-schard*. You were not even a good father, and by the way you were also a very bad husband. You fuck your way through France, through Europe, and now maybe you fuck your way through Africa. You were never at home, you don't even know your son at all. You don't know anything by the way.'

'Well, darling, guess what, *by the way,*' he stood, tucking the ends of his shirt into the waist of his jeans and belting up, 'I'm not giving up my son. I'm going to give up work instead.'

'Don't be stupid.'

'Max is fine with me. Yup, I'm quitting the job to be with him. I love him.'

He ended the call and went out into the kitchen. He lit a cigarette and smoked it hard and fast, then he pressed it out on the dirty dinner plate in the sink and let loose a yellow-grey stream of smoke. 'Fuck you,' he said.

She called back.

'It is so stupid, I mean, how will you live? On what? And what about me . . . ?'

'I don't want him with you and that piece of shit arsehole. You think he's a good example? For my son? No, no way. No, I'm going to give up work, I don't give a flying fuck about it any more.'

'You are being so . . .'

'Yes! I am *stupide*,' he said, imitating her. The phone went dead. '*Stupide*,' he mimicked again, pleased with himself, 'bitch.' He uncorked the bottle of whisky and took great pleasure in drinking from its neck. He lit a cigarette. The phone rang.

'What you are doing is just some kind of pathetic revenge. It is not about Max, it is about you. Jeff, he is saying he wants to meet you in the car park in front of the leisure centre. You are pathetic, you are a pathetic man . . .'

She didn't need to write it down for him this time.

'Tell him I'll be there in ten minutes,' he said.

He wiped his face, and took in as much whisky as he could. He lit a cigarette for the car journey, jumped in, started her up, lowered the window, pulled out. The ground crunched under the tyres. He turned on the radio, and it was Daniel Balavoine, of course.

'*Who is it that can save love?*' he sang.

He had his lights on bright. He put his foot down. He was pure of heart in hatred.

34

✧

WHEN RICHARD PULLED INTO THE CAR PARK, the gendarmes were waiting in their van with only their sidelights illuminated. As he dimmed his lights and turned off the engine, their lights went on full and he saw how it was.

No one else was there, just this young man and young woman, two gendarmes in their dark-blue outfits. They didn't look happy to be there. He was Breathalyzed and handcuffed and spent the night in the cell. The next day, at a tribunal, his driving licence was rescinded for eighteen months when he was convicted for drink-driving. This was the first thing her lawyer raised at the custody hearing.

He was required to see his local doctor for referral to a psychiatrist, on account of the state's concern for his well-being — mental primarily, it turned out — they considered it abnormal to want to kill someone. (He'd admitted his intentions.)

He had given the doc a lot of free samples and gifts in the past. The doc had won the Sanitoxat prize draw last year, a week in Sardinia for himself and his wife. Richard confessed things were bad. He'd lost his wife and now his son. And his home. He'd also lost his driving licence. He was going to lose his job, more than likely. The doc offered to put Richard on sick leave for as long as he could. He offered Richard a prescription for his own products and they laughed about it. *You have to laugh,* the doc said, *you have to be able to laugh, that's what will keep you sane. The rest of it, well, if the drugs work for you, great, but keeping a sense of humour, that's the main thing.*

Of course, a sense of humour would not help him get custody of his son. He told the doc he had some thoughts about madness and sadness, those 'defective' human conditions for which he used to purvey relief. The doctor kept right on writing.

I'll tell you what the problem is, it's the absence of understanding of what love really is, he said, and the doc winced. He saw him hunch over his pad. *Love is loyalty or the presumption of it and that can be quite a presumption, believe me. I know, but that's the point, Jean-Pierre, isn't it? Love is the last delusion of the rational age, the final faith. In a world in which everything is junk, everything is disposable, the idea of love as a fearsome promise is something worth dying for. Worth living for even. Don't you think?*

Well, why not? said the doc, rising and seeing Richard to the door. *You may very well be right.* The doc nodded at the woman at the door. Her husband had died of alcohol poisoning just before Christmas.

'Ça va, Claudine?'

'Il faut,' she said, looking Richard in the eyes. She was the mother of Maxence's best friend. They'd had a few drinks together as couples when her husband was alive. Now she seemed so distant; her pupils were like rafts at sea, the glint of white like the wave of a handkerchief.

He took himself home through the cobbled backstreets via

what they called with good reason 'dog-shit' alley. He left his shoes outside his front door.

Whether love of any kind really did exist or not, he didn't know. But he suspected it was highly unlikely anyone could exist without it.

35

✧

HE WENT INTO ONE of the toilet cubicles and sat there and he took out of his briefcase the print-out of the email he'd saved as a draft to send to Rachel and he reread it.

> In the same way that the development of serious mental illness is a multi-factorial scenario — family issues, impartial mothering, cannabis use at a young age, ostracism experienced through immigration — so it seems to me is the development of the ability to love. To be able to love, you need to have been loved unconditionally during the crucial window of early development. After this point the love module will develop subject to steady acquaintances, familial relationships and friendships with people from the same background set within the context of community acceptance. It requires non-exposure to desertion or abandonment by those who claim to 'love' you. In brief, during the soft phase of development, the 'idea of love' must not be demonstrated to be a lie. This scenario eliminates from the possibility of love all but the most innocent, most remote places. Perhaps it persists in regions of rural Ethiopia.

He sat back. Well, it wasn't much of a love letter. It wasn't much of a letter at all but it had them all covered.

He intended to email it to Rachel for her rebuttal, her holy fury.

Tell me I'm wrong, Rachel, tell me I'm wrong.

He went down to the information centre, took for himself a small sample cup of the coffee, accessed his account, chose the draft he'd prepared, pasted it into an email for her. Then he deleted it and wrote instead:

> Do you believe in love? Write to me, Rachel, most urgently because I need to hear from you. I don't know what to do.

He sent neither. All that was certain was that he didn't know what to do. He'd have to keep listening and hope to hear.

'Please conclude the presentation,' Richard said. 'I apologize for that. I'm fine, actually. Quite fine now.'

They exchanged looks, not mean ones or mocking ones, but looks of concern. The young fellow went through his conclusions and then a senior, older, doctor spoke for the team.

'What are the reasons, we might conjecture, for this low level of depression in such difficult circumstances? Well, we like the term "social capital" here because it seems to us that these very impoverished women are rich in social capital, they turn to each other for help, and share what they have. These informal community-based arrangements act as protective factors in depression and possibly other mental illnesses. Essentially, community — family, friends, and a wider local circle of relationships that are genuinely and intimately co-invested — is a key factor in basic human functioning. Thank you for listening . . . Richard.'

There was some more laughter from the others on the team as the man bent forward to double-check his name-tag.

Richard stood up. He put his hands above his head and he clapped and clapped and clapped. Then he spoke.

'You, in Africa, you have something we don't have! Call it so-cial capital, call it whatever you like. Call it humanity or even de-cency. Call it love! Hold on to it! Hold on to it! Don't let us fuck that up too! My God.'

The room was silent. The plastic water bottle on the present-er's table crackled and popped.

36

✧

WITHOUT A CAR and on long-term sick leave, Richard was a scuttling thing cornered; a beetle in a box.

The stairwell of the block of rentals was pitch black, and it smelt of fried fish. There was a timed light, you pressed a round button on your entry, but it expired by the time you got to the stairs and you were obliged to make your way up blindly. The desperate coughs of a neighbour indicated that he was at the end of his tether; his sputum ricocheted early morning and in the evenings and then lay dormant during the night.

The lettings agent had shown him two dwellings, both at three hundred euros a month, and the one he took was the least dark. Dressed to the nines on a budget, the girl was inordinately professional, her foot on the first rung of the ladder of her career in property. Scrupulously, she'd made an inventory of the single room with its adjacent toilet. She checked the walls for pin tacks, tried the taps, crouched down to look at the electric plugs, opened the shutters and turned the knobs on each of the two wall heaters. The shower curtain was covered in stains, as if someone ran short on the toilet paper. The entire bathroom was about a metre square. It would have been impossible to conceive of one smaller.

Of course the advantage was that you could have a shit and a shower all in the seated position.

The shower curtain was to be retained, it was on the list. She gave a gay little laugh. How was it that in late autumn her face was orange? He decided to examine, he found the cut-off point just before her ears. It was a painted mask. He didn't blame her. He would wear a mask too if he was trying to shoehorn good people into bad spaces.

He settled in, with a couple of bags and boxes and some furniture they'd been ready to throw out or have Guy convert into something else. Possibly a vest.

From the desk at the window he looked up to the bells of the dark church, those great iron testicles of the past strung up as a warning to all would-be romantics who passed through the place from baptism to burial.

Besides floor tiles and the *crépi* roughcast walls that wouldn't stand for him lolling, there was installed a stainless-steel sink and counter. The taps on the sink were vicious things that spouted at angles a tirade of boiling watery abuse.

There was no light in the bathroom. In preference to flaying his back, he showered either in cold water in the dark or increasingly not at all.

He had a coffee machine and its drone punctuated the day as he moved between the computer and its good self. It rattled and shook the corrugated aluminium surface of the sink, underneath which was his fridge. He purchased a futon, the edges of which cut into his calves. There was a sly mattress. They called this minimalism in better circles.

The bells rang at midday; just before the siren went off to remind people that life was lunch.

He went to see his bank manager to arrange the overdraft that he would need. He had never been there before; Valérie and her mother had handled their finances. Under the porch, an old man was sitting on a rug with handwritten posters about him declaring his intention to starve himself to death to shame the bank. He had a cat on a lead for company.

He was directed towards an office. With its transparent sides and cardboard rear, it made the bank manager look like a dolly-man attached to his containment by plastic-coated twisty wires, but one smooth pink arm appeared free enough to move the mouse.

Richard had only ever been overdrawn by a couple of hundred euros. He still had a monthly salary, but a good part of it went to his wife. He had a cheque to deposit from the sale of the four-by-four. He explained that he was awaiting the sale of the house valued at around four hundred and fifty thousand euros which, after the mortgage repayment, would net them about seventy thousand euros from which he expected half. The bank manager smiled damply. His expression seemed to say: *Forget it, pal. The only good man's a gay man these days.*

He noted Richard's good financial behaviour for the last fourteen years there, the regular salary; at times he had had thirty thousand euros in the account. He never put it in a savings account. This was a shame, as he could have had some interest on it. They were offering one and a quarter per cent. He paused, looked up from his computer to see if Richard understood the value of this.

Richard attempted to look blown away with remorse. The young man announced that Richard could have his overdraft of a thousand euros. The printer cheered. He explained — with good reason, given he had before him a man who had just lost his wife and son — how to manage things better from now on.

Richard looked awestruck, grateful, dependent. He wanted the overdraft slightly more than he wanted to maim the bank-boy, but it was close.

He was now occupied for the first time in his life with dealing with 'the little people'. He had ridiculed Valérie for her struggle with France Telecom, the unfathomable invoicing, the contracts due to finish in five years' time for services that weren't supplied or functioning. He'd called her all the names under the sun. He'd even said something he now considered stupid — *'How hard can it be?'*

Simone took him to the doors of France Telecom, but she would not go in. She'd rather flagellate herself with nettles, she said. It was nice of her to drive him to L'Argens. She wouldn't look him in the eyes though; obviously they'd known about Jeff before he did.

The place had changed since Valérie once punished him by taking him in there on a Saturday. Just a year or two ago it was a communist barracks, big grey desks, small rooms with heavy doors. The cast was the same but the place had gone over to consumerism. A tall bald clown and his accomplices, five chunky women in zip-up Terylene navy waistcoats over their mufti, perched on bar stools at kidney-shaped tables with marketing material the bunting around their computer screens.

Holding their tickets, sinners like him sat it out on trendy red pouffes, reading the posters which promised all sorts of things for a modest monthly outlay: clear-skinned children, good looks in old age, companionship. He waited three-quarters of an hour. One man jumped the queue. Sure enough, the man's dreams of a new home/work interface were quickly dispatched and it was at last Richard's turn.

He had come to cancel his mobile phone. The mobile phone could only be cancelled in August 2010. It didn't even work, he said. There was no address for a complaints letter, he should call the helpline. They don't answer, he told the clown. I know, he replied, his eyes twinkling.

Christ, he thought, I wouldn't be surprised if my wife wasn't depressed out of her mind.

He was desperate for a drink by the time they quit the Parisian pretensions of L'Argens for the wannabe chain stores and trashy billboards of the industrial areas. He and Simone lit up. *No wonder people smoke so much round here,* he thought. *The poor bastards are all just trying to talk to each other, and what do they get for their trouble? That circus of heartache, 'Farce' Telecom.*

'How can people live like this?' he said. 'I had no idea it was so awful.'

'This is real life, Richard,' she said. He saw her lean into the wheel. 'But they have a nice new baker's down here by the roundabout and you can just pull into the parking area, it's very convenient.'

He looked at the other side of the traffic queue; at the older angular cars shaped like half-sucked lozenges, Citroëns and the Renaults, the traffic lights changed and they were off.

37

✧

HE HAD BRONCHITIS after just a month in the apartment. It might have been something to do with the smoking. Pale petals of bile burst into his mouth. He got up and went out. He didn't bother to lock the door. He walked in the damp October air to the doctor's.

He was in the waiting room for an hour. Old folk sat ranged against the wall in plastic garden chairs. They contemplated the African savannah the doctor's artistic wife had painted on the wall.

Ten years older than Valérie's parents, the last thrifty generation, ailing now, still traded and bartered in the leftovers from their gardens, haunting each other's bungalows with plastic bags of nuts or plums, some quince paste, a jar of jam; or they drove round to see who was alive and what they had on their trees. In their tracksuits and acrylic sweaters, in their clapped-out cars, they swarmed out in the afternoon, slightly boozy.

Two enormously fat men came in at once, took a plastic garden chair apiece, and one capsized, with the other following suit. It was a remarkable scene; they couldn't raise themselves, crammed into their chairs, they were limbs in the air for a few minutes, six legs apiece, each an octopus. Richard laughed and shook his head, he wiped the corners of his eyes.

A man with his coat buttoned to his chin stood and with *ancien régime* frostiness asked him to stop laughing; it was not the way things were done in France, monsieur.

'I've lived here fourteen years; I'm not some *parvenu*. You people are so racist.'

The stiff old boy insisted, 'It is not dignified, it is lacking in respect.'

The doctor poked his head round the door, and took Richard in ahead of the others.

'How are you getting on with your meds?'

'Famously.'

'You're not taking them, are you?'

He was a very modern man, the doctor, very *sympathique*, on the side of the shirkers, providing sick notes for the perfectly well.

Maybe he has a good sex life, thought Richard, noting the wooden ethnic nudes around the office that suggested someone who has had fun in developing countries. His only weakness, he'd heard in the waiting room, was a sports car and a great impatience with slow drivers.

'You should take them, Richard; the meds. Better than the booze.'

'That used to be my line.'

'You'd find it easier to get on with day-to-day life, you know, if you took them.'

'It's the last thing I want to get on with, day-to-day life. Did I tell you she's taken my son from me?'

'Mmm-hmm. Let me look at your throat.'

'Sure.'

The doc gave him a course of antibiotics and wished him luck with the bronchitis.

'How's business?' Richard asked, folding the prescription.

'Well, good. Hey, you'll like this, Richard. All those people out there in the waiting room? What do you think they've come for?' He rose and showed Richard to the door. 'They're here for your lovely little serotonin reuptake inhibiters. Old age is a depressing time.'

'It's all depressing.'

The doc laughed like it would all be fine, he slapped Richard on the back. A little depression was nothing to him. He saw kids with cancer. *He's so much better than me,* Richard thought, and avoided paying the small charge by stepping outside smartly.

He went via dog-shit alley from the fountain square into the church square and passed by a new estate agent's. There was a cheap little bistro coffee table with a vase of flowers in the middle of it. Beyond the window-posted properties, a fat woman hovered in a woollen poncho. Turning about, she came to the window to face him. It was Adele, the bottom-barer, Simon's wife. And then she saw that it was him; Richard.

Her face fell and she turned round fast. Divorce was, he thought, another disease which is not a disease but which people hold to be catching. Like depression.

One property had caught his eye; his. He read how — just like all the agent's other properties — his own house was 'charming' and 'well proportioned', 'benefiting from three large bedrooms', and, with the possibility to 'enlarge the property', an 'ideal second home'. He considered that a ripe insult. There were three photographs and one of them was of the kitchen, showing the counter he'd installed with the damned salad bowl positioned as part of the 'lifestyle' shot. For the photograph of the pool they'd placed a similar bistro table to the one outside with a Champagne bucket, a bottle of rosé in it and two glasses, just waiting to be filled!

Looking down he saw Adele's thick legs clad in tweed knickerbockers, and he stepped sideways to look at her.

A second home! He rapped on the window. Something in his expression defeated both her professionalism and the spoonful of greed that may or may not be part of the motivation for being a real-estate agent. She turned the key in the door lock. Four hundred and fifty thousand euros! Two hundred and five square metres! A second home!

Now he inhabited an airless hutch. He went back to the studio thinking through the problem of the showerhead. Of all the elements thrown in at the largesse of the landlord, this was significant. It was blocked with limescale and the water emerged at high-pressure boiling hot. The cord was wrapped in metal ringing which was broken in places and showed the yellow plastic tube beneath it. You had to wrap a towel around your hand to hold it, should it be filled with water. He'd used it to scald clean the interior of the toilet.

Since he tried to strangle his wife with it last Saturday the rubber cord was torn and leaking. He'd have to enquire how to go about replacing it. It would be a long litigious ordeal, necessitating a dossier filled with paperwork, he was sure.

38

✧

HIS WIFE WAS BRINGING MAX by after judo so that he could
spend the afternoon with him. She wouldn't let him stay alone
with him more than a couple of hours now.

As he rounded the church he saw her, sitting outside in her
car, a grey Ford Fiesta, waiting for him. She was not wearing
make-up. He was surprised to see her like that; greasy.

'How are you?'

'Fine,' she said, hands on the wheel, not looking at him, tense.
'Apart from the fact I'm the shuttle bus.' Max got out and came
round the back of the car.

'Well, sorry, but you had something to do with me losing my
driving licence.'

'I didn't make you drink. I didn't hold the glass to your lips.'

He put his hands on the side of her car, hung his head, looked
at the tarmac, breathing in the petrol fumes, taking his time. 'Are
you working?'

She made a face. 'No time.'

'Me neither,' he said. 'Have a sense of humour.'

'Your payment never came.'

He drew Maxence into his side and kissed his head. 'I don't
know why. I set it up. Should have happened.'

She looked at him then. 'Lots of things have happened that shouldn't have.'

'I lost my temper. That's all. Anyway, can't your boyfriend help you out with some money? I see the house is on the market. You might have mentioned it.'

'My lawyer says it should be done so that we can share the proceeds.'

'You don't mean share though, as in half, half.'

'I will have to take advice.'

He nodded. He had taken advice too. His lawyer was a first-class bitch. He thought that would be good; imagined, per the televised American model, she'd use that to his advantage. The French model was less customer-service orientated.

He'd made an appointment that week to see her. When he arrived, her secretary was on the phone in a side room. She had crazy hair, multi-coloured, and wore the kind of clothes that frighten men. She was regaling someone with a story about her son's judo teacher. She saw him and nudged the door to with her toe. He stood all the while at the counter, watching the clock with growing anger.

He cast a good look at the bills and invoices on the counter ready to be put into envelopes and sent. The endless formulations which amounted to yet more dejection for the hapless recipients, the original amount, the taxes, the command for payment by a certain date or they sent round the guys to take your microwave. He grew angrier by the second. Eventually, twenty minutes after his arrival, she came out to reception.

'I have an appointment with my lawyer at eleven. Madame Schrecklich.'

'She's not here.'

'But I have an appointment with her.'

'*But,* she's not here.'

'How can that be?'

She poked her tongue through the gusset of the red gum in her mouth, and popped its cherry, leaving in the air a smell of cinnamon. 'We called you. We left you a message, this morning.'

He put his mobile phone on to the counter, slammed it down. 'There is no message on here.'

'She's not here.'

'You didn't greet me when I walked in, you didn't come and tell me this, you haven't apologized at all! Give me a piece of paper, please. I wish to leave my lawyer a letter about this.'

'No.'

'Give me some paper.'

'We don't have any.'

Behind her were reams and reams of printer paper. He pointed to them.

'I'm not giving you any paper.'

'I am paying for a service . . .'

She blew out, bored.

He was going to the door when, like a bucket of blood thrown against a glass window, rage soaked his vision. He turned round.

'You're a rude bitch!'

'And you, you're a bastard! A rude bastard!' she yelled, grasping the edge of the counter and pulling herself over it, her face come alive.

He slammed the door behind him and stood in the street, hyperventilating.

He wanted to get a gun and come back and shoot the place up. He walked up the street. Then he stopped. He wanted to cry, but an old woman had beaten him to it. Ahead of him, she was standing by the tourist information centre reading the charity posters, two shopping bags at her ankles, her shoulders rising and falling.

He was glad he'd taken the company cheque-book from behind the counter while the bitch was on the phone. He went into the information centre and wrote out a cheque for an animal charity there and then.

'I'm through with France,' he said as he wrote it out angrily and handed it to the girl behind the desk. 'Here, have this. Fucking French.'

'*Merci, monsieur, c'est gentil.*'

He slammed down the pen and went out. *What the hell is happening to me?* he thought, walking back to the grey dusty parking lot, between the plane trees.

'I suppose you will not even say sorry,' his wife said, tightening her grip on the wheel. 'You could have killed me, in front of our son. You were like an animal. Meet the real Richard Bird, I thought. Now we know who you really are.' She looked at him, her eyes narrowing, her lips pursing. It was comical in a way.

'Doesn't calling the police on me mean that we're quits? Doesn't another tribunal, another conviction, mean another nail in my ever-growing coffin? Don't you think that sorry would be a little *de trop?*'

'I don't understand you. Why should you have a coffin, now, what is this? Are you planning to kill yourself, *Ri-schard?* Or me? Are you threatening me?'

He'd looked up to the sky. No sun. No rain. A strange day. Nothing at all for anyone. *Nul points.*

'Why don't you get yourself some work, Valérie?'

'How can I work, Richard? I am so busy with your text messages, your phone calls . . . You know, I should get myself a computer. Then you can email me and I can keep it all on file. You never really know people, do you? I should write a book, you know, I really should. They say people like to read about these things.'

'So they say,' he replied. 'It makes them sentimental, I suppose.'

'Ha.' She laughed flatly, then turned a softer face to Max. 'See you later, kiddo. The bus will be back at five.'

'*Ne me dites pas que quand je l'ai quitté ça lui a fait de la peine . . .*' Richard sang out, quoting Mr Balavoine.

She shook her head and took off.

He put an arm around Max's shoulders.

'What do you want to do? I've got no PlayStation or anything.'

'Oh, *putain.*'

He never had to ask where his son got his bad language from. Swearing; it seemed so unimportant.

It was the second time the boy had been to the studio. The first time, just the week before, had resulted in his father's arrest.

'Don't worry, Max, all of that's behind us now. Your mother wound me up.'

Actually it was Max who'd wound him up; he'd thought the kid looked disgusted by the place. Richard had shown him the view of the back of the church, he'd explained how good it was to be close to the village shops and his school and his friends. The boy had said nothing. He seemed to see it how it really was. She'd gone and said something and then the boy had said something about the place not being good enough for Richard. She'd said it again, whatever it was, something about his drinking, about the place stinking of booze and cigarettes; if only she'd held her tongue for once.

He'd taken her by her hair and dragged her to the shower room and forced her head down into the toilet bowl and turned on the shower and let the jet of boiling water burn the back of her neck and her hair and watched her hands, such strong hands, reaching about her, reaching towards the sink, trying to find something to get hold of, going for the plumbing pipes, screaming.

Then he saw it the way his son saw it. Max was standing in the bathroom doorway looking at them.

The father with his chin up, poised, straining to hold the mother down, taking a moment to look at the cord of the shower, about to wrap it around her neck. And then he let go.

It had been a bad month, all told.

39

Rachel and maud went by train from the local station to England. Maud cried with her hands up at the window, her breath obscuring the sight of her father, who stood crying on the platform, waving, with Rachel right behind her daughter, crying too, and mouthing at him, 'Go away, just go away.'

That was the last exchange between them, her saying, but not saying, 'Go away! Go away!' and him miming, 'I love you, Maud,' looking like a wind-up toy, like Pierrot, all down at the mouth as if it were someone else's fault, as if some big bad kid had kept on winding up his clockwork cock.

The train trailed the backyards of the modest houses with the kit swimming pools in their backyards; cement mixers, surrounded by refuse; and the white sit-up-and-beg vans parked with their rears ready for honourable thieving.

Coming into Marseille, birds swooped and swooned, milling around the high-rise towers, flirting with the antennae, dipping and diving, twisting and jiving. Tower blocks fell in, sidling into the city, taking over sideways. There were palm trees between washing lines. Waiting at the station for the train to get its nerve up for the high-speed assault on Paris, she looked at little Maud, at the expression on her face, that pompous disinterest which is the natural expression of the human face at rest. She took Maud's hand in hers.

Outside, beyond the station fences, a yellow-boleroed working man peered into the face-shaped hole of a bottle recycling unit. The man put an arm inside the skip, his cheek pressed against the side of it. Maud pointed him out.

'Yes, darling, he's a French alcoholic, I expect,' Rachel said. She was English. She was going back to England.

As they approached Paris, their eardrums blew in and out through the tunnels, and the long double-decker train eased into the Gare de Lyon and came slowly to a final halt. Its passive people sprang into life, recovering their ambitions starting with their coats and bags, descending the stairs of the train into the smell of someone else's second-hand luncheon meat with garlic, and were held up in their haste the length of the station platform by old women with tight perms.

Rachel had nothing on wheels and Maud liked to walk into her path, which made carrying the big sports bags even harder. She was soon sweating and, as she could not face the Métro, they took a taxi to transfer to the Gare du Nord.

The driver was hunched over what might have been a cloakroom conversation; his radio was either very loud or very quiet, the volume went up and down according to the driver's censorship, which was every time a few seconds too late. *He sees my mouth as something to kiss the children and not to give him a blow job.* (Volume down) *Men, out there, any of you who are listening to the women's show, be brave, be courageous, call in and help us to understand you.* (Volume up) *Now, ladies, something new to the market for intimate pleasure, the vagina kiss, it's a long tongue suspended from lips* (volume drops) *which can give you a lot of vaginal pleasure. We have a caller. Hélène. My partner likes to sodomize me but he is rather voluminous. It's a real problem. Hélène, make this a Friday-night thing, when you can relax and take your time* . . .

Rachel intervened. 'There is a child in your car, monsieur.' She made no condescension to accent now. She added for her own benefit, 'For God's sake.' It was the first time she had used the expression and the first time she had uttered an English phrase in front of a French person, for pleasure.

By the time they reached Waterloo, she had completed her metamorphosis. She dallied ostentatiously in customs clearance, ready to display her baggage purity, a faithful Englishwoman coming home, but they did not bother her.

They stayed a few days with an old friend of hers and quite quickly she found a nice flat in Battersea, with a small garden and a lovely kitchen, just right for the two of them. She went to the bank and collected the cheque-book for her new current account, opened in her maiden name, to which she transferred a useful part of the money her mother had left her.

The first night in their flat she barely slept; she woke, and slept and woke and thought how we are so certain when we are young but doubt becomes increasingly seductive, like going over to comfortable shoes, and she thought about Richard's doubt and then, it came right into her head, a borrowed thought, like eavesdropping at great distance — *Do any of us even know that someone loves us in another place or another time?* — and she sat up and wept, and the tears came horizontally, it seemed.

She could afford some of the small thrilling pleasures of belonging to Britain. She took out a Boots loyalty card and an Oyster card and bought a stack of celebrity gossip magazines, and with Maud enrolled at the lovely Church of England school just over the river she was free to idle in coffee bars.

She was not thinking about Jeff as she strolled. She was thinking about Richard. It was the mother in her, or possibly the English in her — the love of the underdog — she said to herself, as she sat down on a bench right in the middle of Sloane Square and gazed adoringly at the high church of Peter Jones department store.

40

✧

THE BEGINNING OF NOVEMBER; the vines were russet and bawdy; they waved their taffeta at the approach of the cold and violent lover. They drove along the tree-lined road with Richard contemplating the scene. Treasures tumbled from the tree-tops, their rusting scales listing in the wind that shook them with the impatience of a child at a parcel, hoping to hasten Christmas. A cascade thickened and drifted. A leaf came at the windscreen, as if from fingertips, kiss-blown.

He was stuck in the throat of the vision but Simone saw none of it; the windscreen might as well have been a mirror.

He'd called her the night before. He had an appointment with a psychiatrist in L'Argens but he couldn't get there. Would she be kind enough, *given he was Max's father and paid their mortgage and bills* (this he didn't say) would she be kind enough to drive him to see his shrink?

She ummed and aahed and conceded after some talk about bus routes. In the car, she explained that timetables could be had at the town hall. She'd already done her shopping for the week. She posted her letters yesterday. She would drink a coffee in the town to kill time, she'd take a turn round the shops. It was a shame they couldn't do it up in the village. Surely there were enough alcoholics in the village to merit an 'alcologue'. The bars were full from sun-up.

'The price of petrol,' he said.

'What do you say?'

'Petrol's gone up.'

'Yes,' she said. 'That's true. What do you mean by saying that? You're becoming strange. I'm worried about you.'

'There's nothing wrong with me, I promise you. I feel like I can see things clearly now.'

'Well, don't go thinking too much, it will make you ill.' The car was overburdened; restrained to third gear, it groaned. 'We saw Valérie yesterday. We were just out for a walk and we said to ourselves, we should just pop in and say hello, see Maxence, and they asked us to have a drink with them and we couldn't refuse and then you know Guy he drank too much and it was difficult to get him to leave. Once he starts playing the harmonica and going through those stories of Marseille, you can't get him to stop . . .'

'Change gear, I beg you.'

The plainest table. Two chairs either side of tubular steel, plastic seated, with a small peephole to the rear of the seat. There were posters on the wall, against AIDS and alcoholism; there was a photographic image of a liver with a distressed look. Opposite him sat a woman with glasses that were slightly fashionable, slightly sexy, slightly heartless, the sort of glasses that could be whipped off or donned for effect. They were supposed to be a statement of individuality, slightly fifties, pinched-ended, eyebrowed.

He was leaning forwards, as if holding a cigarette down between his legs, but he was holding nothing but his own hands.

On her face was the expression of a slight plea.

He had noticed that morning, as he did his shopping in the

Spar, that so many articles were now labelled 'consume moderately'. Even yoghurts. This had amused him. He had had to share the joke with an old girl. What do they expect you to do? he'd asked her. Gorge yourself on yoghurt? She had taken the product and examined it.

'It's bad for you to eat too much of one thing,' she'd said, and handed it back to him.

This doctor woman was similarly humourless, it seemed to him. He tried out his old smile.

'Well, be gentle with me . . .'

But this woman was like the man who offered Jesus vinegar-soaked bread for his thirst.

'It is not a question of being gentle or not gentle. Monsieur Bird.'

He nodded.

'This is not a punishment.'

'OK.'

'We will be meeting just once every three months to talk, to see how you're getting along. You might even like it, find our sessions rewarding. You never know.'

There was a bright light from the window. He could not resist it, and he looked up into it, taking his share and hers.

'Is it for my own good then, this?' He looked at her very expressly, to remind her that he was no child, no emasculated sadsack, that he was at least a man.

'Yes.'

'Because you care about my health, you care about how I am, in my head. Or is it my heart? You care about how I'm feeling.'

'Both. It's the same thing.'

'That's good. That's much better than I hoped for.'

He bit at a fingernail; he took his time over the operation, noting the little jagged edges that he'd left behind and treating them next to goat-like nips.

'We're here to talk about your drinking, Monsieur Bird. I wonder if you could tell me . . .' He could hear her uncross and cross her legs, the soft buzz of tights rubbing. The woman's smile was fulsome, though no teeth emerged. She was going to try a different tack. What a game it was. This could be her first psychiatric assessment; it could be her five thousandth. She had a good attitude; he could see that they'd been lucky with her. She came to the end of her speech and he hadn't heard anything she'd said.

'Monsieur Bird. I'm afraid time is not accommodating . . .'

'How about you? Are you accommodating? I mean you say you care. I assume you are a Catholic, a good woman, so would you open your home to me, share your food with me, take me in, keep me until I feel better?'

She put her hands on the folder and looked through her glasses at the page she smoothed.

'I know you're just pulling my leg but as I said, we're short on time. So, now, tell me, how do you occupy yourself? I see here in the notes that you are presently on sick leave for depression . . .'

The light from outside was gone, the room grey. He wanted a cigarette.

'Do you know that outside it is one of the most beautiful days I have ever seen? That the natural world goes on and on fighting for life, while we amble along thinking only about ourselves. You see this, here, in here, it's a state-sponsored exercise with the motive of getting people like me back to regular work, to prevent us claiming benefits, to stop us from being any kind of encumbrance, or expense. So, *madame le docteur,* it's as much a nonsense for you to use the word "care" as it is for me to use a word like "free". If there were not a table between us I would be quite afraid of you, I can tell you. You could be quite dangerous, I'm sure. I'm very glad of the table.'

He put his hands on it, and looked at it tenderly, running the palms of his hands left and right along its surface. Then he put his nose to it, then a cheek, and rested his head a moment on it, before sitting back in his chair.

'School-days.'

The woman leant forwards on the table, causing it to creak. She put a wrist under her right breast and ran the fingers of her left hand through the tendrils of hair around her neck.

'You're an educated man. I know you're not a wino. I'm not here to judge you, Monsieur Bird, but the nature of your . . .' she checked the folder, pursed her lips, 'drink-driving offences, and your violent behaviour, two assaults in the last month, well they seem to me to be a cry for help. Your wife has left you. I'm here to help you be happy and sober again because there is a relationship between the two, as you'll know from your profession.' She smiled prettily.

He put a hand over his mouth, cleared his throat. He caught her looking between his legs. 'This is why they have women do so much these days. I take my hat off to you, I really do, you women. You have a way with words. You could sell bacon to the Jews. That's why they give you these jobs.'

The woman coloured, looked down at her file, sucked on the end of her pen, then set it down abruptly.

'Let's get back to the interview. How do you spend your days?'

Masturbating, he wanted to say. He wanted to be the naughty schoolboy, to throw this stagy authority off him. But if only it were that glamorous. Lies, lies, lies in the bar at the *tabac* now or in the ironically named 'Café des Amis'. He was the most drunk in any place at any time. Then when his imagination failed, he had to resort to reality. He told whoever would listen his whole sad story. And then? And afterwards? He sat on his toilet in the dark, holding the door open with his foot for street light from the windows, eating crisps.

'Well, OK then, how are you sleeping?' she said, after a while.

'Not bad.'

'OK, that's good.' She made a note. 'Are you taking your medication?'

He bit his lip.

'I am, yes. Absolutely.'

'And how about your drinking?'

'Doing that too.'

'About how many glasses would you say you consume a day . . . ?' Her pen was tick-happy.

'Oh, just a modest amount, probably precisely the amount that's consistent with being beneficial to my health. You know the sort of thing.'

'How many glasses would you say?'

'About ten. Maybe twenty. It depends on the glass. A couple of litres, minimum. You'd have to check with the Cooperative. They'd have the precise figures.'

She laid her pen down.

'You are very sad and troubled, Monsieur Bird. Even though you're trying to joke with me. Setting all of these pleasantries aside, in your own words, how would you describe your mental state presently? As depressed, or even very depressed? Falling apart? Having a breakdown? Please speak freely.'

'I've lost everything that made me *me* in a matter of weeks; my wife, my son, my job, my house. And I've also seen that the place I called home despises me and possibly always did. Anyone would be upset. All of my so-called friends have turned their backs on me. And I've realized too how much I've let down my son. I'm not stupid nor am I saying I'm beaten, madame, but please understand that for now all I have is wine and cigarettes, and hatred.'

'Who do you hate?'

'I hate my wife, I hate my neighbour. I hate the ex-pats and I hate the locals. I hate your woman on reception who can't address me like a human being. I hate shop assistants. I hate bank tellers. Because they're all dead. Robots. I hate all of you people with your bureaucratic fantasies and your folders and charts, and I thank God for you all, because hating you is what's keeping my heart beating.'

'I am going to make a note that we should work on your sense of self-empowerment, your self-confidence, the way you see yourself. This feeling of hatred you have for these people, who are just doing their jobs as you put it, it's more about you than them. But we can work on that. We can take small steps and help you lift a little of that burden of hatred. I'm sure you don't like feeling this way.'

'No, you're wrong. It works for me. I'm fine with it.'

'We will see each other next on the third of February. In the meantime, try and find a healthy occupation, try and keep the drinking down. And keep taking the meds, as they say.'

She showed her teeth, and good God, it was like a standing ovation, her big white gnashers rose from the plush of healthy gums. He was momentarily overawed.

She came round to his side of the table. Below her shirt and cardigan, she was wearing a miniskirt. All that time, sitting there with her and she was wearing that! He could not help but stare.

'Now, you've heard of "humour" . . .'

'I've heard talk of it.'

'Well, sometimes we all have to remind ourselves that things aren't so serious after all. We have to have a little levity.' She perched her bottom on the desk, leant backwards. 'Next time we'll talk a little bit about your family. You said you've let your son down?'

'Yes.'

'Want to talk about him a little bit now?'

'No.'

She stood up straight. 'Well, that's something I'll have to take note of. It will slow down the process of your rehabilitation, obviously, if you don't fully undertake your treatment.'

'Look, I'd have preferred a public whipping to all of this shit. I'd have preferred to get a good kicking from the police like other people get.'

'It's in your file that you have been diagnosed with paranoia, Monsieur Bird.'

'Who wrote that?' He grinned.

She went back to her seat, checked her watch, made a note, *definitely paranoid, assess for schizotypy* . . . 'Now we've really run over time, so you see we can be quite flexible when it comes to the rules after all.'

He remained seated.

'Are you all right, Monsieur Bird?'

'Yes.'

'Come on then, shake a leg, *coco*. I'll see you next time.'

'I don't think it's fair to classify me. I've lost a lot lately.' He thought of his son. 'I'm only hanging on in here because of my son, otherwise I'd throw it all in, I'd be done with it all.'

She cocked her head. 'Suicidal?'

'No. I'd be going home. There's somebody in England who I care for, but it's not just that, it's all about going home now. I have to work some things out. About the kid. What I'm going to do. It's a stark choice, it's enough to drive you mad. Me or him, that's what it is. Really I just need to be left alone by you people. It's not like you can help me choose.'

'I know. I know. You just want to be left alone. And we just want you to be happy.'

He got up and went to the door.

'And, Monsieur Bird?'

'Yes.' He turned back, hand on the side of the door.

'We're going to win.'

'You won't,' he said. 'I'm not at home here. I'm not welcome. I can't leave and I can't stay. I'm in limbo.'

41

✧

No word from Rachel. He'd emailed her a timid sort of greeting, fishing to see how she felt about him but not venturing much himself, and he had nothing back. So much for that, he said to himself miserably.

Back to sex, back to the old faithful anonymous fuck. He needed contact.

He'd thought a bit about Maurice and the way he managed things, keeping love in a jar and getting his rocks off for a hundred euros in Cannes. Richard had called, but Maurice wasn't taking his calls. He called him all through the night, every half-hour. He didn't want Maurice's woman's number but she was bound to have a friend. It would have to be a woman near a station. Search engines gave you a start with the more genteel terminology—'escort' or 'masseuse'—but you got nothing but highbrow academic stuff if you put in *pute* or 'whore'. All those hypotheses did nothing for his hard-ons. He was not taking the pills.

'Every day, every morning, I am hard!' That was how Guy entertained a crowd, Simone telling a different story behind his back, using one curled little finger.

He arranged an afternoon rendezvous in St-Raphaël. The seaside town, with its *fin de siècle* gentility, all promenade and no action, was exhibiting strolling dolly birds. He took a coffee in the bar where he'd arranged to meet the girl and viewed the passing fare; an old woman in a yellow two-piece miniskirt and waistcoat, with whistles hanging off her bells, another in stout heels, in a gauze jungle-print affair, something toga-like in its arrangement, high over one thigh, low over one shoulder. Transparent bra straps. She was over sixty, a shag pile on her head, rolls of belly. In a place where every woman looked like a hooker, what on earth did a working girl dress like? How could a prostitute get paid work when the competition was giving it away with a free dinner? They'd have to be really good at it, he thought, his hopes also rising. It was quaint really, the idea of the whore.

A young woman in jeans and a white T-shirt came to his table and offered him her hand. Lorena was slim and sweet and he bought her a tisane. She didn't smoke or drink. They talked about her work; she complained that it was like modelling sometimes, you put yourself up for judgement, physically, and often it was hurtful. Nobody liked to be the last chosen. That was why she didn't work in a 'house' any more. Now she worked through the internet, that was her shop window. He brought to mind the dark and purple photograph of her with long hair hiding her face, an arm placed to cover her nipples. A lot of men came looking for love, she said, sipping her tea, which she considered to be like going to a car dealer's to buy a fridge.

So how did she become a prostitute?

She told him. And then there was no way he could have sex with her so he let the conversation continue for a while and then he gave her the money and wished her the best. She protested. He insisted. It had been nice speaking to her, he said. A fellow foreigner; she was Argentinian. A fellow parent; she had a teenage son. She accepted the notes half-heartedly, asked him if he was sure, and then as an afterthought turned back and said: *Look, I'm sure you won't, but please don't go all blue on me. You know, send me flowers or send me texts or anything like that, will you?*

No, he said. *I won't do that.* She'd said to him in mid-stream: *I like rough sex, I like to be hurt because that was what I knew, at home. My stepfather.* It gave a whole new meaning to the cliché — when life gives you lemons . . .

He'd had tears in his eyes so it was not surprising she issued her little warning. Women in her business had to look after themselves in all sorts of ways. He went back to the station thinking that he would take the pills, pretty much entirely for the side effect of the diminished sexual appetite. The prostitute had done what the psychiatrist couldn't do.

42

✧

'I TOLD YOU I LOVE YOU, Valérie.'

'It's not enough.'

'What do you want?'

'It could be anyone.'

'Yes, but it's not.'

'You've changed! You're not the same. You don't want me the same way. You don't hold me.'

'I can't hold you all day long. I have things to do. If you had things to do you'd be happier, you'd stop obsessing.'

'I thought we'd be a family. I thought we'd have lunch together. You're always out.'

'Don't I do things with Max? I don't have my daughter any more, remember? I gave her up for you.'

'You've made me into Rachel already.'

'We shouldn't be doing this. It's too soon for all this. Why don't you go to sleep?'

'Don't speak to me that way! I won't be told what to do!'

'We can't keep going over and over the same stuff.'

'I don't know what to do. I am so unhappy. I thought I'd be happy. You don't love me.'

'You're spoiling it, Valérie. You want so much all the time you're spoiling it . . .'

'It's because I love you so much. I never loved anyone the way I love you.'

'You don't listen to me. You interrupt the whole time. It's just pointless. I might as well whistle down the wind. It's a total waste of time. I'm getting another drink. I hope to shit we've got more cigarettes. Did you smoke the spares?'

'Yes.'

'Oh, great. Can't you buy some when you're out?'

'You're out all the time, you buy them.'

'So we're even arguing over buying cigarettes now.'

'You don't feel the same way, do you? Do you? It's obvious. Not like when I was your neighbour's wife.'

'Don't be so melodramatic.'

'Well, can't you understand why? Think about it. I just left my husband for you, you idiot!'

'Don't raise your voice. You'll wake the kid. Do you want to wake him? Do you want him to hear this?'

'I don't care.'

'Well, I do. Jesus Christ, we've got to have some standards, Valérie. I don't feel well at all. I've got to get myself healthy again. All this smoking and drinking and not sleeping. All these arguments. I'm going to have to go to London, you know, to see Maud.'

'I'll come with you.'

'Oh no. Oh no, baby. No way. That would be a total disaster. It's not too much to ask you, is it, that I spend a few days with my little girl? Why don't you spend some time with Max? God, Valérie. You're like a child. Don't you ever think that what we've done here, it was wrong, or greedy or anything? I mean don't you ever ask yourself if any good can come of this whole thing?'

'I was meant to be with you. That's all that matters.'

'I just feel bad about it all sometimes. Like about two in the morning when I've had a lot to drink, when I'm tired, when you're ranting on at me, when there's no cigarettes. When I want to go to sleep or for you to go to sleep. Or when I want quiet to think a minute.'

'You're out all day long . . .'

'Well, so what? I need to get out.'

'You've been fucking someone else. I know you have.'

'You're ridiculous.'

'I know who it is! It's Adele.'

'Adele! You're crazy. Jesus Christ, Valérie. Maybe we've made a mistake here.'

'Don't say that! How can you even say that, Jeff? I love you. I don't care. I'll do anything, just don't say that, just hold me, just love me, say you love me . . . we can start again, we can have our own children, maybe a little girl . . .'

'Baby, you don't even like children. I guess I'm not going to have a cigarette then. Look, let's just lie down together, peacefully, without talking. I'll hold you, but just keep your mouth shut, please, and maybe we can sleep, maybe you'll feel better in the morning, maybe we both will. Shh. Don't speak, honey.'

'But I need to talk to you. I want to know you. I want you to know me . . .'

'Please be quiet.'

He wished he could take it back, saying he loved her. He'd said it in a way because he knew she required to hear it to sleep with him. He'd said it in a way to enjoy the sex more. He'd said it, in a way, to make sense of what he was doing to Rachel and Maud.

If only he hadn't got mixed up with her.

He found Valérie very sexually attractive; that was the prob-

lem. He was angry with her about it. He'd had the idea to use another woman to satisfy himself and found one just down the road
in the shopping centre. If he could stop being turned on by Valérie, he'd be more able to think straight, to hold himself apart, and
do the right thing. Maybe he could make it up with Rachel and
they'd come back, his girls. He should have just carried on fucking the woman who ran the dry cleaner's. That was easy, that was
a cakewalk compared to this.

He'd taken in some of his trousers. She was a nice woman with
hair like a rat's nest, backcombed right back into the nineteen
sixties. She was long-limbed, kindly. She wore a miniskirt, red
lipstick and could never seem to make her top lip meet her bottom lip. Her small inadequate shop was next to the supermarket.
He bought bread and passed by nearly every day and she would
give him a kind of startled smile; she looked like a cat having its
tail pulled. Her commentary was inane, benign, pleasant. 'So
you're an American, huh?' as she crimped the plastic over his
shirts. He went in there about closing time one Tuesday evening.

'You're an attractive woman. I bet your customers flirt with
you, don't they?'

His bad French was sufficient. She closed the shop, pulled the
blinds to and asked him to come behind the counter. They kissed
at the counter like a happy trades-couple, except he squeezed her
right breast hard and pulled her hair. He popped her up on the
counter-side and brought her down on to his cock a number of
times. She was slender and lusty and these were her qualities so
far as he knew her.

After that he'd skip in with a baguette in the morning and arrange to meet in a lay-by at lunchtime. With the exhaust of her
red Clio going — she had to get home to make her husband
lunch — they met in clearings and had sex on the ground, coughing because of the fumes. His trousers and shirts got flecked with

mud and he set them aside when he got home to drop off at the dry cleaner's.

She got that look on her face one day when he was giving her the lunchtime seeing-to, and she held his head just as he was getting close and kissed him in a different way. He withdrew, got her to suck his cock while he lay on his back thinking, his hands behind his head looking at the sky, and afterwards she said to him, her face on his chest, 'Every time those bells on the door go, I hope it is you.'

His hands made for the dirt, he held himself up and he looked down the line of his nose, his chin on his chest, at her. He thought she resembled Marge Simpson.

'This is not an affair, you know.' Though afterwards it occurred to him he'd used the wrong word. *'Affaire'* in French meant business.

The next morning, he passed by with a *pain de mie* and some croissants and told the woman he felt bad about the whole thing, it was *'pas bon'*, he said to *'baiser une gentille femme comme ça dans la terre'*. What's more his life was *'compliqué'*. He just had the one shirt and a couple of pairs of trousers to collect. She had them handy.

'Donc c'est tout?' she said to him as he handed over the fifteen euros sixty cents and he took the dry cleaning with the wire hangers biting and snapping at the plastic wrap under his arm.

'Oui, merci,' he said cheerfully. The wind chimes clunked against the glass. He held the articles aloft one by one to check through. Yes, one shirt and two pairs of trousers, that was all.

43

$\diamond$

MAXENCE WANDERED INTO THE HALLWAY and sat on the bottom of the flight of stairs that went up to the bedroom suites. He could hear a bed moving. He trod up the stairs, a hand on the banister, his socks slipping on the polished tiles. He liked to wear his socks to bed. His mother said he couldn't but he liked to have warm feet. His feet ached, his legs ached, he was always cold. Growing pains, his father called it. He didn't know the French term.

He put his hands out as he reached the top stair and went on to his knees, advancing on all fours, until he got to the end room. He put his head through the cracked doorway, the sidelight was on, and he saw her feet, the soles of her feet, and he saw Jeff's hairy arse and his two hands on the pillows and then his mother's legs went right up in the air like bedposts and Jeff sat up more and when his mother started to say 'I love you' over and over again, Jeff put his hand over her mouth and took over being the one making the noise, grunting with the bed-head rocking against the wall, and when Jeff's hand slipped off her mouth, his mother cried out, 'That's it, hurt me . . .'

Maxence let his head fall against the side of the doorway, relying upon the contact with the cold plastered wall to help him stay there and stay quiet.

He closed his eyes. He thought of his mother in the restaurant in Cannes, one hand behind her neck holding back her hair in a ponytail, smiling as she put out her chin to eat a *palourde* from the small fork he held to her.

It was only when he heard Jeff make a few nervy snorts that he went. He withdrew on all fours as he had come, shuffling back on the tiles. By the time he got to the stairs, he could hear Jeff snoring evenly, drawing on the night, and he could hear his mother sighing as if there was not enough air.

He went downstairs back to Maud's bedroom, where he slept now, with its neon-pink Ikea rug and floral wallpaper, and he opened the shutters and opened the windows and looked out and saw his grandparents' small bungalow with the TV like a fire in the hearth.

His own house was invisible in the dark; he wished he could sing like his grandmother to call the past to him. He could remember the house when it was alive, the sound of the shutters whining as they swung, the bath emptying, the oven door banging, plates in and out of the sink, the drone of the television, the doorbell going, the stereo chewing on scratched disc, the washing machine in its last violent cycle, banging out a tantrum; a storm in a teacup.

And now he was trapped in the house that he'd watched being built. It took the best spot, it grabbed the best view. And his mother was drawn to it more and more, and his father went along too, and he used to follow in his pyjamas and socks to find them, with his own home less and less inhabited until finally it was only a matter of turning off the lights. A week ago he'd stood with his grandfather, watching him turning off the town water at the supply.

It had all happened as suddenly as if someone had whipped the sheets off them and pulled them by their ankles out through the back door and had put him and his mother in a van, their mouths taped up, their hands tied behind their backs, and taken them a hundred metres up the hill, leaving his father lying on the dirt.

When he closed his eyes and pulled the My Little Pony duvet up around his neck, he could see his father, in their home, sitting on the sofa at the end of a day, lifting a sock from one foot, then the other.

He got up and went into the kitchen. In a bottom cupboard was a box of things his mother had brought to the big house. He took it out and unfolded the interleaved cardboard and took from it the plastic bag of weed. He took the rolling papers from the cutlery drawer and the oven lighter and he sat with all the kitchen lights on, rolling a thick and ungainly sausage of weed. He lit it, it went up in flames and he had to blow on it to calm it down, and then he smoked it.

After he smoked it he went into the living room and took three photos out of their frames and sat holding them over the kitchen bin with the lighter; the neighbours and their daughter, Maud; Maud on a swing; the neighbours with his parents and him at dinner on the terrace. His mother had her eyes closed in every photo. He did not burn them. He let two of them drop into the bin and the third he ripped such that he was left holding only the image of Rachel.

In the morning, at breakfast time, he beat a monotonous noise on the kitchen table with the spoon. She came downstairs, look-ing pale and wretched, and asked him to stop it. He continued.

She ripped the spoon from him and grabbed his arm. 'Listen, you're getting everything you want, you have a quad, you have a PlayStation, Jeff is making such an effort with you, and you're going to wake him up now, you should think of someone other than yourself. I don't know why you have to be so weird all the time. I'm going to take you to see the doctor . . .'

She was tightening her grasp on his wrist. He shouted into her face, 'Why do you let him fuck you?'

She swung her hand to hit him, and the rings on her fingers made contact with the bones in the side of his head and he fell sideways, but it wasn't enough, she grabbed him by his pyjama top and pulled him off the chair and took him through the door outside and she bent him over the walled garden and pushed his face into the soil where the herbs grew, and she shoved his face into the dirt again and again. When his eyes were yellow, when his face was white, when his mouth was loose and open, when he looked a child, just a child, then she stopped.

She put her hands to either side of her face, rubbed her eyebrows, smelt the earth on her fingertips and turned to see Jeff watching her from the kitchen window. But that didn't matter to her at all. Whether he saw her or not, what he thought, that was unimportant. All of that went when her son's face was in the dirt, when she made her child do the crying for her.

44

✧

RICHARD WAS LONELY but he thought he might be hungry. He went to the Spar and bought canned cassoulet, something he'd always thought he'd end up eating one day — he'd given it a cold shoulder hitherto — but each time he'd passed it in the store, he saw it and it saw him; that canned duck and beans in sauce had had him in its sights and won. He bought some cheese too and a bottle of whisky.

Then he went up to the school. The kids came whooping and cheering down the long steps in front of the school with their cases on wheels, a stampede of red-cheeked breathlessness, pigtails and Mohicans, the boys with highlights, the girls in many-buckled boots, their parents waiting, arms folded, smoking, with something on the stove and a letter to post.

He sat on the bottom step, receiving blows from cases and bags, in the back draught of the flapping kids. He finished his cigarette, turned sideways looking up at the school, waiting for the older kids.

His son emerged, almost last, with two or three others, his face dispassionate, and he trudged across the playground in a sort of stupor. He arrived at the top of the stairs, like a diver bored by the board, he seemed to gather himself and took the first step halfheartedly, stopping on each for a moment, the same foot swinging forwards each time, then he just let himself drop, step to step.

'Max!' Richard stood up.

The boy's face was pale, he had rings around his eyes. He came to a halt before Richard.

'Max.' He took him in his arms but the boy remained lifeless, not returning anything, his arms hanging like whole dead fish. 'I've missed you. I love you. Max.' He shook his son. The boy's eyes were on the road, down at the throng of parents, and Richard pulled him close to him, put him under his chin, rubbed his stubble into the soft thick hair.

'I'm not allowed to talk to you. I'm not well, they say. One of us is going to prison or to hospital. I don't know which is which.'

He held him away from him to look at him, to ask what he meant, but the boy's eyes turned again to the road. Richard followed their direction. The town's two fat policemen, who drove round in a car two sizes too small for them, were standing at the front of all the parents. He let Max go on down the steps and into the car park where he found Jeff's car and got inside.

Richard dragged himself past parents with their children, like a leper. He stood on the pavement outside the optician's with tears coming down his face. He knew then how alone he was, how little he had. He felt the absence of Maxence like a physical pain; he thought of the sheep that drag around their prolapsed wombs, the pain was tugging his entrails, as Balavoine had warned.

Plenty of people saw him. No one stopped, no one stopped to say: *Hang on a minute what's going on here? This isn't right, a grown man crying in broad daylight* . . . How had he come to this, so quickly, in a matter of weeks?

After the snack hut which was blowing the smell of old fat up and down the street, he picked his way through the Hôtel Du Parc's painted wicker chairs. He'd stopped in at that bar early evening a few times in the last week, he'd set himself a little routine, telling himself to be there by 6.30 P.M. After a few drinks he felt quite outgoing and was willing to offer friendship and experience, and after a few more drinks it was hard to be humble about this offering. It worked fine for a while, until the barman got irritable and asked him to drink elsewhere. During the off-season, a regular could be like a wife.

He saw Maurice going into the PMU bar and he went in and offered to buy him a drink. Maurice was as uptight as ever, 'Mauroo', his cop eyes permanently wide in shock, his pale face shrunk away from the heat of their terror. He loomed at the end of the bar by the door with an arm across his chest, holding his elbow, looking stiff and in want. 'I can't stay. I've got the ironing to do,' pulling his button collar into a sharp V about his throat.

Nevertheless, they tilted the heads of their glasses together. They ran through their former acquaintances' bad luck. Marc's girlfriend was bitten by dogs and raped on the way to St-Tropez. David had been cheated by a crook from Bargeoles. Bruno had died of alcoholism. Richard said he'd seen his wife in the doctor's. She was probably picking up the same prescription he was, he quipped pathetically, inviting enquiry.

Maurice would not be drawn that way. He was a very hygienic man.

'How's your little woman in Cannes? That still working for you?'

'She's a good woman, an old-fashioned sort.'

'How much do you give her these days?'

'She hasn't put the price up in years.'

'You don't ever think of going somewhere else?'

'No.'

'You don't think of maybe taking her out, of suggesting you see each other as a couple, or that she come and stay with you?'

'She's not that kind of a woman. She's very whole.'

'But you obviously care for her, in saying that. Perhaps she cares for you. Perhaps you love each other and you're mistaking it for sex. If you didn't come to her — what is it, on a Thursday? — she'd worry, she might look for you. And you, if you went there and found her gone — or worse, dead — how would you feel?'

'Look, I can't chat. I am meeting a fellow from the Town Hall any minute now, they want to get my involvement in the elections. He's coming in here to speak to me.' He tipped his head forwards. 'Please don't tell anyone about my getting involved in politics.'

'No, sure, of course not, but who would I tell now? No one speaks to me. I have been cut off all round. Want another?'

'No thank you.' Maurice looked immeasurably demoralized, clutching one forearm across his chest. He did not smoke, and he drank modestly and rarely got drunk, but when he did he'd talk to them about his ex-wife and how he'd made her have an abortion, thinking she'd been unfaithful, which brought him on to the subject of her being the love of his life . . .

'Look, I'm sorry about the dog thing. But we couldn't pay the vet's bills for something you can't reasonably suggest happened at our house.'

'Simone gave him a chicken bone.'

'Oh, come on, Mauroo, even if she did, she didn't mean to harm him.'

'There's a lot you don't understand, Richard. Those people, they are not decent people. They are not much better than gypsies. They are unreliable. Cheats. All the people around here are like that one way or another. Thieves who had the luck to live here. I have broken off with Guy and Simone for good. This dog thing is the last straw.'

'Well, I'm sorry you feel that way. We had some fun together, didn't we? Four in the morning listening to Santana, with Guy on the harmonica. We talked about everything. Wonderful evenings. Remember how Guy used to put on that one song that reminded you of dancing with your wife and you'd say: *Play it again*. Every time, you'd say: *Play it again*. And he did. I can't see myself carrying on here like this, so alone. But I don't want to leave Maxence, you see. I don't want to leave him with the bloody American. So I must stay and wait for what I'm given, I suppose.'

'The American? He's no worse than anyone. Well—and perhaps you *should* go. This is not your home, is it?'

'After fourteen years here?'

Maurice looked at his glass. 'I wish I'd gone back to Alsace, when I had the chance. Those fellows will be here any minute. It would be embarrassing to make introductions since we agreed this would be done on the hush-hush.'

As Richard went off, he saw through the window his former friend, hand across chest, telephone pressed to the side of his face, words being met with words, eye for an eye and tooth for a tooth and nothing more, physically rigid, strained to the limit.

He was surprised to be bathed in light as he went up the stairs to his studio. He looked upwards. Someone had rigged up a construction-site lamp and attached it to the banister of the floor above. Someone had finally had enough of the dark.

There was nothing from Rachel via email.

He sat in the shithole he was renting, drinking, to avoid thinking in any kind of straight direction.

45

✦

SIMONE WAS ON A LIFE SUPPORT of nicotine and smoked emphatically, withdrawing her allocation of oxygen by the tweezer action of her sharp-ended nostrils, in queenly brown shudders.

Last time she was there, she said, was for lunch with the German from down the lane. It had emerged that he was in fact a bereft and bankrupt pensioner with a 'heart of gold'. They'd had a lovely lunch. Simone had done the paperwork for him to get a small state stipend and he'd invited her to lunch as a thank-you.

Breadcrumbs on her breast, grey roots, black chignon, as she sat with Richard and Max now, she'd sat too with the German in happy faux-connubiality, moaning about the waste in the world, the two of them at their best on the bloom of the wine, entering into the mysticism of horticulture, about talking to plants, giving them red wine, and music, singing to them, then getting maudlin, the pear tree that did badly after the man who pruned it badly came back to stay, the orange tree that sulked after the radio broke, how to cajole a tree and how to argue with a tree. The earth, the land, all gone. The bottle empty.

She hadn't meant to talk about Richard and Valérie to him, but she had to talk about it with someone. She couldn't talk to Guy.

'He turns and turns all day long just like his dog, doing nothing. He's completely lost. He won't speak about Valérie. He sniffs the air like the dog, goes in and out morose, he doesn't even clear his plates and cups away. He sits down to do the horses and then he just pushes the newspaper away from him.'

The German had said to her, perhaps Guy blames himself, after all he hadn't set Valérie any kind of example when it came to sticking with things, with working at a relationship. And people these days could so easily walk away from their duty. It wasn't like in their day. Look at you, he'd said, approvingly. You worked so hard, the German said to her. Yes, that was true enough, she'd always worked hard. And as for Richard, he said, it's no surprise he's depressed, but he'd heard the pills help. He was a gentle sort, that German, with hair like a palm tree; handsome once and actually still a fine-looking man. The poor man, a fire burnt down his cabin, and he had nothing. He had a moustache though. Her mother used to say that a kiss without a moustache was like a soup without salt.

'Do you know, I think the German is a little in love with me,' she said, her cheeks pink.

Richard ordered two glasses of Champagne, one for him and one for her, and a glass of Coca-Cola.

'Are you having a relationship with him? This German?'

'At my age?' It was a challenge more than a question. 'The girl at the hairdresser's, her brother's wife saw you at the doctor's,' she said.

'Yes, I've been in there a few times.'

She raised her eyebrows, put the glass to her lips, her mouth flattened as she drank, she looked so disappointed. Their relationship had changed, now he really was like a son to her, he was a burden.

They ordered three menus at eleven euros apiece. It smelt of old carpet in there, and there was something festive about the odour of cigarette smoke and mould.

'I have bronchitis, that's why,' he said, raising a glass.

Simone put her cigarette out in the seashell. It might have been a seashell, or a dried pig's ear. It was hard to tell, it had been well scarred with cigarette stubs.

'I thought you might have been to see him because you were depressed.' She raised her glass. 'Your health.'

'No.'

They touched glasses with Max's. They drank hard, all three of them consuming two-thirds of the glass.

'Bronchitis. Asthmatic?'

'No.'

'Chronic?'

'I don't know.'

'Mine is,' she said, coughing, pausing, swallowing more Champagne, then coughing again, 'it means it's life-threatening, not a temporary thing.'

Max tore off some bread, dipped it in the Coke.

'Go on, enjoy yourself, Max,' she said warmly. 'While you can. Your health is everything.'

'Thank you for bringing him to see me,' Richard said to her.

A plate was put before each of them with celery remoulade, a tossing of grated carrot and three shiny curling pieces of *saucisse*. They each removed the parsley garnish. Richard asked for a pitcher of wine.

'You shouldn't drink with anti-depressants. But you know that.'

'How's Guy?'

'The same. You know, I give him thirty milligrams Paxil in the morning and the evening. I tell him it's for his prostate.'

'He doesn't know?'

'He wouldn't take it if he knew.'

'Jesus Christ.'

'I have to. He's always criticizing me. He's bad-tempered.'

'Even so.'

'It's that or he's on the street.'

'Come on, you love him.'

'Yes. To put up with him I must do. But my health isn't good. I must think of myself, that's what the doc says, but I said to him after a lifetime of putting yourself last it doesn't come easily to me . . .' She finished her glass and brandished it ostentatiously.

The young waitress filled their glasses again and took away the plates; gormless and vacant, a cipher serving, she was invisible to herself. Richard gazed at her.

A group of four bottle-fed British took a table next to them and the largest man rubbed his hands, preparing to lavish the group with rosé.

'Look at them,' said Simone, 'look at their faces, thinking they will get away without getting cancer here. Do you know this is the only village in France with an English-speaking branch of Alcoholics Anonymous? They can't be anonymous. He sleeps sixteen hours a day. I say to him, you're depressed. He says, I'm not stressed. I say, you don't understand what it means, depressed. He goes to bed at seven and gets up at six, then he naps through the afternoon. Do you think it's the pills?'

A meagre steak was served to each of them with fries.

'Bon app'.'

They fell on their plates. It was good to be hungry and good to eat even if it had to be done together.

'Well, I don't know how this happened, how we all came to be here, but I'm grateful for it,' said Max, smiling like the long-absent relative at the reunion.

Richard and Simone exchanged looks.

227

Then after a mouthful, Maxence put his knife and fork down. The boy had tears in his eyes and could barely swallow what was in his mouth.

'What is it?'

'I have a problem.'

'I knew it,' Simone said.

Richard set down his knife and fork. 'What problem?'

'They've put me on pills. For my head.'

'Ritalin,' said Simone, tongue under front gum, reaching for her glass.

From the boy's top teeth two little train tracks of spittle extended across his mouth.

'Ritalin,' she went on, 'it's a good one. Lots of clinical trials. Eat, Maxence.'

'Is it OK to take it?'

'You knew about this, Simone?'

'Yes.'

'It's not OK. It's ridiculous. Valérie wants her son to be on drugs? At thirteen years old? Ritalin is for attention deficit disorder. Max hasn't got that! There's no diagnostic standard for it worth the paper it's written on. Kids have died from taking the bloody drug. She might have asked me about it! I was in the fucking business, for God's sake.' He pushed his plate away from him.

Simone glanced at it. 'Mind your language, Richard. No wonder they've put him on the drugs. Think about it. Think about all he's been going through! And all the things that have happened in the last few months! What you did to Valérie . . . in front of him.'

Max sat round-eyed, his front teeth on his lip.

Richard pointed at him, his anger misplaced, 'You're not to take them. You tell her, you're not taking them.'

The British diners hunched their shoulders, sharing this outburst like treasure chucked amongst them, giving it a rough valuation, finding it quaint.

'Your grandmother doesn't know what she's talking about. Don't listen to her or your mother or anyone. Just me, OK? Those pills aren't bloody sweets or anything. They mess with your mind.'

Simone raised her eyebrows and drained her glass. 'I don't mind it here. It is what it is. There's a nice new little place, run by the Belgian woman who looks like a man, down dog-shit alley. They do little macaroons with your coffee. It's a bit more upmarket. And of course it's nice to go somewhere new.' Her eyes welled with tears. 'Where people don't make comments. I get funny looks in the *tabac,* funny looks in the *boulangerie* and they go quiet in the hairdresser's when I walk in. Richard, she's not a bad person, Valérie. She only wants to be happy.'

'With Jeff? She hasn't got a chance. The man's a liar and a cheat.'

'Rachel was very difficult to live with. All the religion stuff and dragging him off to Africa like that all the time.'

'They went twice! She went to help people!'

'Guy saw her praying in the garden.' She shook her head. 'Africa! She should have been at home looking after Maud. It was such a shame for the little girl. We loved her and now she's gone. That's how life is. One asks oneself why one bothers to love, it's the worst pain in the world.' She sighed. 'We miss the little tap, tap, tap at the door, "Can I come in please, Tatie . . . ?" She was very polite. It's an enormous loss not having them next door any more.'

'And what am I? The cat's arsehole?'

'Oh, Richard!' She found something funny and began to laugh in fits and starts, almost reluctantly, putting her napkin to her lips. 'I saw this tea-towel holder in a kitchen shop, shaped like a cat with its tail up in the air, you just poked the cloth in the little plastic suction thing, right under the tail, it made me laugh. Putting your finger into that hole like that . . .'

'They're getting a trampoline for me,' said Max. 'That will give me some exercise so I can lose weight. I like rhythm. The doctor said it would be good for me to jump up and down.'

'I can't deal with this.' Richard put his hand in the air to call the waitress. Max quickly gulped down the last mouthful of Coke.

Simone ate the last mouthful of steak, and put her knife and fork together. She dabbed at the bags under her eyes. 'It's been difficult. Very difficult for everyone. You will have to let her go, Richard. Everybody wants love. That's all they want. No one used to expect such a thing when I was young. It's like a madness. I don't know where it's all going to end. They say religion causes wars but I say love's worse. They come to me, you know, to have their cards read and all they want to know is whether someone loves them. They get so annoyed when you say something about their work or money or property, important things. They don't want any of that.'

Richard craned his neck to get the waitress.

'Are you OK, Mamie?' Max asked.

She had her hand over her mouth, tears in her eyes. She bent her head to address the boy. 'I pray to the angels for you every night, Maxence.' She finished her wine with her throat trembling.

Richard took the notes out of his wallet and settled the bill with the waitress, holding the bill slip like it was something filthy.

'You don't want your chocolate mousse then,' she said, deadpan. 'It's included.'

'No.' Richard got up, startling one of the British women who'd turned again to ogle them; as he rose he knocked her elbow. Her fork fell to the floor. He stepped on it as she went to retrieve it, by accident. She sat up and put her hand on her heart.

Simone leant across the table towards Maxence.

'Your father,' she said in a hoarse voice, 'is having a nervous breakdown. You might not understand that now but you will when you're grown up.' She got up and stood beside him, putting an arm around him, squeezing his face to her breast. She took a bread roll and slipped it into his pocket.

46

✧

RICHARD STOOD OUTSIDE and lit a cigarette. The Dutch were sitting at a table by the fountain eating panini stuffed with chewing-gum cheese. They seemed not to see him.

They had gone with the Dutch, with Marjolein and Joop and their kids, to the beach in May and lain there with a picnic, drinking wine. Poppies in the sandy grass on the kerb. He could recall Valérie sipping on a Diet Coke, looking sourly at the kids who were arguing and in particular at Max who wanted to go home, and Marjolein sat there too, her breasts hanging like used tea bags in a too-large white bikini top, and Joop had belched or something and suggested he and Richard go for a beer at the beach café and he'd thought, there and then, shit, this is a long business this family thing. But there was always Monday.

The Dutch guy, Joop, he kept himself busy — football, drinking, the kids — and he seemed to love his wife. He had a big jaw, there was something heroic about him, Richard thought now as he put out his cigarette in the fountain.

Something so mundane, something far from anything commonly regarded as any kind of a test of man's heroism, the family unit, what most people would consider normal and right, had beaten him. The nuclear family was set to explode, and no one was clear why, and that was possibly why his pills had sold so well.

Simone finished her own cigarette, twisting her ankle to crush it. She had been lingering next to him while the kid ate his bread roll.

'Écoute,' she said, and she put a hand on his sleeve. He looked at her, at her veiny face, at the mascara that had crumbled on to the bags under her eyes, at the deep brown of them, and at the dry pale mouth that was loose and moving ahead of words, 'Take the boy home with you, Richard. I will get him in the morning. Valérie and Jeff have gone away for the night. Take him. It will give you some time together.' Her eyes moistened. 'You are like a son to me,' she said.

'Are you OK, Papa?' Max said with edgy formality now as they opened the front door. Richard was taken aback by the occasional maturity in his son, it was somehow unsettling. He tried to throw it off.

'Génial, Max. Excellent. It's all going well.'

Surveying the place, Max's face came back blank and uneven as the walls.

'You want a coffee?'

'No thanks.'

'You find it strange, don't you, your father living in a place like this?'

'Not really.'

'We're going to spend some father–son time together in spite of it all. We'll have to get out and about. Maybe.' Without a car it would be hard to do, he reflected.

'Fishing?'

'No. Fuck that. We'll go to Paris, or something on the train.'

'Cool! Can we go to Disneyland?'

'Well, I was thinking, you know, of something more grown up. We could go to London maybe.'

'Oh.'

'Hey, we'll have a really good time whatever we do. Do me a favour, Max, and find your passport. Dig it out, OK?'

'All right.'

'How are things up at the house with your mother?'

He shrugged again.

'Good, bad, awful? Come on, Max, talk to me.'

Richard could see Max's brain working, he was hoeing with his teeth over his lip, raking through the stony ground of things important and things trivial and levelling them. 'Fine,' he said. Then his face came to life, 'Gérard's got a quad.'

Richard corrected him. 'Jeff. Jeff's got a quad.'

'We went down to that rubbish dump place where you and I used to go camping and we just blazed right through it, and the sun came down on me, it was amazing, like it was just on me, it shone on my head, and I felt this energy inside of me reaching up, you know like a snake or something. It was cool. And guess what, Dad?'

'What?'

'They let me drink Coca-Cola at home now.'

Richard put his hands on his hips, hung his head, blew out, like a striker who'd flunked the goal.

'Wow. Well, what can I say? As long as you're happy.'

'Yeah.' The boy's face fell as if he'd seen something else in his mind's eye. After a minute he came to. 'Jeff's got "Grand Theft Auto II". It's violent. It keeps me safe though. I mean it keeps them safe to keep me busy.'

'Yeah? How do you mean?'

'What time is it?'

'Two thirty. Any chance of you sitting down or something? Or taking your coat off?'

Max sat on the bed, a finger in one ear, pondering something, his eyes looking towards the window, an expression trying to form on his face.

'So I'm here for twenty hours?'

'Yes,' he said.

'I'll play chess on your computer then.'

Richard wondered how the paternal love thing was going to work out as his sole motivation for continuing to exist.

47

✧

WITH HER RED HAIR FLOATING in an electrostatic halo, due to the acrylic sweater, Maud gave her mother a small electric shock as Rachel went to smooth down the school uniform. She put a hand on the girl's egg-shaped tummy and Maud straightened. Her breath was of stale milk, her eyes green and her skin pale coral, and Rachel thought she was the most beautiful child alive and told her so.

'I sometimes wonder if I exist,' Maud had said to her at bedtime the night before.

'Yes, I used to think about that when I was little, I used to think everyone else was a robot,' Rachel said, putting her covers around her chin.

'I hope Daddy will be all right,' and she gave Rachel that very grown-up look of both doubt and resignation, and finished with a shrugging smile, as if to say: *But what can we do?*

She took Maud to school across the bridge on the red bus, upstairs at the front, with the smell of steel still on her hands from the handlebar when she left her.

Within a month she'd collected England past and England present. She went to her local pub there most days at eleven for her morning latte and pomegranate juice with a celebrity gossip magazine that she grabbed from the newsagent's next door, her attention usually diverted by the headlines of the top shelf — *Top Brit Clit* had her in a wide-mouthed grin as she handed the old man her five-pound note. You could get anything you wanted in this country now.

She listened in the pub, lingering till lunchtime, to builders talking like aristocrats with their long-winded parenthetic conversations and formulae, 'I suspect that . . .' and 'swapping paradigms'.

The British seemed to have the best of everything. She was proud of her greedy little country packed with foreigners practising plumbing. Big girls exaggerated around a trestle table outside the pub, enjoying the Indian summer, with their lower-back tattoos in ethnic patterns signposting acres of backside for development, fur on their collars, baubles on their bags. Passing them by, she paused to appreciate the black in their language. She had the sense of being evicted from her time, she had no idea whether she was 'stylin'' or 'wack', 'dope'.

She was meeting an old friend for lunch. They were at school together; sixth form college in Hove. It was seven years since they saw each other, when Binda came to New York to stay with her and donned a builder's white mask to tour the neighbourhoods. Lemons and boiling water to start the day, and the pained anticipation that Binda might just sanction the moment to eat as being one without greed as its motivation, as they sat with hot plates of food going cold.

'Are you and Jeff the only ones who use this shower?' she'd asked imperiously one morning, quivering in her camouflage pyjama bottoms and ribbed vest, the hairs on her arms standing out on goose-bumps.

'Yes.' Jeff had looked up from his cereal.

'Because I found a small shit in it.'

'That would be something to do with our cat.'

'Oh. Well. I didn't know you had a cat.'

They'd laughed about it, she and Jeff, they'd laughed so loudly in bed that night that Binda told her the next morning she could hear every word of it. She said she'd come for some sympathy. She was going to leave her husband. She wanted to be heard, not mocked. She hadn't brought the right shoes, it was a shame Rachel hadn't told her about the hills. No one expected to come to New York and find hills. It was not a good stay and Rachel was glad when she went. But that was a long time ago, and now Binda was divorcing number two.

A cabbie sat outside, head against the window of his vehicle, scrolling through messages on the mobile phone. Flipped open it was like a powder compact of old. She asked him to take her to Speakers' Corner. She was going to walk along Oxford Street to meet Binda on Duke Street.

She sat in the cab with a strange foreboding. Binda knew her when she was shabby, or at least shabbier. No one else in her life knew the extent of it. The men. All the men she'd loved without being loved. She'd not been able to understand why they didn't love her so she didn't accept it, no matter the evidence. She had ignored their failures to turn up, the nothing for her birthday, the other women, their deprecation in front of friends. She saw handsome men where there were none, she invented for them a future magnificence and a past glory, she told them so, she helped them sober up or get drunk, find their socks, eat their dinners and she let one literally piss on her. *Don't leave me. Do you love me?* It was a shabby business and she couldn't get away from it. Jeff was the last in the line of naked emperors who'd proved she was ugly, common and worthless.

She got out of the cab, swapped a pound tip for being called 'darling' and stood a minute watching a Socialist Workers Party speaker holding a small happy crowd in his thrall. She was pleased to see the romantic old fool.

'*They've told you you're ordinary. You've accepted that. But the fat cats, the people who think they're powerful, they want you to believe that.*'

The crowd withdrew, gingerly, individually, one by one: *We are all fat cats now.*

She dawdled through Selfridges, passed along perfumery, looking at the veiled Muslim women, fingering the perfume 'Insolence'. The word 'luxury' was stickered on every surface and people must be pampered and titillated, such that a coffee éclair was an erotic promise.

When she was a girl, there were still people who died in their homes after living in them all their lives, possibly being born in them, certainly being bored in them. People still made diary entries of two to three words pertaining to the weather. There were reliable seasons, the cuckoo in May. The smell of currants in the larder. Home knits. Moth holes. For dinner — mince, mince, mince. Square ice creams in square cones. Rice pudding with a leather skin. The advent of the aubergine and the mystery of how to cook it, how to eat it and why. Mother being anti-men, the lesbo-wok days, short hair and brown rice, broccoli. All the gay boys postered around girls' bedrooms and kissed goodnight. When a pierced ear on a chap was something to write home about. Fear of credit cards. The Filofax, the mention of the wine bar, something French. How they shoved grapes and cheese in sandwiches, then they shoved foreign cheese in foreign bread and it all went haywire. You never threw out knickers. You walked like a duck at the time of the month. Before they went over to panini and panty liners. Then they began to invest in having better things that would last longer, that was the idea. Going upmarket on the escalator and finding the mezzanine, cold and stark and lonely. Everything in aluminium or steel. Industrial, built for the last hoorah, the triumph of the machine age. Stone flooring. Wood not plastic. The excuse for the expense; it will last. It will outlive me, that kitchen. As if that's a good thing or worth anything at all, the idea that your kitchen will outlive you. Incest in books and on the telly, brothers doing sisters, then upping the ante with your auntie and, when it all fell apart, dads doing daughters. Such a shock, such a terrible shock to the system and rife; everyone at it like knives.

She went to work as a temp, and she went out every night on the same basis, going to strange places with amorous lively men who turned to stone in the morning. Then she went to the same house twice, with a different man two years after the first time. Though her maths was poor she understood the probability of this, that the odds were long and her chances uneven, so she decided to leave London, to leave all of that behind and never to go back.

But now she was back, and now she was a mother and Maud was her talisman. Maud made her better, not Jeff nor God but Maud.

Binda was waiting for her in Carluccio's, squashed between a stack of festive cakes and a wire rack of jars of pickles at eleven quid a pop. She rose to give non-contact kisses.

'I don't know if it's sencha or just green tea, but I'm buzzing.'

Binda had married a banker and she was so *over* money. She wore an array of friendship bracelets around her wrist, a vest and loose parachutist pants, with a shiny silk bomber jacket. She had some illegible script tattooed on her neck. She looked beautiful. Her forehead was lined but handsome, her eyes bright, her skin was tanned and her hair pale and short.

If Rachel was going to tell someone about her husband's affair, a nearly twice-divorced friend seemed a good choice.

Binda began; she had spent the last ten or fifteen years on her self-development. They ordered antipasti and water. She barely mentioned her husband, in fact she mentioned no other person at all.

'Life is not personal, nothing is personal, if someone says something to me, a criticism, it is not personal . . .'

'No, it's more about them,' said Rachel quickly, thinking this might be a two-player game.

'There are three rules for living,' Binda went on, 'the faithful word, absolute honesty, and the present moment.' She would elaborate.

A half-hour passed or more and Rachel sought desperately around for clocks, craning her neck to see their neighbour's wrist. The bastard was having a glass of red wine and chocolate cake. Binda never took sugar, it was an addiction and all habituated attachment is bad. Binda's soon to be ex-husband lived a deluded life, his head full of trivia like money, ambition, and he lied, he lied to himself, and so of course he lied to everyone. Binda never told a lie. 'I know that it makes people uncomfortable to be around someone pure. They see themselves reflected like in a mirror. It makes people very nervous.'

Rachel could see that. She wondered if this was how she'd sounded at her high point, on her high horse. She wanted to go.

'I'm not perfect, Rachel.' Please God, thought Rachel, do not let the next word be 'but'. But Binda was better than buts, and much, much more long-winded. The bill came. Binda paid with Amex and Rachel put in a note and fiddled for a tip. She might have said: *Listen, love, my husband's screwed my next-door neighbour, I've moved country and I'm a single mother to a five-year-old girl who cries for her father and I'm broken-hearted that the family I made is dead, but I'm fine thanks.* But there never seemed an opportune moment.

The next time they met they would talk about Rachel. Binda said life was great when you learnt to let go.

'Be like a child.' She had no children; she considered them exemplary. 'And be honest.'

'I am!'

'No, I mean in general. Live an honest life. Be true to yourself.'

'Oh. That.'

Honesty seemed to be a luxury afforded by people who didn't have to work for a living.

Binda's T-shirt bore the slogan *Nobody's Perfect*. 'And another thing . . .'

Shit.

'. . . Enough with the "love" stuff. It's such a delusion. It's to keep people from really living their lives as fully actualized persons, the whole concept, Barbara Cartland you know. It's a silly thing really. For spiritual cripples.'

'Wow.' One religion or another, different name, same game; consolation. 'Hey, Binda, do you still have the cactus-shaped travel dildo?'

With Maud watching telly that night, she drank a couple of glasses of wine. Then she lit a cigarette and stood outside in the communal courtyard, smoking it, watching her neighbour through the window arranging cereal packets in her surgical gloves. The woman paused to cry out, 'The disgusting smell of cigarettes.'

She looked at Maud sitting so devoutly at the TV screen, a primrose in her yellow pyjamas, sucking her thumb, her small blanket in her grip, and felt lonely, and then she felt guilty at feeling lonely with her lovely girl right there. *Why isn't it enough? What's wrong with me?*

'I am a bad mother. I am a terrible mother,' she said to herself.

She began to cry, sugaring herself in self-pity. 'And no one's going to rescue us.'

While she was putting Maud to bed, too heartsore for story time, making an excuse, downright lying in fact — 'I have things to do, sweetheart,' (like crying or watching *Extreme Makeover*) — the phone rang, and for a minute she thought, she hoped, under the influence of the wine and the cigarette and the tears spilt, it might be Jeff. She was not a spiritual warrior. She took the stairs two at a time, the noise of her descent telling her all she needed to know.

'Rachel. It's Richard Bird.'

'You sound so formal! Is that your phone voice? Richard Bird. I know who you are. Oh, I'm so glad to hear your voice. I'm feeling like shit.'

'Well, you're not alone.'

'Oh, good. Good. God, it's good to hear your voice. Are you OK?'

'Yes. OK. I got your number from Simone. She said you called her.'

'That was weeks ago, just after we left. To explain things a bit. So how are things?'

'Bad.' He laughed. 'My wife's a nightmare. I can barely see Max at all. I'm wondering what the hell I'm doing here. It's weird, but I can't fucking stand the place now, or the people. The people are shocking when you get to know them. I've been losing my temper. Shit, what am I even pretending for? I've been losing my mind. And you? How are you?'

'Oh, OK. Dreadful. I don't know what I'm doing here. I was thinking about you today.'

'Were you?'

'Yes. I was thinking you were right about me, you know, that I wasn't to be believed with the God thing, that I wasn't up to it. I suppose if I'd never gone to Africa, if Jeff hadn't had his thing with Valérie, I might have gone on with it. I might have thought I knew something. Anyway, now I know you're right. And I feel a total failure.' She gave a short laugh.

'You shouldn't.'

'Well, I do.'

'There's so much I would like to say but now I'm on the phone I can't seem to think.'

'Oh. I wish you would. *Extreme Makeover*'s finished.' She laughed again.

'Did it go well?'

'Yes, she gave the twirl, you know, hands-on-hips-look-at-my-tits. She looked just the same as they all look.'

'Well, I suppose we all have the same fantasies.'

'Yes. We do.'

'Rachel.'

'Yes.'

'Rachel.'

'Yes?'

'Are you having a glass of wine?'

'Could you hear my elegant slurping?'

'Yes. I wish I was there with you.'

'Like the good old days,' she said drily.

'Rachel . . .'

'Yes.'

'I miss you.'

'I miss you too.'

There was a pause. Rachel took in the stairwell with clouded eyes. She was done with it there.

'What's your email address? Do you have one?'

'No. I don't. Well, I do, you know, the same one but I don't have a computer here. I just haven't got myself sorted. I mean I'm still deciding who I'm going to be.'

'I wanted to write to you. It's easier, and less embarrassing.'

'Give me yours. I'll work something out. An internet café or something. Go on, spell it out slowly, letter by letter, no I missed that bit, start again.'

She wrote it on her arm in big black Biro letters and when they finished speaking, she sat looking at it.

48

✧

THEY ATE IN SILENCE; Valérie, Jeff and Max. Sometimes Jeff would take head of table, other times he'd abdicate and sit slightly apart, off to one side, his chair back from the table. He had bad table manners, he'd sit with his fork in the right hand, no need for the knife, he cut his food with the back of the fork, a crust of bread in the left hand, elbow on the table, drearily picking through the plate as if going through litter, and he'd leave his fork as it fell just before he lost interest and get up and saunter off, mid-thought supposedly.

She suspected his 'creative' impulses were a way for him to do as he liked. It turned out they had little they liked to do in common, besides sex. And the sex was taking longer and reaping fewer rewards. She liked to go shopping; Jeff disdained it and one of his pet quotations was: *Shopping is not creating*. 'So what?' she asked him and he had no answer for that. She went alone, wandering, thinking underwear, thinking she could lose weight, thinking she could have her breasts done.

Maxence sat ready for the meal even while she was still chopping the vegetables, watching her. She had a glass of wine next to her, doing no good. She was slicing the carrots roughly, she noticed all the faults of her work, the lack of care, the dirty peel on the dirty chopping board going in with the slither of the garlic's outer coat, the root of the onion and a piece of its brown wrapping.

'I saw a man in the house. Going about the place, picking up things and putting them down,' said Max. He helped himself to some peanuts from the saucer on the table and ate with his mouth open, looking at her.

'You mean in the other place?'

'Here,' Max said. He put a wet fingertip into the salt on the plate and pushed it round, making a trail like a road in the snow. 'Some guy just walking round like he owned the place.'

She nodded; she used the wooden spoon to stir the vegetables in the pan. She was thinking of Rachel. She said to herself, nearly daily being in that woman's place, *you were a fool, Rachel, a fool.*

Rachel said a lot of silly things: *We have too much so now we're going to share.* Well, she took her up on that one. *All children are all of our children.* Sure. Until you have to choose who gets the seat belt. Or the daddy. And she ran away as soon as it was out, their affair, she gave Valérie free rein, not even confronting her — as Valérie would have done — not even trying on some rhetoric or show-violence. Rachel took her moral credit and ran. It was a rout. And now Valérie had assumed her spoon. She used it to free the long slices of onions that were burning.

'Max, go and do something. We're not eating for an hour. Just go and do some homework or something and leave me alone for a bit.' She took a sip of her wine and rattled about her for her cigarettes.

'Ugly guy,' he said.

'You're talking rubbish. Go away.'

'Who is he then?'

'You know who it is.'

'Gérard.'

'Jeff!' she shouted, opening the pack and seeing it was empty. 'Jeff! His name is Jeff. Stop all this Gérard rubbish.'

She put three skinned dead rabbits into the pot with a litre of stock and put the lid on it, and then she left the kitchen as he would not.

An hour or so later they sat down to eat.

'Sit at the head of the table,' she said to Jeff. She'd redone her mascara and lipstick and changed her shirt for dinner. Jeff was wearing a woolly hat, dirty jeans and a sweatshirt. He did not take the hat off. He sat to the side instead, facing Max, and so she sat at the head.

She served them the food and they ate without looking at each other as she went between them with questions and ideas, 'I thought we'd have goose for Christmas . . .' which went unanswered. Max belched explosively at one point and Jeff merely raised his eyebrows without looking up.

Max put two elbows on the table.

'I think it would be better for everyone if you just left now,' he said to Jeff, with dignity.

Jeff took his hat off, laid it beside his plate, and looked at the boy. 'But you see, kid, this is my house.'

Then the man got up and went past the oven, adding with his characteristic flexibility, 'Well, in theory anyway, until Abrams boots me out of course.' He knelt in front of the bottom cupboard. He slid half of a cardboard box out of it and felt around inside. It was there and then he recalled a fragment of a dream he'd had about Don Abrams. In the dream he'd been in a room with other people, and he'd known that Abrams was sitting in the wings, watching him but not saying anything.

'The dope's gone.'

'No, it's not possible,' said Valérie, rising.

'Yup, it's gone,' said Jeff. He didn't make anything of it, he simply stood up, walked out of the room and went into the TV lounge and they heard the raucous cheers of a rugby-match crowd.

When she went in, he was sitting on the sofa, he had his feet on the coffee table, his back to her and he put a finger to his lips, without looking round.

'Shh,' he said. 'Not a word.'

'Jeff. I know you miss Maud . . .'

She saw his shoulders tense. She wanted to touch him. She looked at her outstretched hand; the fingers trembled. She thought about telling him she felt for him; but she'd given him too much already and none of it was enough.

49

✦

VALÉRIE PUT ON JEFF'S OILSKIN COAT and went in her slippers across to her parents' house. Perhaps Simone had taken the dope back.

Just before she stepped on to the terrace she recalled that today was her father's birthday and she went to turn round again and go back, but she was caught; a light went on.

Her father was sitting at the table he'd made. He had the olive-wood ashtray before him, and the box of red wine was on the edge of the table, a black stain on the terracotta beneath its nozzle. There was a red tinsel garland around the box.

'I see the festive spirit is here,' she said.

'It comes free with the box this time of year.'

'Is Simone up?'

'No, she's on the sofa, sleeping.'

'Right.'

He was wearing overalls and a cardigan. His dog, so permanently favoured, nestled her head on his crotch. He stroked the dog, 'Oh my beauty, oh my girl, yes, I'm here, yes . . .' Then he added, 'Have a drink with me now you're here.'

'OK,' she said.

He lurched as he rose, against the table, and went sideways to the cabinet for a green-stemmed wineglass. He filled it with red.

'Weather's fucked,' he commented, making a circular movement with his head to take in the whole world. There were some crisps on a plate and a jar of pickled mushrooms open, next to a tube with toothpicks in it. He pushed them to her with the back of his arm. 'Help yourself.'

'*Santé.*'

'And yours.'

The old man coughed and it reminded him to light another cigarette. In the manner of the heavy smoker, he didn't offer her one.

'Can I have one?'

'Oh yes, excuse me,' he passed her the pack and went to ignite the lighter but his hand was shaking so he passed it to her. She lit up. 'So you've got rid of your husband.'

'Yes.' She took a sip. 'Did you only just notice?'

The old man swallowed half his glass.

'You like your new one?'

'But yes, of course.'

'Mmm-hmm.'

'Well, in fact. I don't know.'

'I see things, I see how they are.'

'It's not easy.' She felt a tear at the side of her nose and stopped it with a fingertip.

The old man saw. 'What are you going to do about it?' He looked at his hands around the glass, not at her.

'I don't know.'

'You've got a problem. Maybe more than one problem.'

'I've made a mess of it all. It's not that I want Richard back. I don't. It's just that Jeff isn't very kind.'

'We're worried about the boy,' he said. 'The boy's got something wrong with him. He's got no manners. I always did say that he had no manners and we thought, well, kids are like that these days, but it's more than that, he's not right. You should talk to the doctor, that's what your mother thinks.'

'Yes, I know. I have. But he's just a boy. It will get better.' She shivered, looking at her wine. 'I know I'm not a good mother.'

'No one's saying it's your fault. There was a kid like that on the farm at Nancy. Strange kid. Shot the priest. He was never right.'

'It's not like that.'

'No, maybe not. No. Anyway what do I know? I know shit compared to what most people know these days. I read the books but I think what's the point, it's all just words. We all need the rain and the sun, we can't live without them, that's something you can't argue with. The trees need it, the animals . . . it's been too long without rain now. Well, what's it going to take for you to be happy?'

'I don't know.'

'You're not a young woman. You're a mother. You have a problem with that kid and you need to get yourself straight. You ought to leave that guy out of it, get back into your own home, get yourself together. You need to be proud of yourself. You need to be strong. Instead of mooning around that American all day, doing nothing but crying or drinking or whatever else you do.'

'Ha. Great. Thanks. Thanks for the drink.'

'It's nothing.'

She pushed the empty glass away. 'How you think you're able to give me fatherly advice, I don't know. You've become like a wino, you're filthy, you're useless, you don't do anything any more, you just sit drinking all day, you're just rotting. *"Ordures"*—that's what she calls you behind your back, did you know that?'

252

The white of his eyes was yellow, the pores on his nose were large and the end of it purple, his eyebrows trailed as unkempt as his moustache. 'I know,' he said. His eyes filled with tears. He sniffed, raised a smile. 'I could do things, you know, back in the day. I had some success. I knew people, and the little place I ran then in Marseille it was always full, and I was taking so much money I didn't know what to do with it, but I sent most of it home to your mother. I never paid my taxes.'

'So why did Mother have to work a market stall?'

'She only did that for the show of it. She had a fur coat. She had dresses. She went out. You had clothes, didn't you? And you never went hungry. And yes I drank, I've always drunk. Always will. It's like diesel for my engine. I've drunk since I was a boy. Down in Marseille, I'd have my first brandy at six in the morning when I got up. I'd drink until I fell over, but I worked, I did something like two hundred covers in that place. I didn't get to bed until two or three, then up at six. People these days don't know anything about work. Or drink. Now I get drunk on the smell of a cork.' His eyes were wet and he wiped them. 'I sit here all day like an old cunt doing nothing.'

'You're depressed.'

'That's what she says. I'm not though. What have I got to worry about? She does all that side of things. Me, I have nothing to think about. I've been reading one of those books on corruption, you know, by what's his name — you know the one.'

'Chirac?'

'That's the one, but he didn't write it himself. What a rotten stinking carcass it is, this government. It's all backhanders, everywhere . . . You get to thinking, what's the point?'

'You gave up long ago anyway, when we went over to computers.'

'People were kinder before. The postman used to bring the old folk a baguette and a bottle of wine when they couldn't get out, and their cigarettes. Now he'd be sued for it. Well, we all give up some time. Not at thirty . . . what age are you?'

'Thirty-three.'

'Not at thirty-three. No. That's too soon. Still, maybe it gets sooner with every generation. Maybe Max will give up at sixteen. Your mother went to bed with a friend of mine, just after you were born, and I caught them and I took offence.' He touched his beard. 'I say offence but the truth is I was heart-broken.'

'So in revenge you went off with every tart in town . . .'

'No, there were a couple who wouldn't . . . Catholic sisters, though I dare say back then, a nod and a wink, Holy Mother, and you know, but no, everyone knew everyone and married women didn't screw around. We would have given you a brother or a sister, you know, but well, I lost the taste for it all, family life, and I went away and made a living . . .'

'So it was almost *Little House on the Prairie* but Mother blew it.'

'That's right.' He licked his lips and served both of them a top-up of wine. Glass in hand, he fell to crooning to the dog . . . 'We used to sing that with Maud. I don't understand all of this, I don't know what you call it — sex, love — I don't know. I'm too old. You explain it to me. What's it all for?'

There were other things he didn't understand, the principal one being why his mother had turned him out of his home. He'd got stuck on this question and it stopped him getting round to the others. But there was no answer for any of his questions, and for every question for which there was no answer there was a glass of red.

'I don't know if I ever did love Richard. I never knew him. I used to say to him, *I don't know you,* but he didn't seem to mind. And he was never here, remember? Max was very difficult and I felt lonely, that's all there is to it, and you and Mother were always prying. I had no private life. Then, I fell in love with Jeff . . .'

While she spoke he sat seriously in imitation of a sober man listening hard. Under the cover of the conversation, they'd been stealing glances at each other, working out where they stood, who remembered what, circling each other like two boxers.

'You're a lot like me, you know.' He filled her glass with more red, and set it back down on its sticky stain; drunk now, he pointed to the lawn in the dark. 'The robins are confused. They don't know whether to stay or go. I give them birdseed right down there on that bit of lawn, and they bob around and bounce right up to my feet. Even your mother says she's never seen that before, but they trust me . . .' He held aloft one hand as if there were a bird sitting in it, then eventually saw he was looking at an empty space. 'I shouldn't have gone and left you both. I thought you'd be happy to see me when I came back. But you weren't. So I came back less and less, but you were such a good-looking girl, you had *my* nose, though not as big nor as broken, and I thought, well even if she hates me, even if she wants to kill me, I'm coming home to keep an eye on her, to watch out for her, because she's all I've got. She's my blood.'

He put a hand over his mouth and they both sat there in silence for a moment, then he spoke again. 'What I want to say is that I know you never had the love you needed.'

He went at his tearful face with his sleeve. His hands were so big and crippled up, it was like trying to put out a candle with a spade; he cuffed himself.

She stood. She looked down at him and felt her throat tighten: *He's crying for himself.* 'I should get back home, it's late. It must be midnight. Thanks.'

'It's nothing,' he said, 'a glass of wine or two for your daughter, that's nothing, nothing at all.'

'I feel so . . .' she put her arms about herself, to warm her upper arms with her hands, 'hated.'

The chair made a noise as he went to stand, and he fell back against it. The back of it was tipped against the wall, the two front legs off the floor; the plate of crisps fell to the floor and smashed as his stumpy hands made for the table to steady himself and in a half-rise, aghast, his face looked like a gargoyle in the swinging lamplight.

'Are you all right?'

'The table's slippery, it's just difficult to get a hold of it,' he said.

'Well, go to bed now, go to bed, don't sit here drinking,' she said. 'Happy Birthday.'

50

$\diamond$

INSIDE, SIMONE WAS LYING on the sofa, smoking. Unobserved, her expression was one of profound loneliness, her normally buoyant cheeks hung low, unmuscled, unpacked. Her legs came together, swinging round as if tied and lifted by a small crane; she put a hand to the small of her back, sighing, and withdrew from behind a cushion the little purple pony with gold hair. Maud's. She put its muzzle to her lips. 'Ah, *la petite Anglaise,*' she said, smoothing the acrylic toy hair, 'she was our angel.'

'I know. I know,' said Guy, his own eyes red at the sight of the pony, 'every day — tap, tap, tap — *can I come in, oh Tonton Guy, show me the harmonica, no not like this, like that, you're doing it wrong,* always commanding me . . .'

'I know. She had you around her finger.'

'Do you want a hot drink?'

'It's late. But I won't sleep anyway. Yes, I'll have a coffee. Make yourself one of those drinks the doctor gave you.'

'Yes.'

'You were talking to Valérie.'

'Yes.'

'And it's your birthday.'

He looked up at the broken roof tile with the rustic scene painted on it, clock hands glued on, 'No, that was yesterday.'

'She knew it was your birthday and she came to see you.' Simone sat up.

He put the kettle on and looked at the tea bag on a string. He turned it around his crooked finger. 'She's worried. This thing with Jeff, it's not working. He'll go.'

'Did she say so?'

'No. But I know. He'll go.'

'Oh, you know yourself, more like. No, he won't. He loves it here.'

'She's my daughter but she's hard work.'

'She's your daughter all right.'

He filled the cups, spilling more than the cups gained. Simone raised herself and went for the cloth, hearing the pitter-patter of the water on the tiles. She wiped.

'I'm worried about Richard,' she said, holding the cloth still for a moment, leaning on to it. She looked out through the window into the dark.

'We can't worry about everyone. We should just worry about our own. Valérie and Max.'

'He has been like a son to me. He's been good to us. This Jeff, I don't like him. I don't sleep, I just stay awake worrying. That's what old age is for. You do the worrying the rest are too busy to do. I was born an old soul. My grandmother said . . .'

'"You will carry a cross all your days . . ."'

'Yes. And it was true, wasn't it?'

'You have big arms, my love.'

She made a face. Her arms were large, it was true. 'Well, I need them, with you to carry home.'

He sat in his chair, she went to her sofa, they never swapped places. Both of them moved their feet to feel for their slippers.

'Let's watch television. I can't sleep now, I'm thinking about Valérie and what's going to happen next. If only I could protect her. I would have shot the person who ever hurt her or the boy, that's why I keep the gun. I would shoot them and take the consequences. But who do I shoot here? Jeff?'

'Poor Richard; all alone, no job, no car, no family, nothing, not even a pot to piss in. *Nichts. Nada. Nu-ssing.*'

'Maybe he will come back if Jeff goes.'

She squeezed her nose, considered. 'And then they would go back into their house, and everything would be the same again, if they could forgive each other. Maybe she could drive him to work, this sick pay will run out next autumn, there's that to think about. How will the mortgages be paid then? But we wouldn't have Maud back. These religious people are so black and white. That's the last we've seen of Rachel, I don't doubt.' She sighed and lit a cigarette. 'Anyway Richard's not the same man he was, he's lost his mind.'

She pressed on the volume button and sat back, biting a finger and holding her cigarette off while she did. Telly Savalas was worried too, and his problem was a double murder, but that problem could be solved within forty minutes. It gave them some relief to see him do it.

51

✧

SHE SUBLET THE FLAT. She packed the bags. She put the
school on notice. She got everything out of proportion, on the
basis of his email to her and the email she sent back and the many
others that followed in the same day, going from polite enquiry
to lightly sexual teasing, to revelations, to distress and culminating in the plainly stated need to see each other as soon as possible. She got everything out to pack and was then awed by the ab-
surdity of it. When she might have been doing useful things, she
was standing gazing gormlessly into the fridge.

She peeked at Maud here and there as if to check how much
she loved her; Maud sitting on the toilet, swinging her legs. Maud
with her tongue out colouring the insole of her shoes with a felt-
tip pen. Maud sitting with her thumb in her mouth in rapt en-
grossment with the television screen. She peeked at her for clues
to right and wrong. She sat and held Maud to her and kissed her
head, not thinking, just feeling whether what she was doing was
right. She had to go fast and go slow.

After Ashford, the train went at such a terrific speed, faster
than the trucks and cars on the motorway, into the limbo of the
tunnel, the long pause, where no one dared to think about the
water around them, and then the train went through the auburn

landscape of northern France, through fields washed too often, the fabric of them pilled and worn thin, and on the horizon the grey and apricot tones of later afternoon, the clouds moving above the fields, the low sky licking its hide.

In the Gare du Nord, a freezing cold came up from the ground. 'This station must be the coldest place in the world,' she said to Maud, and mooted the idea of a hot chocolate before departure.

Upstairs in the Eurostar hallway, couples kissed goodbye, young and matching, blonds with blondes, brunettes with brunettes, boys with girls. She watched a couple French-kissing. She could stand and watch as long as they could keep kissing. She saw how they had their hands in the backs of each other's sweaters, how they moved their tongues in each other's mouths, eyes closed.

Watching them, she took a sip from each hot chocolate in turn. 'Too hot,' she said to Maud, 'too hot yet.'

Maud was speaking but Rachel was listening to the couple, she was close enough to hear the sound of their kissing. She could hear the tiny wet lapping slaps, the flimsy sighs and miniature groans and the breath that became a sigh in another person's world.

'It's not hot now,' said Maud, poking her staring mama.

After Avignon, through the window again, the brown fields looked damp at the thought of snow in distant mountains, and though there had been no rain here, the lesser-windowed houses kept an eye open just in case. An olive orchard was like a hundred ghostly harpies, hair-strewn, all the trees leaning the same way.

'Oh God, I'm scared,' she said, taking Maud on to her lap and kissing her.

'Mummy, you're hot, your hand is hot.' Maud put a hand on

her mother's forehead. 'Your head is hot. You must be ill. Are you losing a tooth?'

'I'm fine, darling,' she said and drew Maud to her just to smell her, to smell her breath, to hold her, to feel her, how little she was, how squashy she was with her plump tummy and bottom, and she smelt her neck, and brought her hands to her nose and smelt the odour of the girl's thumb where she sucked it.

'You're all mine,' she said.

'And a little bit Daddy's too,' said the girl and went back to her thumb, keeping an eye on the window, keeping an eye on her own interests.

52

✧

THAT EVENING, Richard drank six beers in the Café des Amis and then instead of going back to the studio he walked the four or five kilometres towards his former home. The long roadway out of the town was well lit now, offering as it did access to new villas, to vineyards and a restaurant with a helipad.

He addressed himself fondly as he walked, he had a little chit-chat with himself, he quizzed himself on this and that, made a joke at his own expense, avoided a difficult question with a sly poke at the questioner, gave himself some paternal solace with a few old wise saws. He considered how odd it was to have this otherness inside of him, and to rub along together, not always as a team, but more, much more, provocative than that; this internal noise of contradiction was life, the bang and boom of being only assuaged by the palliatives of drink, sleep, death; slightly less immanent thanks to 40mgs citalopram and 3mgs risperidone twice daily.

He was not taking the meds for their prescribed purpose. He was using them to reduce his libido and to decrease his desire for drink and, as a bonus, he was quite happy.

He looked back over his shoulder before he left the long

straight. Powerfully lit at night, the great old church next to his studio was shaped like a big thumbs-up.

He slipped over the rough stone wall along their lane, catching his backside a little, and dropped on to the grass. He smelt the thyme and walked through the lane of cacti on to the gravel driveway, going past his house and towards his neighbours'.

He saw the fairy lights at his in-laws' windows. Christmas was approaching with a snarl, the hyena season of goodwill, going for the straggler separated from the herd. He walked in through the front door, which was open as always.

'Pack your bag, I've come to take you away.'

Maxence turned round. He had used his mother's lipstick to write on the overmantel mirror: *There is no love here.*

'Max. What the hell are you doing?'

'Writing. So they all can see it. So they'll know.'

'OK. Well, it's strong.'

'Yeah. It is strong. It's powerful. It's a spell. A curse.'

'OK, now put the lipstick down. I've come because I decided to take you to London tomorrow. We'll see the . . .' he saw himself in the mirror, looking a bit lopsided, 'the Christmas lights. And Rachel. We'll see Rachel and Maud. That will be nice, right?'

'OK, we're going away.' Max smiled and put his hands out to his father rather in the manner of the romantic heroine. 'All my life I've waited for this.'

His eyes looked glassy, his smile was wistful. He reminded Richard of the girl with acute dystonia in Nyeri.

'Max. Are you drunk or something?'

'I've been smoking Gérard's weed.'

'Shit, no. You've been smoking grass! At thirteen years old? Shit. Let me make some coffee. Where's your mother?'

'Upstairs getting pumped by that guy.'

'Hey. Watch your mouth. Christ, Max, we've got to get you

into Catholic school. What have they done to you, your mother and that arsehole? They've completely dropped the ball. You were such a . . . a kid, you were just a kid. Now, cigarettes, dope, and all of this . . . !' He gestured at the mirror to mean everything, the fact that his son was coming undone in his wake, and he ran out of words and he felt like he might break into tears so he went to the kitchen to make them coffee. 'Come and help me then, Max, will you?' he asked him weakly.

In the kitchen he watched the boy go from cupboard to cupboard seeking the coffee; he threw a door open as if trying to catch someone out, then peered into each saying, 'Anybody home? Hello? Anyone in? You think you're pretty smart, hiding in there while your old pal Max needs a cup of coffee . . .'

Richard blew out. His son looked back at him. 'What?'

'Why did you write the letters, Max?'

'What letters?' He put his hand on a jar of Nescafé. 'There you are.' The jar fell and he caught it. He bounced it in the palm of his hand.

'The ones your mother and I got. You wrote them, didn't you?'

'Yeah, those ones. Yeah.'

'They were disgusting.'

'Yeah. Simone helped me.'

Richard shook his head. 'You're lying.' He put his hands on the counter.

Max turned round, he put his hands out and shook his sleeves loose. 'Actually, Dad, the truth is it was all done by magic.'

'OK, let's just get the coffee made.'

'And you'll never guess what, but I can fly.'

'Dear God.'

'I can.'

'OK. So show me then.'

'It doesn't work all the time.' Max gave him a roguish look.

Richard set to making them both large cups of sweet coffee, which they drank in silence. Then he put his son to bed and sat down on the rug next to him, waiting for his breathing to change.

He felt the two tendons at the back of his son's head, in the soft hair.

He put his face next to his son's. 'I made you. You're not me but you're in my care.' He put a knuckle on his son's cheek and stroked it tenderly. 'I love you so much. I'll put us both back together again, I promise you.'

In his heart, he felt that he might not be able to and he wept. He wanted help. He prayed for it, he said in his mind over and over again, 'If there's a God, then help me, please.'

Max was smiling in his sleep, his expression lordly.

53

✧

AN EARLY RISER, Guy had already given handfuls of seed to the birds, going from the tobacco fug of the interior into the cold harsh air outside in his cardigan and underpants and slippers, feeling the wet of the grass seeping into his toes. It had rained all through the night and stopped at dawn. Guy went outside with his coffee to admire the effects. He stood for ten minutes, sipping the bitter drink, looking at the boy jumping on the trampoline.

Maxence was in pyjamas and a hoodie, going up and down monotonously, his hands in the pockets, hood up. There was an ember glowing at his mouth.

Standing with a rucksack, also watching, was the boy's father. He wore a baseball hat and Guy could see he was rough-shaven and thin and that he looked a few times at his watch.

At the front door of the big house was Jeff, with a towel around him, smoking, watching the boy too. Valérie came to the front door, dressed in a sweater and jeans with a coffee in her hands. She stood back from Jeff.

'What's going on?' Simone called from their front doorstep.

Guy gestured towards the boy.

'My God,' she said, stepping forwards.

'He's on the trampoline.'

267

'It's not even seven.'

'Seven, eight, nine, what does the time matter?' said Guy. 'He's a boy, time's of no importance to him.'

'It's strange,' she shivered, pulling her dressing gown tighter.

'We're all watching him, you see, that's what he wants, that does him good,' said Guy, coming inside and rubbing his hands together, following her in through the door. He went to the window to look again. 'We think our bodies are our own, our hands we think we own, we work, we drink, we fight, but that's of no importance, we share more than we know . . .'

'Take your pills. We're going to have some horse-meat for lunch. It will do you good.'

She pushed three pills towards him and he took them obediently without water.

'Do you ever listen to me, Simone? Do you hear me when I speak?'

'I hear you. Mostly you say the same thing.'

'Richard's making the boy get off the trampoline.'

'Good. That's good. What's Richard doing out there?' She pressed the button on the coffee machine and went to the small kitchen window. 'Are they going somewhere?' She reached for the phone and pressed in six numbers. 'Valérie. What's going on? Is Richard taking Max somewhere? London! Have you lost your mind? He can't take him anywhere in his condition!' She put the phone down. 'She's thinking of herself. She's only thinking of herself and Jeff. Just them. All she wants is to be happy even if it hurts other people. It's gone wrong, everything we hoped for, and I can't do a thing about it.' She raised her swollen eyes to the ceiling. 'God knows how much I've tried for everyone's sake. I've fought all my life, but I can't go on fighting.' She shook her head and lit a cigarette.

'Don't work yourself up. You'll make yourself ill.'

She gave a curt laugh and dabbed at her eyes.

Guy went on, from the window. 'Max is dressed now and they're going down the track together, he and Richard.'

'Well, stop them! He's abducting him!'

He came away from the window and sat in his chair and lit a cigarette. 'He's his father.'

'He's a mental case. The doc said so. Can't you stop them? Why aren't you stopping them? Oh, Guy, you're no use to any of us . . .'

She went into the bedroom and opened the wardrobe. She brought out his gun and held it in front of him. 'Stop them!'

'I'm to shoot one of them, am I?'

'Just frighten them,' she said, shaking the gun, holding it with two hands in front of him. 'Just shoot it into the air to scare them, make them come back. I'm exhausted with worry. I need a night's sleep. Please, Guy, please do it for me.'

Guy extinguished his cigarette, took the gun and smelt it lovingly. 'No, those days are gone and we're left behind, that's all. We can only watch.'

'My God, you're useless! You're nothing more than a lump, a lump of . . .'

'*Ordures*,' he said. His brow gathered. He put the end of the gun in his mouth.

'Guy! Don't.'

He took it out again. 'Don't worry, don't worry.' He laid the gun on the coffee table and it knocked to the floor the little Moroccan brass tea set. 'My little girl,' he said. 'Gone.' Then he put his head in his hands and cried.

She went to him and put his face to her breasts as she always did. 'Darling boy,' she said, into his filthy hair, kissing him.

269

'Don't leave me,' he murmured, 'I won't live without you.'

'I'll never leave you. Yes, you'd die without me. I love you. Don't cry.'

The boy and his father set to a fast pace going down the hill into the next village, enjoying running where the descent was steep, laughing, each with his rucksack bumping on his back.

'Are we running away, Papa?'

'Yes, yes we're running away.'

'Just you and me now!'

'Yes!'

'Then let's run fast,' and Max skipped and skittered into the shingle where the road made a steep bend down into the valley. He skidded to a halt, and sat down and took off his shoes.

'You need your shoes, Max,' but Max ran ahead again and so Richard stooped to pick them up and he carried his son's shoes all the way into the village at the bottom of the hill.

They managed to thumb a lift from the village to Les Arcs, the last stop in the Var on the high-speed line to Paris.

They ambled down the broken hill to the station, picking their way through all the potholes and gravel into the parking compound where no one could park since the Var was determined to be worthy of terrorism too, where the police kept cars moving and booked them for not stopping at the stop sign that their van obscured.

Students and old people wandered in and out of the Eastern European–style building, setting a-rattle the pamphlet holders that were empty, as they passed through to stand on the platform where old newspapers blew up and down the train tracks.

It was a place where bad news was broken, and one saw occasionally the rebuttal of the information, the fumbled protest before the slump of acceptance into the arms of the messenger.

The back draught of a departing train smelt like dog's fur and the two of them closed their eyes and held their breath.

It was Max who saw them first.

54

✧

'RACHEL,' MAX SAID. 'And Maud.'

Richard checked the kid's face, saw the blank expression in it, and the fine white hairs on the boy's upper lip. He thought: *What now?* And also: *He'll be better after a few days away.* And then he saw just across from them on the other platform Rachel at the top of the steps trying to deal with a rolling suitcase.

'Oh, my God,' he said to Max.

Max went and sat on the orange plastic seat with its small seat-hole and put his legs out. He looked across to the distant shape of Roquebrune.

Then he got up and went inside the station to see if there was a vending machine. He bought himself a Coca-Cola.

He was halfway through the can when he noticed his father gesturing for him to come up to them. He was smiling with ex-hilaration. Both of them, he and Rachel, were red-faced, and the little girl was wheeling along a suitcase that matched Max's bed-covers.

'We were going to Paris, then to London,' Richard explained, clasping his son's far shoulder, embracing him. 'But, we can go tomorrow, or whenever, can't we, Max?'

'No,' said Max. 'We have to go now.'

'We can go another day.' His father squeezed him hard, then let him go.

Richard took off his baseball cap and ran his hand over his lower face. Rachel, flushed, put her hand through the back of her hair. They were paused there together, on the platform at Les Arcs, adding everything up.

Max began to hum a song that had been in his head for days and although he was looking at them he did not bother to listen. The song was important. He liked Justin Timberlake. The guy seemed to know something.

'*Don't be so quick to walk away, dance with me . . .*'

When he replayed a song in his head it was precisely like the original recording; it was another of his powers.

Soon they were in a taxi, all their bags in the back. They'd struggled a little in trying to lower the handle on Rachel's case. She tried first, then his father took over, then the driver and then they took everything out, piece by piece, each rucksack, the pink case, the large black case with wheels and they laid that flat and put everything else back in on top and Rachel was explaining the suitcase's failings and shaking her head and saying, 'I still can't believe it, such a coincidence.'

The Justin Timberlake track stopped inside of Max's head.

'There's no such thing as a coincidence,' said Max.

His father took the front seat next to the driver. His father was English again, and he turned to address Rachel in his language. The children sat and watched the two adults undertaking the ex-cruciating business of being careful when much is at stake, the very English way of doing things, the tight faces, the short sen-tences, the polite enquiries as the car crept sluggishly through the roadside village that at midday was abandoned. In the winter nothing much was reliably or consistently open, apart from the *boulangeries,* advertising in neon, three hundred and sixty-five days a year: 'PAIN'.

'Well, I'm assuming you were heading to the house . . .' said Richard, and he gave that little laugh that was not really amusement and Rachel returned its notes, beat for beat.

Facing forward as the car rounded the summit of the hill, Richard said, 'Did you get my last email?'

'I got it.' The children looked at her. She averted her face, looking out of the window. 'That little chalet house is still up for sale then.'

'Yes, it will never sell. It's too gloomy and there are even more new houses now.'

'Really?'

'Yes, even in just a couple of months.'

'Goodness.'

Richard put a hand on the back of the driver's seat and glanced back. His face fell, eyes first, right into her lap. She reached to cover his fingers with hers and swaddled them tight. They looked at their two hands and then at each other. Neither withdrew their hand until the taxi pulled into the grounds of Abrams' villa.

There were two phallic conifers either side of the gateway; one was brown. Other trees had failed to take; one, a great palm tree that Jeff had bought for eight thousand euros, came up the hill like a sedated elephant on the back of a circus trailer and was planted into a cavernous hole, exposed to the winds on the hillside, and died. A magnolia in front of the house withered on one side and lost its leaves; ambitious flowers were rooted out annually, desiccated, defeated, and finally all that remained was what had been there before them; lavender, cacti, some straggling roses, the same as those that guarded the vines opposite.

The villa they'd had built for Abrams was grand, in its white eminence with its olive-green shutters and hacienda-style rear extending over stone terraces, but the grounds were bedraggled and recalcitrant and it seemed that here as elsewhere in the Var, nature resisted imported ideas.

On the hilltop, nothing moved, nothing stirred and it was silent. The car came to a halt before the front door. Rachel held her breath. The driver cranked the handbrake. When she opened the door and stepped outside, the true cold shocked her.

55

✧

Simone was bent over a flowerbed, extracting dead dahlias, her hair in a topknot, wearing her sleeveless jacket over a thick sweater and knee-length leggings with cross-stitching at the knee, reminiscent of corsetry, but the sexy black was an expired grey.

Guy was soaring across the paddock on the ride-on mower in his cardigan and pyjamas, like a tramp come into his kingdom on a chariot of fire, an ashtray affixed to the bonnet.

After Rachel left, Jeff had asked them for help and paid them a small wage, which they accepted since Simone was worried about their finances with Richard's change of circumstances.

Guy cut the motor and stared. Simone stood straight, then put her hands to her hair; she dropped her trowel and ran to the white Mercedes taxi.

Maud released herself from the seat belt and got out of the car. She and Simone embraced, Simone in tears, cooing and clutching at the little girl, while Guy came up behind, his slippers grassy, his face perturbed.

Richard and Max got out and Max dropped his rucksack to the ground and went inside the house.

276

'We met at the station,' Richard explained, though neither of them heard him.

'Oh, how we've missed the little princess! Come in and see how I've still got all your playthings, I've been keeping them for you all nice and safe for when you came home, my own little French girl,' Simone insisted with heavy propaganda. 'You're not English, are you? No! Come to Tatie. Oh, what's happened to you over there? You look so thin! Tatie Simone's going to fatten you up with some of her cake . . .'

'Can we watch television?'

'Television!' Guy said, with mock indignation. 'You've come all this way to watch our television?'

'Of course you can, *ma puce.*'

'I'll do the washing-up after I've seen my programme. And I'll make you lunch, Uncle Guy. I'll make you a *croque-monsieur.* But don't get it in your beard.'

Guy laughed and rubbed his beard.

'Come and have a drink with us. Come on,' said Simone to Rachel and Richard, wiping her eyes. 'Are you staying a while?' She looked from one to the other. 'We've been helping in the garden. For something to do.' She raised her shoulders, wrinkling her nose. 'That's all. We barely see either of them.'

'Well, I haven't come to see them,' said Rachel. 'I came to see Richard.'

'You can stay with us! We'll make room. Will you be here for Christmas? I should run down to the shops . . . but come on, come and have a drink, let's open a bottle! Champagne? Oh, this is such a good surprise.' She took Rachel's hand in hers.

Rachel looked at Richard, 'Shall we have a drink then?'

He shook his head. 'No, I need to be with you now.'

Simone looked from one to the other. Her mouth moved but she said nothing.

The taxi driver got out of the car. 'So?' he asked. 'Christmas is coming. Maybe I'll miss it standing here. I turned the meter off. I'll have to start it up again if we're going on. I'm not doing this for my pleasure.'

The little girl was almost at Guy and Simone's house, holding Guy by the sleeve, pulling the long cardigan arm down. 'So, the princess of the Var. Or are you now the princess of London?' he was asking her.

Simone glanced at them, and a smile broke out on her face along with a little shimmering sweat.

'Christmas, yes. The man must go. That's good. So, go! Go on. Have fun!' Simone said to the adults, waving towards the taxi, breathless suddenly, perspiring and rosy-faced. 'Go on! Go and do what you need to do, we'll look after Maud.'

Inside the house, Max sat down on the sofa. His mother had cleaned the mirror. She was in the kitchen, he could hear her moving pots and pans.

'Max?' she called out, and came through with her sleeves rolled up. Her eyes were puffy.

'I'm back,' he said. He put his legs out, his dirty shoes making marks on the Persian carpet.

'What happened? Where's your father?'

'With Rachel.'

She knelt before him. 'My poor son. It's all my fault.' She said, 'Let me make you something to drink. A hot chocolate.' She put her arms around him and screwed her eyes shut. 'I love you.'

'You love Gérard,' he said. 'You can't love this one and then that one, this one and then that one . . .' and he sighed heavily like an old man getting bad news. He got up and put the television on.

Jeff came in through the French doors. He'd been in the vineyard. His woollen hat stood high on his head. 'What the hell's going on? What's the kid doing back?'

'Rachel loves Richard and Richard loves Rachel,' said Max, not looking at him, changing channels. 'Your daughter's over at Simone's house.'

'You lost me there, pal,' said Jeff. 'Say that again?'

Valérie was kneeling on the floor by the boy, who was moving sideways to sit farther away from her.

When Jeff saw Valérie there, defeated, he knew it was true and he found the pure clean warm smile he'd looked for everywhere in those last few weeks and he took it and wore it and dashed out, leaving the double doors wobbling in his wake, letting the cold blow right through Abrams' house.

56

✧

IN MAÎTRE KANTER'S TAVERN, satisfaction runs to several variations sausage-wise. The *choucroute* comes heaped high, damp and cold, along with boiled potatoes. As for the Master himself, according to depiction here, there and everywhere, he remains young and virile, the eternal German, with his wide-brimmed hat and braces, one arm out, open-handed, the other offering a great big jug of beer.

The aluminium plate of standard restaurant design sat atop the gas burner between them and sizzled. The rain was lashing down and this was a good place to be.

Rachel looked at Richard. He had seedless-grape green eyes, his blond hair was shying away at either temple, his long nose was thin, but when he smiled his cheeks were full.

She was not really listening to him, she was watching him speak. (They were waiting for the Riesling to be served and the six *'fines de claire'* apiece.) A comma in his sentences was marked with the lift of his right eyebrow. He was telling her that he'd stopped working, and that he'd enjoyed being with Max. When Max went, he had nothing to live for.

She drank down her glass of wine.

In his recounting of the events leading up to his diagnosis, there was apprehensiveness to his eyes, which told of what was to come after the humorous account of failure; intimacy.

There are many side effects to losing your mind, Rachel, and the one that's not printed on any leaflet is living in a shithole. The state psychiatrist tells me I am in the grip of depression with schizotypy affect. She's hedging her bets. The depressive blames himself for his unhappiness, but the schizophrenic thinks he's not so much responsible for his own state as he is for other people's. I'd rather go with the schizophrenia than the depression; the voices and the magical thinking. I mean I think there are some delusions that are necessary if one's to make it. I took the pills to sort myself out, though not in the way they'd think. I used them to take sex off the agenda. I think a spell of abstinence has done me some good actually. I don't want to lie to you. I don't want to lie any more, at all. I took the pills, Rachel, the very ones I used to sell. Now that's irony. Jeff never did get irony; everything that was sheer bad luck he called ironic. Not good for a cartoonist. Still he had the right profession, quick sketches of 'funny'. I think everyone chooses their profession pretty well. We all find our cover. But when I began to sell pills to people who were quite plainly not unhappy or mad, my cover slipped and I saw myself for who I was. In Africa, instead of looking at the punters, which was what I was out there to do, I saw them looking at me. It all came at the same time, you know, that insight and losing everything. I can't tell you which came first but they came together. There you go. Talk to me, Rachel, you have no idea how I've missed you.

I've been sleeping so badly, Richard, the street lights and of course I had no curtains, and one night, it came right into my head this phrase — 'Do any of us even know that someone loves us in another place, or another time?' In the daytime, when I wandered around London, by about three or something I knew it was you. So I just started packing. I did. The vicar at Maud's school's church in London told me that communion is the great metaphor. He said to me — He takes you, He breaks you and then He blesses you and gives you. That's what's happened to us, Richard. He took us and broke us at the same time, in the same place . . .

'You are lovely, Rachel, but how can I be sure? Of you? How can I know nothing bad's going to happen? How can I just hand myself over to you?'

'You just do. It's a leap of faith. I'm not talking about God. Faith; it's all we can have really.'

His eyes were hooded, and a single vein to the left of his left eye flickered blue. He put a fist over his mouth. He nodded.

Then he spoke. He told her that he'd done it; he'd made the leap. Right there and then. He'd done it.

'I'm yours,' he said.

He sat beside her on the bed in Room 118 in the hotel next door. He took off his shirt slowly, button by button, flexed each shoulder in turn, left then right, and let his shirt slide.

'Pour water over me,' he said. He gave her the water bottle from on top of the minibar. 'Pour it over my head.'

She knelt up behind him, her hands on both of his shoulders.

'All of it.'

She poured it and he shook at the shock of it.

'Everything is you and when I look at you, I see everything,' she said, looking at the both of them in the mirror, her hands about his waist, her face on his wet shoulder blade.

'It's all about us now,' he said, holding her hands.

The resuscitation; mouth to mouth. The years slid off the scales, the future failed to weigh, there was nothing in the balance and the two of them were poised, touching in two places.

57

✧

'I DON'T MIND THE BOY jumping up and down on the trampoline half naked every morning, I don't mind that, that's fine, I haven't got a problem with that . . .'

Maud was standing on the pedal bin coating the kitchen counter in arcs of bubbles, Simone behind her, her hands twitching, ready to catch her fall. Guy was at the kitchen window.

'But I don't think it's good for him to be up on the roof with no clothes on. It's winter.'

'What time is it?' asked Simone.

He checked the clock, screwing up his eyes. 'Nine.'

'How long's he been there?' She pushed past Guy to the window to look. 'My God, he's naked.'

'He has a baseball cap on.'

'This is ridiculous! You watch Maud for me.'

'He's not happy,' said Maud, shaking her head as Simone left, the glass-fronted doors shaking in their frames.

Jeff went out on to the balcony of a guest room and stood on the ledge of the balcony, holding on to the edge of the roof. Max was sitting cross-legged on the apex, looking at the sun. If he'd cared to, he'd have seen Jeff's bald pate, with its genital frizz and blotchy marks, and he'd have heard the rolling reason of his American inflection, but he didn't.

Jeff rested the side of his head against the *crépi* of the wall and rubbed his few days' growth of beard against it like an animal. He heard the kid begin speaking.

'In the beginning was the word. There was no God until then. The words are the magic. Not the cards, not the cups, not the balls, not the wands . . .'

'He's up there talking shit,' Jeff said moodily when he came back down into the kitchen where Guy and Valérie were both drinking a consolatory glass of red. 'He must have been reading Rachel's books. He's spouting on up there like a preacher man.'

Simone came in with Maud. Jeff took his daughter in his arms and made a fuss of her. He'd been disappointed when she chose to stay the night with Guy and Simone. He'd been very irritable that evening, and kept going to the front door and looking across to their house, thinking how once he'd stood there, and not so long ago, looking the wrong way.

'I'm going to call the fire brigade,' said Simone, hands on her hips, slightly excited, as ever disaster-hungry. 'My God, he could fall and kill himself.'

'Good that it's rained, the ground is soft,' Guy reflected, finishing his glass.

Valérie went out on to the lawn to look up at the roof. She put her hands to her mouth and called out, her voice uncertain as if she were reading for a part, 'Max! Max! What are you doing? Come down . . .'

He was looking towards the Mediterranean, his mouth was moving.

'Max! Is this to punish me?'

Jeff came out and stood by her. His daughter followed. 'Max. Don't be a screwball. Just get your butt down here. You could kill yourself . . .'

'Don't say that, you might make him nervous, you might upset him . . .'

'I know what I'm doing. Look, all of this, it's all about getting our attention. He's on a roof, he's like I want you all to look at me, to look up to me. All the magic and the Bible stuff it's to compensate, isn't it? For not being good at sport, for not being good at school, for not being good at anything really, and you and Richard splitting up. That's what's going on here. You don't need a degree in psychology to figure that out. You can play along if you want but I'm not going to. He's still a kid. Come down, you little screw-up! Come down or Gérard's going to come up there and whup your ass . . .'

'Oh, stop it, Jeff. Stop it. You're not helping.'

'Little shit! He's just holding you to ransom, Valérie.'

'He's not a little shit.' She was crying, she turned to him with her hands balled, angry. 'Like mother like son, you think! You don't love me at all, you're a liar, Jeff, a liar. You should never have said it if you didn't. What are you? What are you? Nothing. It's you, the shit!'

'Oh, wow, that's good, that's really fucking good. You crazy bitch! Love you? You're impossible to love, you don't give anything and you talk all the time. No wonder your kid's on the roof. You don't know how to love anyone. You totally fucked up my life! I oughta be up there with him.'

Guy came over to them, holding the ladder; he put it down on the driveway, then, the cigarette still between his lips, he walked across the grass to stand squarely in front of Jeff.

He showed him a finger and almost touched the end of Jeff's

nose, his eyes dark. 'Just be quiet. Just hold your tongue. Be cool, be very cool. Or I swear I'll kill you.'

Jeff put his hands up. 'OK, grandpa.'

'You should have kept it in your trousers,' Guy said sullenly, turning to go back to the ladder. Simone was standing in the front porch of the villa.

'They're coming, the fire brigade,' she said. 'I told them the house was burning down and there was a kid inside, otherwise they wouldn't have come. What's he doing now? Max.'

Guy looked up, squinting. 'He's just sitting there, listening to us. It's a good view. You can see for maybe a hundred kilometres. You can see the hills of Canjuers, you can see the Mediterranean on a good day. It's a good place to sit. And he can hear everything that's being said.'

Simone let him position the ladder against the wall. 'Maxence, you want a coffee?' she called out, stepping back.

'How about a cigarette?' Guy added, stepping back too.

Valérie went and sat on the trampoline, with Maud behind her going gently up and down, pitter-patter, singing a school hymn.

'Dance then, wherever you may be . . .'

Jeff stood moving his hand across the bristle on his pate. It comforted him. His heart was racing and although it was bright and sunny nothing felt clear to him; he was stuck. In the chill air, he felt the little goat-teeth of conscience nip, nip, nip on his collar. He had so wanted to be a good father. He felt his arms loose, his hands unheld.

The fire engine, a great red truck, hauled itself in through the gates with a burly thick-set man leaning out of the window, looking every inch the gay pin-up.

'Which house has the fire?'

'This one.'

'Where's the fire?'

Simone raced forwards, letting the sleeveless jacket part, presenting her woolly breasts. 'Oh, *monsieur le pompier*. There's no fire. Forgive me, but we're in such a state here. There's a child on the roof.'

'Well, tell him to come down.' The man put his head back in to share this with his comrade, who broke into a handsome smile.

'It's not funny, monsieur. The child has been up there all night,' she touched her nose, 'maybe longer, we're not sure. He might have hypothermia. He could die.'

'Who is the kid then, madame?'

'He's my grandson. He's not well in the head. He's on pills for his head.' She pointed at her own. 'You've got to get him down, monsieur, I beg you.'

'Here comes the punch line,' said Jeff, as a taxi pulled in through the gates.

'*Ma foi*,' said the taxi driver, getting out, following their gazes, looking up. 'There's a kid on the roof.'

The back doors slammed as Rachel and Richard got out.

'We've got a hose,' said the fire-engine driver, descending. 'We could soak him a bit, he won't like that.'

'You don't go soaking kids,' said the taxi driver. 'He could fall, then you'd have a dead kid.'

'I'm a part-timer.' The driver shrugged, looking at everyone, recognizing Guy and giving him the *bises*.

His handsome comrade in the crisp uniform came round and greeted them all with handshakes, ending with Simone, whom he gave the *bises*.

'Simone? I thought I knew you! My mother's still doing the Rotary club.'

'She's not!'

'She is. Eighty-five next March!'

'Guy. This is Guillaume . . .'

'Dutouquet.'

'I knew it was something like a parrot.'

'Well, I think the best thing is if one of you could climb up and have a chat with him,' said the big driver.

'Tried that,' said Jeff.

Maud ran across to Rachel. 'Max is on the roof. He's been reading your books, Mummy. That's why.'

'He'll jump for sure if this guy goes up to reason with him,' said Guillaume, pointing at Guy, grinning.

'I don't mind going up,' said Guy grimly, focusing his eyes on the boy.

'You're no good with heights,' said Simone.

Richard stood at the front of them, his hands sheltering the sides of his eyes. He relinquished Rachel's hand though she'd come up behind him to hold his.

'I'll go up and talk to him.'

'The kid's a psycho,' said Jeff. 'He'll come down when he's hungry, he eats like a horse.'

Richard turned round to look at Jeff. Jeff held out his hand for him to shake.

'I'm not shaking your hand.'

Jeff held it there. 'I'm saying sorry, man.'

'You're saying it to the wrong person.'

'He hasn't eaten for days, not properly,' put in Valérie.

'He might be malnourished,' said Simone, shrugging.

Richard went inside.

'There's something wrong with the kid,' said the burly fireman, hand at the peak of his cap. 'I mean to be sitting up there arsenaked on a day like this, there's got to be something wrong with him, that's all I know.'

Guillaume saw Valérie. 'Sorry for your troubles,' he said.

'Can't you guys go up there and bring him down?'

'We haven't got that kind of equipment. We have been known to do cats as a favour, though according to the rules we're not supposed to, if the cat got hurt we could get sued, you know. It's ridiculous, isn't it? But you know, one thing I do know is that you get up there and they come right down anyway.'

'He'll come down,' Jeff repeated. His face was without any trace of mirth. He needed the boy to come down, to release him; he felt vulnerable standing there, as exposed as if it were he on the roof. He hadn't even looked at Rachel, but he could feel her looking at him and it was an unpleasant feeling. *It's not my fault,* he said to himself. *None of this is my fault anyway.*

'He'll listen to Richard,' said Rachel. 'Richard will know what to say.' She said it with such a sure warmth that at last Jeff ventured a look at her. The expression on her face made him feel sick. They were lovers, then, she and Richard.

Richard had climbed on to the balcony wall and stood with his hands on the bottom ledge of the roof, where Jeff had been before.

'He wants to be careful,' said Guillaume, wincing. 'You see, we can't do anything like that really, not without being roped. I don't think of myself, I mean if I weren't wearing this uniform that would be me right there. It's right that it's the father though. He is the father, right . . . ?' He looked quickly at Jeff.

'They shouldn't have asked you to come out. You're only supposed to come out to put out fires. I know. I did a volunteer stint myself down in Cogolin in eighty-three,' said the taxi driver.

'Would anyone like a drink?' asked Simone.

'Sure, just a small one.'

'A schnapps or something.'

Richard spoke to his son. 'Come on, Max. I'm back now. Come

down, son. I love you so much, Max. You're my best pal. You know that. Come on, Max. I need you. Come down.'

Max put out two fingers and moved them in the air between them, making the V of the sights of a gun, then closing them and making a circle as if anointing his father. His right foot shifted and displaced the corner of a tile. Richard caught his breath as his son's trainer-clad foot failed to find a place to rest; it seemed to hang and shudder. Automatically, he put a hand out. 'Careful, kidder, it's wet, the roof, from the rain.'

'This is not good,' Guy whispered. He had the ladder against the wall but it didn't reach high enough to be of any use. He stood by it, tense, his hands in their fixed shape.

'Come down, sweet boy,' Rachel called out. 'Come down. Let's get you warm and safe and we can all talk.'

'Listen to Rachel,' said Richard, 'she's right.'

'Happy families,' said Jeff sourly.

'Oh, Jeff, you're such a fool,' said Rachel, turning to him suddenly. 'You're such a hypocrite, you don't have a conscience.'

'Oh, don't be all highfalutin, woman. Call me an asshole or something, will you?' He kept his eyes on the roof; he did not look at her.

The taxi driver clapped his hands together and blew on them. 'Is the guy on the roof going to pay me? There's no point in me waiting here watching it get dark, he could be hours up there, you know.'

'He could be,' said Guillaume. 'You have to take these things slowly. It's psychological. It's a game of nerves. You get the big tough guys like Hubert here, who want the action, but me, what I find interesting is watching the thing unfold, you can soon see what's going to happen.' He put out his cigarette. 'I don't like the look of this one.'

'People just don't know how to raise kids these days,' said the taxi driver.

'Here's your money, fella,' said Jeff, taking a couple of notes out of his pocket and striding towards him. 'There you go. Merry Christmas. That should cover it. *Connard*.'

'I'm not the one with my kid on the roof. *Connard*.'

'He's not my kid.'

'He's a nutcase. What's he doing—welcome party for Santa Claus?' he snorted and got in his car, waiving Simone's offer of a glass of schnapps.

'The kid's not a nutcase,' said Guy, still looking at the roof. 'That's one thing he's not.'

The firemen were each given a small shot glass of schnapps by Simone, who wiped her hands on her trousers and bristled in the cold. 'I don't know what's going to happen any more,' she said.

'Shh. *Calme-toi*,' said Guy, 'it will be all right. He's not mad.'

Richard was speaking again, addressing his son. 'Max. We've been selfish, all of us. We've been thinking about ourselves. None of it matters now, it only matters that you are safe. You're a special kid. I love you, Max, I'd give my life for you. I'm coming up there.' His hands got no traction on the damp tiles and he wondered how he was going to do it. He called down to Guy. 'How do I get up there?'

'Try the back balcony,' said Jeff, 'go to the other side, that's how the satellite guy got up there, there are some steps. You want me to come show you?'

Richard got down and went back into the house.

Valérie stepped forwards, cupping her mouth, shouting up to the boy, 'Max! Your father's going to come to you. Just stay there.'

The boy's left leg slipped and he looked slightly surprised; as he put his hands flat to steady himself, he dislodged a couple of tiles and they dropped to the ground.

'Max!' Valérie called again. 'Just wait there, your father's coming. Oh Max. I'm so sorry, Max. I'm finished with Jeff. I don't care about that now, it's all over with, it was stupidity . . . Please forgive me. I've been a terrible mother. Give me another chance, Max.'

Jeff went into the house, shaking his head and laughing without feeling.

'Come down to us,' said Richard softly, coming up the back roof, gripping the upper side of each tile, his cheek pressed to the tiling. 'We can make a new start.'

Max was speaking. 'My grandmother prophesies. My grandfather reads from nature. My mother is a demon. My father is a stranger. I am a servant of God. He wants me to be the bridge for you to meet upon.'

'What's he saying?' Rachel asked.

'He's talking about my gift,' said Simone, shrugging over at the firemen. 'He might have my powers. I'd never have imagined it, but it's possible. It can skip a generation, that's quite normal.'

'He's talking about nature,' said Guy. 'Listen to him.'

The firemen lit cigarettes.

'He's telling a story,' said Guillaume, smiling as guilelessly as if it were snowing.

'. . . his politicians told the king that his people were dying every day, of a disease new to them. The king said to himself, "But I am alive and well and happy. If they die it won't matter to me for I have stored up everything I need. If they die, even better, I will have everything to myself." And a voice in his head said, "Yes, but you won't be loved." But he answered it, "That doesn't matter to me." The voice spoke again, "But you won't have anyone to talk to." And he thought about that too and answered, "I've done a lot of talking. I have had enough of it." Then he heard the voice saying to him, "But, King, do you not think you *ought* to save them?" And he replied, "No, I do not. And I do not believe in you." And he drank a lot of wine on his own, the best wine he had. He made sure to smile at everybody and to say things to trick them about what he was thinking so they wouldn't rise up against him and kill him. He had the storytellers put out stories of his ancestors and their terrible evil doings, so that the people would say, "Well, in our time we have a much better king, we're very lucky." He surprised them at times with a little kindness. But even the smallest kindness hurt him, and he felt unhappy and his desire for the deaths of the people grew stronger until he went mad with longing for their destruction and tore at his chest to try to rip his heart out.'

The two firemen had been giving each other comical looks during the boy's story.

'It's a Perrault,' said the driver. 'It's called "The King and the Flute", isn't it?'

'There was no flute in it.'

'No, he forgot that part.'

Simone and Maud and Rachel held each other's hands. Valérie had her hand over her mouth. Guy remained standing behind, his hands on Simone's shoulders, a serious expression on his face.

'That's my story,' he said, 'that's my story.'

'I couldn't hear half of it. What was it about? Some king eating his heart out? Is it an English story?' Simone frowned at Rachel.

'It was like a parable,' said Rachel.

'There wasn't a happy ending,' said Maud.

'Look!' Guy raised a finger.

The boy was no longer there.

Richard came to the front door with his hands on the boy's shoulders. 'I'm going to get him to put some clothes on,' he said, wheeling him round again. Max looked unperturbed; glassy-eyed and vacant, his cheeks were peaky from the cold.

Valérie ran to her son. 'Oh, Max. I meant it, everything I said,' she said. 'Let me love you, Max.'

'Let him get some clothes on, Valérie, he's freezing cold.'

Max looked at his mother. He took her face in his hands and kissed her on her nose.

'Well, thanks for the drinks.' The firemen handed Simone their glasses. 'Good luck to you all. Call the doctor out maybe, to check the kid over.' They got into the cab of their truck and the noise of the unleashing of their amusement was only just caught in time by the electric windows. They drove off, laughing about it all.

'And what about the old man saying, *that's my story . . .*'

'And the taxi guy calling the American a prick . . .'

'You know they've swapped wives, right . . .'

'Who?'

'The two couples.'

'They drink too much, they laze about around the pool, looking at each other's wives half naked, they get everyone doing everything for them and then they wonder why they've got a kid on the roof.'

'She's had a breast job. Corinne told me.'

'Sure, they got it half price, he's in the business, that English guy.'

'He used to go hunting with the Vidauban crowd.'

'Yeah. I know that. He used to get drunk and go on and on about his work. A cosmetic surgeon. Down in Nice. It's why I like this job, you see, you get to see people in difficult situations, you know. That's how you get to see what a person's like. I used to want to be an actor.'

'Did you?'

'Maxence! My grandson!' Guy called as the boy, now clothed, came through the front door. 'From this day I will not drink a drop of wine again!'

When they each tried to embrace him, he looked at them in turn. They clutched at him and said his name, and told him they loved him. Then he went with his grandfather to his house and the first thing he did was to pick up the ten-litre wine box on the outside table and brandish it.

The old man assented.

Max took it and stood on the back doorstep, he held it low between his legs so that it seemed like he was urinating, and he turned the tap round to make the flow louder and faster and they both had a sly laugh about it.

'Genius!'

'I know it!'

'Good man!'

'A cigarette!'

58

✧

THE WINTER ADVANCED AND RECEDED in a war of attrition with the summer. One day the daffodil soldiers emerged with their long green-leaved spears, the next they were heavy-headed, struggling against the cold. There came first the white wild flowers and one or two white butterflies, and then the cold wind would blow them away. The next day the yellow dandelions broke cover, and they were matched by yellow butterflies, then blossom burst like popcorn popping on the branches of the cherry trees, infant fig leaves uncurled and blue flowers dared a dome-head here and there, and at last there came a poppy, just one, but the next day there were three, and then with a great hoo-rah nature chucked everything she had at summer and the poppies raged across the fields like measles.

The ex-pats had spent the cold months taking a turn here and there at somebody's house, comparing prospective summer rental incomes, now in jeopardy *'thanks to fucking Tuscany'*, playing board games with petulance.

The morning after Maxence was on the roof, Valérie was in the kitchen, cooking her son pancakes with tears dripping off her chin, a wad of kitchen towel in one hand, a spatula in the other.

When Maud came to breakfast and saw her, she fled to the front door in her nightdress and stood on the doorstep calling out, 'Daddy! Daddy! Daddy!'

Jeff was gone.

'What are you doing?' Richard asked Valérie at lunchtime, finding her alone in the kitchen. She was sitting at the round dining table, holding the roll of kitchen towel between her hands. 'Come home with me. I have bought some bread, some cheese and ham. I'll make us lunch.'

'What home?'

'The old one.'

'It's rented.'

'No, they've reneged on it. I didn't want to upset you.'

'Oh. They seemed nice people. They were French too.'

'Yes, I'm sure. They probably were. It's not important. Come on. Get some clothes on.'

She bridled. 'You don't tell me what to do. Just because Jeff has gone.'

'Listen, Valérie, I completely understand you.' He said it gently because he was tired. He sat down. He felt exhausted and was ready to give up. 'I feel the same way,' he said, flicking at the Marlboro cigarette pack with his middle finger and thumb. It hit her forearm. 'I'm done with being married to you too. The only good part of it was laughing at the kid together, or sometimes at other people, and now and again the sex, or what I can remember of it. I just want to offer you lunch, that's all.'

Max came in, dragging a backpack across the floor. He sat at the table with them. 'You don't want me to smoke, but you smoke.' He withdrew a cigarette from the pack on the table and Richard smacked his hand to stop him and held it with his own and shook it.

They went down the lane, just a few hundred metres, and opened up their old home, and took to their old dining table; they sat in the same chairs they'd always sat in.

Richard made them all a sandwich and Max withdrew to his old room; he was reading *Fifty Great Religious Thinkers*.

Valérie had the remnants of make-up in the corners of her eyes, her face was puffy. She ate. She fell upon the sandwich, which was thick with butter and the soft ham fat and the gum-caking cheese. She was hungry. Richard poured them mugs of red wine and stood by the back door, drinking his with two hands around it like it was soup.

Outside Guy was walking up the road, almost gingerly, pointing each slipper before placing it, his arms shunting like a marionette steam train, compelled by some inner tune, his mouth moving, the dog wagging its tail alongside him. His face shocked Richard. It was as red as a baboon's bottom, high and puffy, like a punching glove; he looked like he had alcohol poisoning. Richard thought, he might be quitting the booze just in the nick of time.

'You know, I wasn't exactly a saint myself. So I can't hold this thing against you. There were other women. Just sex though.'

'I know,' she said, 'Jeff told me.'

'Did he? Yes. Well. I know what you are and what you're looking for because I am a lot like you. More than I would have guessed, I suppose. Why don't we both stay here for a while until things settle? I'm thinking of our son. You do as you like. Come and go as you like. We'll keep the kid safe, to make him better. Just until he's better. We'll give it six months. And then we'll go our separate ways. I think that's the best we can do. On the one hand it seems so much, on the other it seems so little. We'll just live like lodgers in the same space for the time being. For the kid's sake. He'll pull himself together. But no pills. That's what I'm going to insist on, no pills. We'll keep him off school for a little bit too.'

'OK. Fine. I don't know what else to do in any case. But what about Rachel?'

'Rachel? I love her.'

She raised her eyebrows. 'How amusing.'

Rachel had told him to stay on for a while, for his son's sake. Otherwise, she smiled, 'it will bite us in the arse.' She told him this time was their safety net. 'Do you really want to mess things up again? To have another failure?' She'd put a finger on his lips to stop him saying anything. And that was that.

'Hey, it won't be so bad, Valérie. We'll have my sick pay. As I said, you do as you like. We'll be OK. I won't give you a hard time. Maybe we'll even be friends?'

'I don't want some kind of cheap comfort.'

'I just want to do this for him, and to call it quits. I'll forgive you if you'll forgive me.'

'Is this some kind of Rachel-Christian thing?'

'No, it's not. I can forgive you because I don't love you.'

'Oh well, that's fine. So what are you going to do about sex? Obviously this is something that has been very important for you.'

'I'll make my own arrangements. You make yours.'

'What happened to the machismo?'

'I'm taking a pill for it.'

She ate the last piece of the sandwich from her plate then took the plate over to run it under cold tap water. 'But Richard, I don't know if I can make it through another six months without killing one of us. I don't want to have you so much as look at me. I really don't like you. When I think of you, I think of how

300

insincere you can be, and cruel, the games you play . . . how false . . .'

'Yes, you hate me. So, what are we to do? Give up on Max? You think suddenly you're going to be able to mother him?'

'I think I can do it now, the mothering.' Even as she said it, she brought Jeff's face to mind; it was as if he were always by her side, she saw him at the third chair, he was absent when present and now he was present when absent. 'But you, you can have your fresh start, Richard. With Rachel. You can make everything new and perfect so why don't you go, go away, with her.' She looked at him and her face was ordinary, it was not contorted or contrived or play-acting, it was bare and plain and without beauty or ugliness. It was the face of his old enemy. He had thought the mess he had made of his life was something particular, but he had the feeling now that it was nothing to do with events or circumstances, it was simply what weak, foolish, beliefless people did. Day in, day out. They couldn't care less about each other.

He went outside and called Rachel on her mobile phone and spoke to her, smoking a cigarette.

'We seem to have some sort of understanding, she and I,' he told her. 'I hope we can make it, for Max's sake, but it's going to be hard. Rachel, how do you know that it will work between us? This way? With the distance?'

'Don't doubt it. You're wasting time. Don't think. Just stand up,' she said.

'That makes it sound simple.'

'It is simple.'

He saw Simone's car slow down as she passed Abrams' villa, and looked through the open gates of the empty home.

Her face shone from her morning ablutions and potions, but

her mouth was like a dam, holding back a natural force. Seeing nothing to cause her to stop, she applied a little pressure to the accelerator and the old hopeless car that was hers, complete with filled ashtray and two pairs of cheap sunglasses rattling in a side pocket, lurched into the loose gravel.

59

RICHARD FOUND MAX peering over their rear fence. 'I wish they had kids next door,' he said. 'This is shit, living here, all alone.'

It was not a good time to say it but there was never going to be a good time. He sat Max down at the picnic table.

'Max. I have to tell you something. I'm going to leave France. In a few months. Not now, not until I know you're happier. In a while though, I will. I should never have come here. It's not your fault, or anything to do with you; the fault was mine. I made it a long time ago.'

'You were greedy,' said Max, solemnly, 'really greedy.'

'In a way, yes. They call it ambition,' Richard admitted, 'but all I can do now, to put things right again, is go home to where I came from.'

'To Rachel, because you love her. What about me?'

Richard went on, looking at the grass. 'You belong here. This is where you come from.'

'The son of Man has no home . . .'

He pulled his son to him and put his head under his chin. 'You will visit me in the holidays and I'll come and see you. But it's right you stay here. You're safe here.' He held him off and looked at him from under his brow, 'Hey, you know, your grandfather thinks you're very special. He thinks you're some sort of genius.'

The boy shrugged again, but there was a flicker of interest in his eyes and he put his nose in the air. 'Yes, I have saved him, you see.' The grin was devilish. 'I told him he owes me his soul now. But I don't really want it.'

'You are a very special boy. That's the truth.'

'No. I'm not well in the head. I'm nutty.'

'That's shit. That's just shit, Max.'

'I killed Gérard, you know.'

'Stop . . .'

'No one will ever see him again.'

'OK . . .' Richard sat back and blew out.

'I don't mean I shot him or stabbed him or anything. But I killed him. I was stronger than him in the end.' The boy nodded slowly and his eyes were bright. Dimples appeared in his cheeks. He stood up. He climbed on to the picnic table and stood looking down on his father. He closed one eye and pointed at him. 'I'll save you now.'

60

✧

RICHARD WENT IN THE LATE AFTERNOON to pick up some things from the studio. He stowed them in Valérie's car, then told her to go home without him. He wanted to walk back, he said. In fact, he went into the church that had so dominated his life physically for the last three months.

The church was like a cathedral, imposing and assuming, a cold goofy place; alien. It was dark; light came from a couple of candles, and the octagonal stained-glass window on high. The only sound was the cooing of the pigeons outside.

Along the side, he could pick out the various shadowy side-shows of piety. It was a frightening place in a way. It was not frightening in the way of horror films, in the way of the skeletal hand touching a neck, it was frightening in that it paid homage to pain.

There was a painting of the Garden of Eden. He considered it, he considered the two rounded bodies, with the serpent between them, their eyes large with apprehension. At issue in the Garden of Eden was not sex — it was love, he thought. The temptation of Eve was surely to see Adam as an object of devotion. As to whether they were shagging or not, God didn't give a fig.

He looked then at the single modest carved offering of the

Son, gaunt-faced, stricken at his bad luck, the cross behind him like a hammer knocking the sense of the world into his petalled head. Evidently God's little homunculi wanted to love someone who looked like them, so He sent Himself in their garb, two legs, two arms and the rest and the bastards killed him. He wasn't *enough* like them. Richard smiled: *We want dirty little failures capable of loving dirty little failures, that's all.*

As he stepped down the hill, he tried to bring to mind all the disappointing things about Rachel to make himself feel better, to be better able to manage her absence, but by the time he got to the roundabout and waved down Simone's car coming out of the supermarket car park, he was thinking about having a child with her.

61

✧

JEFF WAS RENTING a highly angular studio apartment. The last occupant, the realtor told him, had hanged himself there. It put some folk off.

Jeff considered what he was going to tell Don about the last four years. He'd confine himself to generalizations, he decided. It would be best to be cut and dried, he might imply some bad business but he would not dwell on it; there was a whole vast American literary, cinematic and musical canon in such a vein.

In the last months he'd noticed this black fleck in the vision of his right eye so that wherever he looked he saw a dark comma. He'd spent the first few days with it batting the air as if he had a mosquito familiar. He went to the optician's and was told it was retinal debris; he'd always have it. To him, it represented Africa. In his summary of the last four years he omitted that part of the story, reasoning with himself that their patron might not have been pleased to have shared by proxy in their charitable endeavour.

He appreciated being back in New York. 'Wow. Europe's way different to the States. They just can't leave a person alone,' he said to himself. 'Who knew?' But it was he who knew. He had no illusions about himself and what he was, not deep down; he knew he was a drifter, beyond the reach of any judgement, even his own, but still, it did not sit easy with him, the African experience nor his time in France. He preferred not to think about it.

'Thank God I'm back.' He loved New York, with its prim grid under a grandiose sky. There was nothing to get worked up about in private, everything was out on the street. A man with a rubber elephant trunk strapped to his face rode past the glass window.

Don's great bulk moved across the café floor; he coyly held the sides of the long navy-blue coat together as he came swishing between the tables. The two men shook hands and Jeff ordered two lattes up at the counter. He glanced back to take a peek at his patron, his friend, his one-time partner. Don was sitting back, looking right at him. Jeff faltered in response to the barista's second request for five dollars sixty.

He set down the coffees and took his place. It was a mistake, going to Europe, he said. Rachel got all riled up over the Twin Towers, like America was the problem, but now he knew he should have stayed put. This was his hometown.

'You know what, Don? Being here I just feel like I'm me again.' He checked Don's face. 'And, you know, the way those people carried on over there, it was totally unacceptable to me. You know, there came a point where I was just like, "Stop; enough of this bullshit." I mean you wouldn't believe it, the last day I was there, there was the neighbours' kid on the roof. No, I'm serious. There was no way the kid was going to kill himself, it was just a stupid stunt. But, you know, it was like no one was happy unless they were fighting. Oh the countryside's beautiful, sure, and I thought I really could live there, you know, but it was hard to get any peace. Isn't it always the women who mess things up? I'm gonna miss my little girl of course, but Rachel'll bring Maud out next summer, or I'll go see her. I kind of think character's formed anyway by the time a kid's five. She's real cute. Hey. By the way, your house looks great, man, you should go and see it. Really. We did a good job. The photos don't do it justice. You have to kind of feel the space of it.'

'No. I'm going to sell it.' Don's eyes looked into his coffee cup. 'My heart was never in it after Tyler died. It kind of felt contaminated to me. I never thought any good would come of that place. But listen, you're back now, buddy, and it ain't all rosy here I have to tell you. I had to let go thirty people this year. Old-school types. But look, if you want to have a go doing some web design freelance, be my guest. It don't pay much, the day rates are half what they used to be, maybe less.'

'The advertising side of things, it's just gone? Print? TV? No way? Wow. That's a blow. I sort of thought I had a share in that business. As a partner.'

'You did. You got your share paid to you in France, bud. Monthly and then some. You're lucky you didn't share in the debts.'

'Wow. OK. I can't believe you didn't tell me any of this.'

'Yeah. I wound it up a year or so after you left. I thought you might notice I wasn't sending you any work. Liked the wine by the way. *La Bête Noire*. The black beast. You bet your ass. Funny.' He nodded without a trace of humour. 'Well, you've probably lived every motherfucker's dream making your own wine. But you're back now. Take the job, use it as a base to look for something else. The glory days are over though, they're long gone.'

'Sure. Sure.'

'Hey, cheer up. You're back in the city, like you said, that's the thing.'

'Man, I really screwed up leaving this place. Anyhow,' he slapped the table with his two hands and replaced his dismayed expression with his old trusty grin, 'let's go out and get blasted tonight, should we? Like the old days? Fuck the rural idyll and pastures green and all that. And fuck women as well. Next time I'm going to get me some eighteen-year-old Hispanic or something.'

He looked about him. The café was filled with the semi-artistic hippies of the area, vitamin-starved. A preppy-looking woman sat askance, made notes on a pad on her lap with her eyes bouncing about the place. Once or twice he caught her eye. Across from her, closer to the mutual table, another woman was breastfeeding. They were all just sketches. Amused, benevolent, Jeff the cartoonist sat there surveying it all. He had solved the problem of pain long ago.

Don stood up. He shrugged his coat on to himself, his hands emerging last from his sleeves. He dipped them into his long, long pockets. His upper lip snagged.

He put a hand on Jeff's shoulder. 'It's all come full circle, it's all how it should be.' He turned back before he got to the door. 'Can't do that drink tonight though, buddy.'

62

✧

A HANDSOME YOUNG MAN with tight glossy curls, Middle Eastern, tight blue T-shirt and jeans leans into the fourteenth-century fountain; his arms back, he drinks.

Old grudges unfurl in the sunshine. The waitress admits her son will have to take the school year again. The restaurant owner shrugs over the graffiti that won't wash off. The mayor strides round, grinning. Those English who have crossed the street to avoid each other no longer do so, but fall back on the unfamiliar greeting, 'Hullo.'

The siren sounds twelve and the florist lifts the hanging basket from its hook and takes it inside. The shopkeepers next door, a dapper couple in baggy fine linens in natural hues, lift hangers off the racks of linen trousers and shirts and carry them inside. The postcard racks are wheeled into the *maison de la Presse,* the lights go off inside and cigarettes are extinguished, then the sign is turned on itself. *Fermé.*

An old couple hasten down the steep cobbled alley, holding on to each other. The greengrocer considers rebellion; quiffed, he stands with an arm leaning on a rack of aubergines, tomatoes and peppers, and faces down the town at 12.30.

Grinning tourists with baskets pick their way towards the

pizza café, settle in, and sit like Peeping Toms getting a look at other orders, taming their saliva with swallowing, until it's their turn to smile the smile which had been already forming in the queue for security at Gatwick.

Three years before, the pizza man's wife left him to start her own restaurant elsewhere, and the little woman who ran the tea shop took the risk of going from knick-knacks to *gourmandises*, and the greengrocer expanded his range to include dried pulses and pastas, cheese and eggs and they all wondered whether they would make it through the winter; now they had made it through three. The ex-pats were leaving but the tourists were still coming.

The owner sets the pizza down with pride. The little black wet marbles, the picholine olives, roll forth, the pizza crust is lighter than a crêpe and wood-smoked dirty enough to push the confection beyond sanitary into something far more pleasurable. He's been good-natured to the odd customer through the winter months, he was good-natured to the crowds through the summer. He's taken it all in his stride. It isn't so much, but it's something.

After three years of building works which jeopardized the commerce of the town, a week of free events has been organized by the municipality and so the town is unusually full as people come and find a table for the music this lunchtime.

Richard nods at the winegrower from Château Thuerry, the vineyard on the road to the motorway; a man with walnut skin, wearing today, in place of his blue overalls, a cowboy hat with studs, a nylon shirt with a Japanese tiger prowling down its side.

Out of the backwoods they come in from the winter in denim shirts for the men and elastic-waisted long skirts for the women, the less judicious with short skirts, fags in gobs, singing along.

With his equipment plugged in, up and running, the lone

young singer, bandana Springsteen-style, gives it emotion, the tendon on his neck taut.

'*Wiz or wizout you . . .*'

There they are — Richard, Simone, Valérie and Max, having lunch. Valérie keeps a seat free opposite her and leans forwards to touch it when other would-be lunchers enquire. She shakes her head and says it's taken.

It's the first hand of summer, there's drink and talk, and they stay away from anything difficult, just as they always had done, only now they know it, and now they know it's not for ever.

Guy emerges from the photographer's two doors down where he went to ask after an old black-and-white camera, and takes the free seat opposite Valérie. She reaches forwards to touch the camera he's holding and the two of them dip their dark heads to the prize.

Simone is smoking and watching the human traffic. Richard has an arm around Max's seat and he's keeping time with his hand to the music, but he's playing and replaying in his mind excerpts from Rachel's email of the morning.

He kisses the boy's head. He kisses the boy's head again. He smiles at Guy. His eyes prick. He is full of gratitude to him for helping him make Max better. For insisting he's special.

They go home in Guy's other new acquisition, a clapped-out Nissan truck. Guy pulls over after the first roundabout and offers a lift to Jacques, who squats down in a derelict van in the woods just past the German's place. Many times on her way back and forth from shopping Simone has passed him and not once has she stopped, though, like her, every day he goes to the village for his wine and bread, only by foot.

Max turns to look through the rear windscreen and sees the man, his hair and beard blowing, crouching, holding on to the sides of the truck and he smiles at him. Jacques smiles back, risks a tentative thumbs-up, almost losing hold. Max returns the thumbs-up. He is sitting behind his grandparents, between his mother and father.

Thrilled with this exceptional show of neighbourliness, when he bids them farewell, Jacques, against his own interest, enthuses about the land he's squatting on and explains how Richard would be able to snap it up for next to nothing as the owner is desperate to sell.

'I could help you. I could speak to him for you. I could arrange it. Man, I'm hungry. And lonely.'

He looks from face to face, keenly. He is trading his shelter for something he has not defined. They turn him away.

'You're a good man, Guy,' says Richard.

'No,' Guy says. 'No, I'm not.'

As he goes on his way Guy says that he hopes the fellow won't misunderstand the gesture. Simone scorns him, she insists the man will be round in the morning, bothering them; this she foresees with conviction.

Standing outside their back door speaking to Rachel on the phone early in the morning, Richard sees Guy giving Jacques his marching orders from their terrace. Jacques tramps down the slight hill from their bungalow towards the grassy alley that separates the three houses, looking scalded.

'I thought we were friends! A little *tartine!* A lousy piece of bread! For pity's sake. A small glass to warm a man!'

'I'm not drinking with you. Go on with you. *Fous le camp!*' Guy calls after him.

'Some people don't know anything about brotherly love.' He gestures at Richard. He puts his hands on his hips. 'One lift! One measly ride on the back of a truck and he thinks he's Jesus Christ.'

Guy sucks on his cigarette, squinting after him until he sees the man diminished by distance. Then he sits back down at the table with Max for their early-morning game of chess.

'I know that I'm lucky,' he grumbles in a low voice. 'I could be him.'

He moves his moustache with his nose and cheeks, considers the chess pieces. His brow floats as surreptitiously his eyes take in the double doors behind his grandson. Catching Max's eyes, he nods at the chequered board to confirm it has his attention.

When the door opens, when the wind chimes tinkle, when Simone emerges in her buttoned-up housecoat, his whole face changes.

ACKNOWLEDGEMENTS

With regard to the study of mental illness in rural Ethiopia, I draw upon ideas in papers given by Dr Atalay Alem and Dr Negussie Deyessa. With regard to the experience of immigration and the association of dopamine levels with the presence of the symptoms of schizophrenia, I refer to papers by Dr Gerald Hutchinson and Dr Jean-Paul Selten. Any errors in interpretation are mine. I make reference to Richard Bentall's witty paper 'A Proposal to Classify Happiness as a Disorder'. I refer to Julian Jaynes's book *The Origin of Consciousness in the Breakdown of the Bicameral Mind*.

Thank you to the World Psychiatric Association for allowing me to attend the 2005 conference, and to Downing College, its Master and Fellows.

Thank you to two good shrinks who became two good friends: Dickon Bevington and Bedirhan Ustun.

Inspiration came from Joop de Jong, Sir Richard Gregory, Tim Crow, John Read, Steven Rose, John Searle, Trevor Robbins, Barbara Sahakian, Barry Everett, Geraint Rees, Chris and Uta Frith and Nick Medford.

To Gill Coleridge, Juliet Annan and Rebecca Saletan, for your generous patience, my heartfelt thanks. Also to Jenny Lord, Shân Morley Jones and Cara Jones for the kind support.

To Marcus, thank you for giving an idea a life.

LOUISE DEAN
March 2008
www.louisedean.com